The

Woman

who took in

Parcels

and opened one

PENNY KLINE

Published by Accent Press Ltd 2019
Octavo House
West Bute Street
Cardiff
CF10 5LJ

www.accentpress.co.uk

ISBN 9781786156518
eISBN 9781786156525

Printed and bound in Great Britain by Clays Ltd,
Elcograf S.p.A

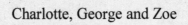
Charlotte, George and Zoe

ONE

'We call them "serial offenders",' the tall, and rather alluring, delivery man explained. 'People who order goods when they know they're going to be out all day. This one's for number thirty-four.'

Neither of them smiled. It was not a joke. For her own part, Jane never ordered anything online, preferring to visit the shops and check goods face to face, so to speak. Presumably, her neighbours sat at their computers, clicking away, without a thought as to when the garden lights or digital pedometers or babies' play centres would arrive.

'What's your name, love?'

Jane opened her mouth to say "Seymour", but the word came out differently. 'Marple.'

'Initial?'

'J.'

'Sign here, please.'

Taking the stylus from his outstretched hand, she

signed "Jane Marple" with a flourish, and took the package – it was lighter than she expected – speculating as to what something so large and bulky might contain.

'I'll leave a note at number thirty-four.'

'If you must.' The package was addressed to Willa Molloy. Last time it had been number twenty-one and the owner had rung Jane's bell when she was in the bath and she had been obliged to dry herself hurriedly and open the front door in her dressing gown. Her hair had been wet, and would not have looked its best. Once auburn, it was now a steely grey, although the freckles on her face and hands were a reminder of the colouring she had inherited from her father. In her youth, she had been what people call "a fine-looking woman", with her high cheekbones, and lacking the glasses she now wore, more as a defence against the world rather than because she was unable to see in the distance.

The parcel had been badly wrapped, either that or someone had tossed it across the sorting room and it had landed awkwardly. Ripped paper, and sticky tape that was coming away at one end. Why had she signed "Jane Marple"? So silly, but one made these gestures to keep up one's spirits. *One's* spirits? She sounded like the Queen but, as well as leaving you at a bit of a loose end, retirement meant losing your status, something she was finding a little hard to bear.

Miss Marple. The Miss Marple Day. She had enjoyed the books, preferring unassuming Jane Marple to pompous Hercule Poirot, but later she would look back on that day with a faint shudder. Of regret? Or was it guilt? How little control over events one had and it was easy to see how one thing led to another. Easy with hindsight.

Just now, Rousseau was writhing round her legs, demanding food. According to a website she had visited, cats' purring lowered your blood pressure, and certainly Rousseau had one of the loudest purrs, jumping onto her knees and purring like a ... like a what? In the past, she had thought of herself as something of an expert in similes and metaphors, but recently her brain produced only clichés. Purring like a steam engine. Gorging like a pig. The thought that the tabby cat had no knowledge of his namesake, Jean-Jacques, made her smile.

'I have never shared Rousseau's belief that human beings are good by nature, but I did believe in my pupils developing a healthy sense of self-worth.'

Rousseau looked up, with traces of meat on his whiskers, and she felt obliged to explain. 'Self-worth, Rousseau. All this depression and anxiety is the result of low self-esteem. People rarely suffer from it in times of severe stress. In wartime, for instance, when the wish to survive is stronger than the wish to compete.'

She had put it badly so it was not surprising Rousseau's tail was disappearing through the cat flap. She picked up Willa Molloy's parcel and gave it a squeeze.

If it had contained any small items they would have fallen out through the rip. What was it? Willa Molloy went in for ethnic clothes, brightly coloured and not very flattering, but she thought she could feel something hard.

Shoes? No, normally they came in boxes. A close neighbour ordered numerous pairs and the parcels were marked with the name of an expensive store, one into which Jane had never ventured.

Taking a pair of scissors from a drawer, she cut through a short length of sticky tape – it would be simple enough to re-stick it – and dragged four polythene-wrapped objects through the outer packaging. The invoice that accompanied the items fell to the floor. Jane retrieved it and checked the contents, and how much each item had cost. A fair bit, but that was true of most things these days.

The description, "pink fluffy handcuffs" was self-explanatory. Of more interest were the teacher's outfit, mortarboard and black patent leather underwear. Not real leather, of course, and consisting mainly of strips and buckles, together with a pair of knickers that would be extremely uncomfortable, but perhaps that was part of the fun.

The fact that fetishists liked teachers amused her. Freud had explained it as an association between an object and a first sexual experience. That thought was less appealing. *Sit down, child, and do as you're told.* The boy's hand on his groin – was that what Freud had meant?

Willa Molloy's husband, Brian, was Jane's doctor, a decent enough man, if on the dull side. Or so Jane had believed. Unwanted images sprang to mind. Willa cavorting in the teacher outfit, and Brian dressed as a schoolboy, in shorts and knee socks. Stuffing the

4

mortarboard and patent leather back into their respective bags, she snipped off a small strip of fresh sticky tape, and returned the package more or less to its previous state.

Parcels were often damaged in transit. When she delivered it to number thirty-four, Willa would be none the wiser.

As it turned out, it was Brian who answered the door. Still dressed in the casual outfit he now wore at the health centre, in place of his grey suit, he gave her one of his benign smiles. 'Jane – what can I do for you?'

'Parcel for Willa.'

'Ah. Thank you. She's at her Zumba dancing.' He gave a little laugh – because he knew what the parcel contained, or was it the dancing class he found amusing? 'Birthday coming up. I was hoping for binoculars, but this is the wrong shape. What d'you think? I know, a kite. I mentioned how flying a kite might be good exercise.' He fingered his thinning hair. 'I expect you take in plenty of other people's parcels.'

'I do.'

'What would we do without you?'

'What indeed.'

He hesitated and she was afraid he had noticed the damaged state of the package, but he was only preparing to ask after Eddie.

'She's fine. Much the same.'

'It's a good place, The Spruces. You were fortunate they agreed to take her. But I expect you know that.'

'I do.' How crass he was. At one time, she had thought

5

doctors the crème de la crème, but, according to Willa, Brian had only gained a place at medical school because his doctor father had been a rugby blue.

'You look tired, Jane.'

'Didn't sleep terribly well.'

'Of course.' He had adopted his professional GP's expression. 'Missing your friend. Grieving. These things have a tendency to manifest as physical symptoms and the symptoms are telling us—'

'Goodbye then, Brian. Enjoy the rest of your evening.'

He pushed up the cuff of his green sweatshirt. 'Programme about breastfeeding and hypochondria in ten minutes' time. Fascinating.'

'I'm sure.' Jane turned her back on number thirty-four and made for home. How did Willa stand the man? On the other hand, Willa would not be the easiest person to live with. With whom to live. In spite of the changing directives of whichever Education Minister was in office, Jane had insisted her pupils became familiar with at least the rudiments of good grammar.

Lost in thought, she reached her house, put her key in the lock, entered her sitting room, and was stopped short by a dull thud in the pit of her stomach. In the centre of the cat basket Rousseau normally scorned, lay the fluffy pink handcuffs.

TWO

While she was tipping the contents of a waste-paper basket into her black wheelie bin, a familiar voice spoke Jane's name.

'Oh, good morning, Noel.'

'How are you?' He was wearing a red T-shirt and those trousers people called jogging bottoms, although she had an idea it had changed to "trackies".

'I'm well, thank you. How's Corinne?'

Noel jerked his head in the direction of his house at the top of the road. 'Still applying her warpaint. Says she feels naked without it. Lacks your confidence.'

'I'm too old to be concerned about my looks.'

'Nonsense. You're a very attractive woman.' He stared deep into her eyes and she experienced an involuntary twitch in her groin. At her age, she was supposed to be past such sensations. A myth.

No doubt, women had always fallen for his looks: hair like a raven's breeding plumage; handsome features;

bright blue eyes. She wanted to tell him about the teacher's outfit. Ask his advice. But it would mean confessing she had opened someone else's parcel. She had considered throwing the handcuffs in the bin but, in the meantime, had hidden them in a kitchen cupboard, behind the herbs and spices she rarely used in her cooking.

Noel gave a theatrical sigh. 'Do you find, as soon as one problem's solved, another rears its ugly head?'

'I do.' Could he read her mind? Much more likely he was thinking about Corinne, his new paramour? Well, newish, since it must be getting on for six months since her arrival in Faraday Road. Stories abounded how she had deserted several children to move in with Noel, although recently Jane had discovered it was *one* son, in his last year at school. Bad enough if you were inclined to pass judgement on people, but that was something Jane tried to avoid since rarely did you know the whole story.

'Eddie getting on all right?' Noel sat on the low wall, and began re-tying his laces. 'You must miss her.'

'I miss how she used to be.'

His smile had a hint of sadness. His own, or because of Eddie? 'Rousseau was in our garden earlier, stalking a pigeon.'

'I hope you shooed him away.'

'Name suits him. Noble savage – that *was* Rousseau's idea, wasn't it?'

'Rousseau himself never actually used the term "bon sauvage" but he did believe in man's innate goodness.'

'Jolly good. Rely on you, Jane, to keep me informed

8

on such matters. Hope next door's loft conversion's not disturbing you too much.' And he bounced down the road in the trainers he believed made him look like a young thing.

In less than a week he would be dead.

The Jane Marple day. Later, she would pinpoint it as the time it all began – the turning point that led up to the tragedy, and its alarming aftermath. But did anything have a genuine beginning and end? Life was a string of events, most of them random, like Eddie's dementia, although one day they might discover a way of preventing it. Eating large amounts of beetroot or standing on your head for ten minutes, morning and evening.

Building materials cluttered up the pavement, and a large skip took up two valuable parking spaces. She ought to be used to it, but when she and Eddie arrived in Faraday Road there had been hardly a loft conversion in sight. Now the vans – Noel's vans – were a familiar sight. Pale blue, with identical pictures of fluffy white clouds on either side, the company specialised, it said, in high-quality conversions. Not *that* high quality if some of the building materials she had observed were anything to go by, but Noel himself was high quality, and he had a high-quality partner now too. High quality *and* high maintenance, that was dear Corinne.

Next door – the home of Dave and his young daughter Simmy on the ground floor, and Gus on the first – was having a loft conversion and on weekdays the noise was more or less continuous. Hammering, shouting, electric drills and a local radio station. Dave was at his workshop during the day, but since his camera shop closed, Gus was at home, and Simmy too, now the school holidays had begun.

Rousseau had joined her and was inspecting a container with the remains of some chicken wings in a spicy sauce. It was not to his liking. Like all cats, he had an inquisitive nature, something, had she but known it, that was to provide her with a vital clue in her coming investigations.

What a racket. It only needed a truckload of scaffolders to come up the road for the cacophony to be complete. Above the noise of the drill, she could hear Simmy shouting at her father. Isolated remarks floated through next door's kitchen window. *Don't believe. Why not? No, I won't.* Jane worried about the child who, now she was a teenager, must be suffering from the lack of a mother. Still, in spite of adverse publicity, single parents were frequently a good deal more conscientious than two. Something to do with having sole responsibility? Dave was clever with his hands, but hardly the creative type, so presumably Simmy had inherited her imagination from her dead mother. When she was a year or two younger, she had insisted she saw a ghost coming down Faraday Road; a nice one, she said, not frightening at all, and with a baby in her tummy. Jane was no psychologist, but she was familiar with the way children – and not just children – invented stories to try to communicate something that was too difficult to express openly.

Best not to think about it. One of the drawbacks of living alone was that it allowed you too much time to think. Best to keep busy, keep your head down. *The unexamined life* might not be worth living, but it was a good deal easier. A twinge of pain in her upper chest. Heart disease or indigestion? On television, it was Cancer Week. During breakfast she had stuck it out as long as she could bear it then switched to the other side where a female celebrity, with lips like Mick Jagger, was being interviewed about her divorce. Cancer or cosmetic surgery, or switch off the television and try the radio.

Gus had appeared, still wearing his pyjamas and with a tartan rug draped over his shoulders. 'Morning, Jane.'

'Good morning.'

'How's Eddie?' He was standing in a patch of sunlight and she could see the small square of white paper on his neck where he must have cut himself shaving. 'Settled in all right, has she? How long is it now? Must be getting on for a month.'

'Six weeks.' It was good that people still asked after Eddie, even if it was in much the same tone of voice as mentioning a death. Would a mercy killing have been preferable to The Spruces? Not her place to play God, but were the same fate to befall her, she would have no wish to be resuscitated from a heart attack or stroke.

'I miss her too,' Gus said. 'She had a refreshing habit of speaking her mind.'

'That was the dementia.'

'No, long before she lost her marbles she told me if my

11

shop wasn't doing well I ought to retrain as a plumber. Called me an idle old bastard.'

'I'm sorry.' Jane was thinking that perhaps she should make a living will. But that would mean asking someone to witness her signature. Brian would do it, while telling her how sensible she was being. Or Noel, who would have a jollier approach. *You're not going to die, Jane. People like you live forever*. 'You and me, Gus, we're both in the same boat, on the scrapheap, retired, at a loose end.'

'I saw you talking to Noel. Runs five miles a day. Likes to keep fit so he can hang onto all his bits on the side.'

'Surely now he's got Corinne …'

'Oh, her.' Gus' eyebrows twitched with amused surprise. 'You think Corinne will satisfy his need for admirers, do you?'

'I've always found him very kind and empathic.'

'Empathic eh? So you're another of his fans. Right, why did I come down from my flat? Oh yes, I know. Thought I heard the postman but it was some flyers jammed in the letter box.' He waved at a woman Jane had never seen before, who was unlocking the door to number twenty-two. It had a "Sold" board in the front garden.

'You know the new owner?'

'Just being neighbourly.' His fingers fidgeted with the top button on his pyjama jacket. 'Take no notice, just envious of Noel's flashy good looks. And his relative youth.'

Poor Noel, destined to be cut short in his prime.

THREE

Mondays, Wednesdays and Saturdays, and sometimes in between. The visits were a duty, not enjoyed by either of them, although who could tell what Eddie enjoyed? Still, if it put the handcuffs out of Jane's head for a while it would be a blessing. During the night, she had tried to decide what to do. Wrap them in a separate parcel and push it through Willa's door. No, that would be a give-away. Post them. No, the rest of the stuff had arrived via a delivery company.

She could tell Eddie about it, in the knowledge the crime would go no further. On second thoughts, Eddie had a way of picking up on stray words. *Handcuffs. Pink fluff. Someone else's parcel.* Matron was normally too busy to listen to the residents' ramblings, but the word "handcuffs" might make her prick up her ears.

When was the precise time her friend and companion had disappeared and been replaced by a zombie? Horrible word, "zombie" – she would never have spoken it out loud – but things had a way of springing to mind long before you had time to censor them. Was it the night Eddie ran down the road in her nightdress? Or the day Jane hugged her and received a hard bite? Could she have kept her at home longer? Had she arranged to have her admitted to The Spruces because she was too lazy to get up for her in the night? No, she was being unduly harsh on herself. The confusion had been something she had adjusted to, along with finding various objects in unexpected places. Her precious tablet in the washing machine, only discovered when it crashed around among the jumpers and knickers. And by then it was too late.

The sun was shining on the neat little front gardens in Faraday Road. And on the scaffolding, of course, and the skip, overflowing with off-cuts of hardboard and empty paint cans, and quite a decent shrub that had been broken off at its roots. Apart from the building materials, the road was looking attractive, with its front doors painted tasteful shades of green and blue and grey, and its bay trees and window boxes. Recently, house prices had soared and were a constant subject of conversation. Prices and home improvements. Jane had no intention of moving, or improving, but pretended to be interested in extensions and the paving over of front gardens. Had nobody heard how, since the rain was unable to soak in, paving stones led to flooding?

The two student houses let down the "highly sought-after street" somewhat, and Jane often picked up empty baked bean tins and beer cans and deposited them in one of the black wheelie bins, but she liked the students and they provided a touch of *real life*, whatever that was supposed to be.

Coming out of her front door, she bumped into Simmy, and the child let out a small squeal of alarm as though she had been caught in some nefarious act.

'I'm sorry, dear, I didn't mean to make you jump. Summer holidays at last.'

Simmy sucked a strand of her hair.

'How do you plan to spend them?'

Simmy flicked up her fringe, a pointless gesture since it fell straight back over her eyes. Recently, the girl seemed to have lost her tongue and Jane hoped she was not being bullied although, if that were the case, the holidays would have come as a relief. When things went wrong, parents imagined it was something to do with school, and teachers assumed there were problems at home.

Like all the best people, Simmy loved animals. Perhaps, if she invited her round to see Rousseau, the child might open up. Just now she was standing on one leg like a flamingo. Bad simile, since her colouring was dark – brown hair, brown eyes and olive skin. Still, her legs were long and thin. Normally, she wore shorts and a T-shirt, but today the arms of a shapeless sweater hung to the tips of her fingers and the heavy chain round her neck had something black on the end of it.

'New jumper?' Jane asked brightly. 'What's that on your chain?'

'It keeps evil spirits away.'

'I see. I rather thought worry dolls came in sets, little bags with a drawstring.'

Simmy gave her a slightly pitying look. 'It's an amulet.'

'I see.' Jane studied the slightly unpleasant-looking creature with its one baleful eye. 'I'm on my way to see Miss Knox.'

'Oh. Is she all right?' Simmy's narrow-eyed expression had changed to one of concern.

'Yes, thank you, dear.' According to Gus, Simmy and her father were not getting on, and this was borne out by the shouting. Simmy, still only thirteen, wanted to stay out late? Or find boyfriends online, or whatever teenage girls got up to these days?

'Miss Seymour?'

'Yes, dear?' The rosemary needed cutting back. Rosemary for remembrance. *Do you forget where you've put your keys? Do you find television programmes hard to follow? Do you sometimes find a word is on the tip of your tongue?* Yes. No. I don't remember!

'Do you know what happened to my mother?'

'Your mother?' Jane was unprepared for the question. 'I believe you were very young when she —'

'Two and a half.'

'I'm sorry, it's sad for you. You must miss —'

'No, because I can't remember her.'

Jane opened her mouth to say she meant she must miss not having a mother, and thought better of it.

'Dad won't tell me why she died.'

'I see.' Perhaps talking about it upset him. Unlikely, since it was eleven years ago and Dave was not the emotional type. Although one never knew what went on in other people's heads. Cheerful, open people could be hiding a dark secret, and the gloomy buggers, like Dave, could have a tempestuous love life, carried on away from prying eyes.

Simmy had screwed up her face, a warning that Jane was not responding adequately. 'I think she ran off to live with another man. Some mothers wish they'd never had a baby. I saw this television programme about a woman who wanted a career and —'

'Oh, I'm sure that's not what happened, dear. I expect she was ill.'

'If that was right, Dad could tell me. I thought she might have done a murder. It would mean she had a life sentence so she wouldn't come out of prison until I was twenty-two, unless she was allowed out on parole.'

'Talk to your dad again. Perhaps you caught him at a bad moment.'

'No, I've asked him heaps of time.'

'I see.' What was Dave playing at? Surely the child had a right to know. Was Simmy correct when she suspected her mother had walked out on the marriage? 'Do you have an aunt, someone who might —'

'No, and I haven't got any cousins either. It's only me and Dad and you know what he's like.'

Jane did know what he was like. 'Next time I see him,

I'll have a word.'

'You promise.'

'I do.'

'I think Mr McNeill knows.'

'Noel? What makes you think that?'

'I asked him if he did and he winked.'

'Oh, I wouldn't read anything into that, dear. He winks at everyone.'

'So you'll ask Dad why he won't tell me?'

'When it feels like the right moment.'

With a look that conveyed the belief all adults made promises they had no intention of keeping, Simmy stumped back into her house and slammed the door. What *had* happened to her mother? Hardly a mystery of "the body in the library" variety, but at the very least, when she lay awake at three in the morning, it would provide something to think about other than the fluffy pink handcuffs.

Tricia Tidewell, Jane's other immediate neighbour, had appeared, plus buggy containing Ada, strapped in and screaming, and Liam and Pippa aiming kicks at one another. The woman looked at her wits' end and Jane would like to have provided her with some parenting skills, but suspected the offer would not be welcome.

The houses in Faraday Road were solidly built, in the late eighteen nineties, with thick, relatively soundproof walls, but the Tidewell children were particularly unruly. Not that Jane would dream of complaining. Sandwiched between number twenty-five and number twenty-nine, she liked to think of herself as an oasis of calm. Not that twenty-five was normally so noisy. Mrs Garcia owned the house – Dave and Gus rented their flats – and presumably the new loft conversion was so she could acquire another tenant.

'On our way to the shops.' Tricia released her hair from its white band, and scraped it back again. It was something she did often, symbolic perhaps of a fresh start. 'Sandals and trainers. Cost a fortune. Ian's away. Pippa, for heaven's sake! On business, he *said*. Liam!'

'What is it Ian does? I'm afraid I've forgotten.'

'Spare parts.' Tricia blinked several times. 'For the motor industry.'

'And he's required to travel extensively.'

'You're so lucky, Jane.'

'Am I? In what way?' She was going to be late getting to The Spruces.

'You had a career, used to be a head teacher.'

'Head of English.'

'Liam's learning to read. Phonics.' She had to shout above the noise of the baby and the hammering in the loft conversion. 'And sometimes they memorise whole words. Liam can read elephant and skyscraper.'

Jane was thinking that perhaps she ought to offer to look after Ada while Tricia took the other two to buy new shoes. No, it would be the thin edge of the wedge and she had never been good with babies. Besides, Eddie would be expecting her. One of the staff would have told her what day it was. *Your friend will be here soon.*

Tricia was looking up at the loft conversion. 'Ian says the weight of them makes the house sink. He doesn't like Mr McNeill, they had an argument, but I think it's because he's losing his hair. Ian is, I mean.' She released her own hair again, struggling to catch the escaping wisps as she pushed up her band. 'It's always been a problem and I'm afraid Pippa may have inherited it.'

'Your hair? It's a pretty colour.' Most people had an irrational dislike of at least one part of their body. With Jane it was her teeth, which were nothing like the ones in toothpaste ads. Did it matter? Probably not. So why did the ads make her so cross?

'Right then, I'd better be off. I'm on my way to The Spruces to visit Eddie.'

Tricia put her head on one side, in a gesture of sympathy that made her look like a bird listening for worms. 'It must be a relief you've found somewhere safe. I mean somewhere where they know how to care for people with … no, what I meant, where you don't have to worry about her, if you know what I mean.'

'I do.' Jane moved on, ignoring the chorus of "it's not fairs", the familiar cry of siblings asserting their rights. A sense of fairness was innate. Strange really, when so few things in life were fair, but perhaps the wish for justice was a survival strategy. Marjorie Underwood, head of Science, would know. Jane missed the staffroom discussions, almost as much as her English classes. Reading and listening to the radio was not sufficient. One required the stimulation of others in order to keep one's brain active. And crosswords, of course. She only needed one word to complete last Sunday's. *Conceal about old amplifier for crime.* Eight letters. Conceal. Hide. Amplifier?

With a heavy heart, she set off again for The Spruces. Conversation would be limited but some of the other residents were more *compos mentis* than Eddie, and the staff were friendly – mostly foreign but why not? They were glad of a job, cheerful, kind, patient. Jane's eyes filled with tears and she brushed them away with her sleeve. What on earth was the matter with her? It must be the weather, overcast and muggy. Removing her cardigan, she hung it over one arm. *Put your best foot forward.* Or some such nonsense. *I never saw a wild thing sorry for itself.* Thomas Hardy, she thought. No, D.H. Lawrence. If Tricia Tidewell wanted a career why on earth had she had three children in quick succession? And why, for heaven's sake, was Dave refusing to tell Simmy what had happened to her mother?

Had she but known what was to come, the Tidewell children and Simmy's mother would have been the least of her worries.

FOUR

Eddie was sitting on her bed, with her hairbrush in her hand. Since moving into The Spruces, she had put on weight and Jane suspected that, given half a chance, she helped herself to the other residents' sweets and biscuits. In the past, she had been fussy about what she ate, taking notice of the constant supply of information on the media. Drink a glass of red wine for your heart. No, don't. Eat low-fat products. No, don't – they're full of sugar. Eat five a day. No, eat eight.

For a time, they had consumed vast amounts of broccoli until one day Eddie had asked her why she kept cooking such a disgusting vegetable. *But you said we should eat it three times a week. No, I didn't!* Had that been when it all began? Small inconsistencies that gradually turned into larger ones, like the time Eddie had accused her of stealing her raincoat, an absurd accusation since Jane was four inches taller and had a perfectly good raincoat of her own.

Something that had always irritated Eddie, was Jane's liking for Beatrix Potter. *Squirrel Nutkin – oh, for heaven's sake. Jemima Puddleduck? It's just a duck, Jane, you're so sentimental, you've never grown up.* But after the illness took hold, it was a different matter. Eddie had studied Jane's collection of Beatrix Potter books, pointing out particular illustrations and insisting Jane take in the details. Tom Kitten's buttons or Mrs Tiggywinkle's basket of washing. Jeremy Fisher's galoshes or Squirrel Nutkin's missing tail.

'Are you ready?' The bristles of Eddie's hairbrush on the back of Jane's hand had put an end to her trip down memory lane. 'Shall we go downstairs?'

'No!' Eddie scowled at her so Jane concentrated on the wallpaper with its pattern of orange and white flowers on a pale yellow background. When the house was a convent, the walls would have been plain. No wallpaper, no pictures, but possibly a crucifix. The scent of holiness still lingered. Or perhaps it was air freshener. Holy water fragrance?

Eddie had a few items from home, unbreakable ones, a velvet mouse, a small wooden box with a carved lid, a pot of hand cream and a jar of moisturiser. Jane doubted if she noticed them any longer, but they made the room feel a little homelier. Taking a box of fruit jellies from her bag, she removed the polythene, and handed it to Eddie, who ignored it.

'Where's Biddy?'

'Biddy?' The polythene had reminded Jane of the

fluffy handcuffs and made her flinch. With guilt? No, it was fear. 'Sun's out, we could have a stroll round the garden.'

Eddie stayed where she was so Jane sat down again. 'It's a comfortable bed, not too hard, not too soft.'

'Shut up!' Eddie flung out an arm, narrowly missing Jane's glasses.

Taking one of her soft little hands – her own were more like eagles' talons – Jane pulled her up and guided her towards the door. No need for her jacket. She was wearing the green cardigan she had knitted for herself several years ago. Her light blue trousers had a stain on the back. Blue and green should never be seen. Jane could remember her mother reciting the adage, one today's fashion icons would find absurd.

'Down we go.'

'Get off!'

'What did you have for breakfast? Do they give you a cooked one? I always enjoy a cooked breakfast, provided someone else has cooked it.' Keeping up a stream of chatter seemed to work best. 'I was looking at your painting, Eddie, the one with the three cats. Rousseau's well. Eats like a pig.' Not true – he was finickity and turned up his nose at inexpensive cat food – but, in Eddie's company, Jane found herself mouthing mindless platitudes.

'Where's my comb?'

'You want to comb your hair?'

'No!'

'I saw Simmy this morning. Simmy who lives next door, you remember.' *Simmy, whose father won't tell her what happened to her mother.* 'It's the school holidays, six whole weeks. I don't think they're going away. Dave's too busy.'

'Dave's workshop.'

'Yes, that's right.' Something had clicked in her brain, possibly because she had liked Dave, who she once described as a "no frills" person who called a spade a spade. 'Dave is Simmy's father.'

'No, he's not.'

Negotiating the stairs was tricky. Eddie clung to the rail, and Jane clung to Eddie. She smelled of talcum powder, something a care worker sprinkled on her when she helped her to wash? 'It's a nice, warm day. I saw Tricia Tidewell when I was leaving and the two older children were wearing shorts and T-shirts, and the baby had her sun hat.'

'Shat.'

Jane laughed and Eddie turned her head, surprised. 'Oh, Eddie, I do miss you.'

'Where's Biddy?'

The garden was well kept, too well for Jane's taste, with large patio slabs at intervals, and the minimum of plant life, but it felt cool and fresh, compared with the stuffiness of the house. The Spruces was a well-run home – Eddie had an *en suite* bathroom – but Jane's heart sank at the thought she might end up in such a place.

Did Eddie mind? Who could tell? Since she had

always been mildly eccentric, Jane had failed to notice her early symptoms. Or refused to accept they *were* symptoms. Lack of concentration was not unusual. She was an artist and artists were allowed to be in a bit of a dream. The memory loss had come later, and followed a small seizure. Not Alzheimer's, as Jane had feared, but vascular dementia, the result of a stroke or several strokes, when the blood supply to part of the brain was cut off and caused permanent brain damage. Multi-infarct dementia, the hospital doctor called it, following cognitive tests and a brain scan.

The previous summer, Eddie had started to look vacant, and stopped painting altogether, and later she had refused to buy new shoes even though the ones she wore every day had soles that were coming away from the uppers. On the other hand, once, when the sink was blocked, she had become very active and managed to unblock it, thereby avoiding the expense of a plumber.

During her last year at the school, Jane had worried how she was coping with her classes, but art was a subject where you could get away with murder. Loud laughter had come from the art room. One of Eddie's funny anecdotes about her childhood, or Eddie saying or doing something inappropriate? Jane had prayed the Head was not walking past.

'Look, Eddie, a thrush.' Up in the maple tree that stood out from its neighbouring pines, the bird was singing, blissfully unaware of the nature of its chosen location.

'I'm cold.' A hand clutched at her skirt, dragging her

back towards the house.

'A new person, a woman, has moved into number twenty-two, Eddie. I've seen her but we haven't been introduced. Nothing as bad as a ring in her nose, but not far off. Black leggings and a woolly hat, pulled down over her ears, and it's not as though she's young. In her forties, I'd say, but reluctant to join the adult world.'

Eddie had stopped listening. No, she had never been listening. Before she became ill, she had talked too much so that Jane had sometimes felt she "needed some space". Now the house felt so quiet she was sometimes obliged to go for a walk, in the hope of seeing someone she knew, if only by sight. As the person approached she would plan a way of starting a conversation. *How big the children are growing. Your wisteria is doing well.* Or, when all else failed, *Very warm for the time of year – or cold, or wet, or windy.* Acquaintances said "hi", something Jane had never managed, although these days even "hello" sounded a little formal.

'Rousseau sends his love,' she said, painfully aware it was the kind of thing people said to very young children. 'I bought him some cat treats but they were not to his liking.'

Eddie's lips moved and Jane held her breath, but she was only gathering saliva in her mouth so she could spit on a patio stone.

'I saw Gus when I was coming out. Gus, who used to run his own camera shop, you remember. Oh, and Noel sent you his best wishes.' Not true, but mention of Noel might divert her from pulling leaves off a plant. 'His loft conversion company seems to be doing well. They're converting next door's.'

'My loft.'

'Yes, where you did your painting. All your paintings are still on the wall. I often look at them. D'you remember how we went up to London to the Summer Exhibition and they'd hung your picture in a corner and you were afraid nobody would notice it, but they did?'

'A landscape.'

'Yes, that's right.' So she *did* remember. 'It sold for quite a lot of money and we had a little celebration.'

'I'm cold.'

'I took in a parcel for Willa Molloy. You remember Willa, bushy hair and brightly coloured clothes.'

'I'm cold.'

'No, you're not.' She had spoken too sharply and poor Eddie was looking puzzled. 'Yes, all right, we'll go inside again. I was telling you about Willa's parcel. Willa who's married to Brian. The paper had torn and the packages inside … a teacher's outfit, Eddie.' Jane started to giggle. Nerves, rather than because it was funny.

'Brian.' Eddie was refusing to let go of a shrub.

'Careful. It looks prickly. Yes, Brian, he used to be your doctor. Brian and Willa. Handcuffs, Eddie, aren't people odd?'

'I'm cold.'

Back in the dayroom, Eddie sat down heavily and kicked off her slippers. Jane wished they insisted on shoes. Shoes gave a semblance of normality. Slippers were more comfortable but Eddie's feet, unlike Jane's, had never caused her any trouble, and slippers felt like stage one of a decline that culminated in a walking aid.

The dayroom was pleasant enough. Comfy chairs and coffee tables and an enormous television attached to one of the walls. Just now, there was one of those consumer programmes. The sound was turned down too low to hear what the participants were saying but, because of the display of gadgets, Jane guessed it was about cold callers. The correct response, when a voice told you your computer had a fault, was to ring off. Normally Jane did just that, but yesterday she had asked the caller if he believed in God and, when he said "Of course, Madam", she had suggested he must be worried what would happen when he went to heaven, or the other place. So silly, but it had given her a modicum of satisfaction, although later she had felt sorry for the man. Perhaps it was the only job he could find.

Matron was approaching and, by the look of her, it was not good news. She was dressed informally but her dark blue skirt and blouse would have passed as a uniform. Her bronze hair was short and wavy and she had a silver brooch in the shape of a fish, with matching earrings. 'We had a little incident, Miss Seymour, someone's valuables dropped down the toilet.'

'By Eddie? Oh, dear. Had something upset her?'

'Something or someone. Anyway.' She licked her lips in anticipation. 'Part of the frame is rotten so we're having the window in Edwina's room replaced, and since the carpenter is willing to work at the weekend, Doctor thought it might be a good idea if she went home.'

'To my house?'

'She has her new tablets and we're hoping they'll help. One night would be sufficient. You could collect her first thing on Saturday and return her on Sunday evening.'

'This coming weekend?'

'I'll make a note of it.' The matron drifted away, doubtless relieved that Jane had raised no objection, and aware that she had the whip hand since if she protested that Eddie was in no fit state to go home, it could be used against her. *In the circumstances, I'm afraid we may have to ask you to find a different care home, Miss Seymour.*

Looking back, Jane would curse herself – and the gimlet-eyed matron. Of all the weekends she could have chosen, why, oh why, had it been *that* one?

FIVE

Once, Gus had run his own photographic shop. Now he spent most of his time watching sport on a widescreen television. The loft conversion above him must be driving him insane, so it was not surprising that, when Jane decided to go and buy a new light bulb for her fridge, she found him standing staring up at the scaffolding. He was dressed in baggy trousers and a brown pullover, and, in spite of it being well after lunchtime, was still wearing his bedroom slippers.

'Good morning, Gus.'

'Jane.'

'How's the conversion progressing?'

'You may well ask.' Gus had an interest in wildlife, but Jane doubted if many birds nested in Faraday Road, or were starlings and sparrows immune to the noise of loft conversions?

'Has Mrs Garcia been round lately? I wonder who she's planning to let it to.'

He gave a sour laugh. 'As if we'd have any say in the matter. I chose a top-floor flat so I wouldn't hear footsteps tramping up and down. That Noel has a lot to answer for.'

'His are not the only loft conversions.'

'If you say so. As a matter of fact, I've been thinking of moving. Finding somewhere —'

'Moving?' Jane's stomach lurched. 'Oh, you don't want to do that, Gus, you might find the new place was even more noisy. Besides you have friends in Faraday Road. You like it here.'

'If you say so.'

'We'd miss you. I know Simmy would. Only last week, she said you were like the bear in a favourite picture book she had when she was small. She meant because you hibernate in the winter. Not that I blame you. My windows let in awful draughts. I ought to do something about them. One of Eddie's is being replaced at the weekend.'

'Are you all right, Jane?'

'Me? Why do you ask?'

She had said too much, shown herself up. But why not? Why pretend? Gus was her friend and having him living next door was important. They were on the same wavelength, had the same sense of humour. At least, she liked to think they had.

A familiar four-wheel drive was coming up the road, black with tinted windows, an absurd affectation and highly inappropriate when it came to finding a parking space.

'Talk of the devil.' Gus whipped off his fisherman's cap and gave an ironic bow. 'Here *comes* his lordship.'

'Is Corinne with him?' Strictly speaking, Noel and Corinne's house was not in Faraday Road. It was right at the top, on the corner, and its front door was in Vernon Road, where the houses were semi-detached and double-fronted. Four bedrooms or, if a loft conversion had been added, five, not to say, six. Why had Noel bought a four-bedroom house when, until Corinne turned up on the scene, he had lived alone? So many lacked a decent home, while others saw property as an investment. Still, for all she knew, he had inherited the place.

'I suppose she must be good in the bed department.' Gus gave a disparaging laugh. 'How long do you suppose it will last?'

'Apparently Corinne abandoned her husband and son to move in with him.'

'More fool her. Where did she meet him, d'you know? If she'd taken the trouble to find out …'

'Find out what precisely?'

Gus smiled to himself. He liked to give the impression he was the easy-going type, but his darting eyes gave him away. 'Rumours abound, Jane, rumours abound.'

'But they *are* only rumours.' Why was she defending Noel? Perhaps it was poor Corinne she was thinking about. *Poor* Corinne, who had left her husband and child.

Gus was muttering something about an airhead.

Jane looked up at him. 'I've never known what that meant.'

'Yes, you have. Nothing between the ears.'

'She's nice-looking, takes trouble with her appearance.'

'If you like that kind of thing.'

'Don't all men?' It was a ridiculous conversation, one she wished she had never started. *Had* she started it? She felt upset, out of all proportion. She had let Gus know she would miss him if he moved and he had not responded how she hoped he would.

Noel had pulled up close by, and Jane noticed how the passenger seat was piled high with supermarket bags. His job to do the weekly shop? Surely not. No, she was in danger of gender stereotyping, not that Corinne was likely to have been chosen for her housekeeping skills, although she could well be someone who shopped locally for particular delicacies, a special kind of cheese or those melt in the mouth tarts from the Portuguese café.

Eddie had always loved sweet things. Country walks had usually ended with a self-indulgent afternoon tea – scones with cream and jam, followed by home-made lemon drizzle cake. Memories of Eddie, before the illness took hold, should be happy ones. In the main, they were, except the contrast between then and now was ever-present, and sadness as everyone knows is a far stronger emotion than happiness. That was why the soap operas were always full of misery and pain.

Gus was pointing at Rousseau, strolling down the road. 'Been sniffing that clump of weeds.'

'Has he? Cats have a superior sense of smell, but not

as good as dogs' I believe.'

'Cats are killers. Millions of feathered victims every year.'

'Rousseau's too well fed.'

'Oh, it's nothing to do with hunger.'

'Yes, well, I know how you feel.' Rousseau was rubbing his face against Gus' shoe, moving on to Jane and curling his tail round her leg. Noel had joined them. He bent to stroke the cat but Rousseau turned away, letting out one of his ear-splitting yowls.

'Discerning creatures, cats,' Gus said.

'How right you are.' Noel snatched Gus' cap and crammed it on his own head. 'How are you, you old reprobate? Used to sell cameras, Jane, but we're all photographers now.' He patted the phone in the pocket on the leg of his trousers. 'Guess what I did in my younger days?'

'I've no idea.'

'Male model.' Noel smoothed back his hair and walked a few paces, pretending he was on a catwalk. 'What do you think? I was slimmer in those days, a slip of a thing.'

Gus was laughing, and Jane felt put out. The times she had listened to his complaints about Noel's loft conversions. Now he was giving the impression the two of them were good chums.

'Need to be fit to be a model.' Noel returned Gus' cap and leapt in the air, clicking his heels together before coming back to earth, or rather pavement, with a bump so that one of his legs gave way beneath him.

He rubbed his ankle. 'With deportment like yours, Jane, you could have been a model yourself.'

'I think there's a bit more to it than good deportment.' She had to raise her voice above the barking of the dog at number twenty-six. Its name was Lucky. Lucky for some perhaps. Still, the poor little chap was not taken for enough walks. Perhaps she should offer. No, perhaps not.

'Have you always worn glasses?' Noel peered at her face. 'They suit you. Last time I had a check-up, it turned out I need them for reading. *Anno domini* and all that. Getting past it.'

'That I would doubt.' Jane picked up Rousseau and put him under one arm. 'Eddie's coming back at the weekend, while they repair the window in her room.'

'To your house?' Noel looked genuinely concerned. 'If you need any help.'

'Thank you, Noel, but it's only for one night. And two days,' she added, attempting a cheery smile. 'I don't know about you two, but after I've taken this creature home, I'm thinking of visiting the Portuguese café to indulge myself with coffee and one of their delicious pastries.'

Neither of them offered to accompany her.

36

SIX

On the way back to her house, a voice called Jane's name and she tensed. It was Willa. Not the parcel, the missing handcuffs. Would Willa be prepared to admit to what she had ordered? Possibly. Perhaps such outfits were run of the mill these days. Should she feign ignorance, or admit the guilty truth and collect them from behind the herbs and spices?

'How are you, Jane?'

'I'm well, thank you.'

'It must be a relief not having to get up early each morning and go to your school. Apparently, teachers burn out with all the stress. Is that what happened to you?'

'No, I retired at the correct age.' A multi-coloured scarf had been wound round Willa's bush of wiry hair. Some of her clothes were from the Turkish shop. Her round face was not unattractive but, in Jane's opinion, she applied rather too much lipstick. Today it was fuchsia pink.

'It's Arthur.' Willa let out a long, dramatic sigh.

'Your son?' Jane pictured her, dressed in the patent leather knickers. Not a pretty sight.

'Say if it's out of the question but I was rather hoping … I thought …'

Jane waited but all Willa managed to produce was another heavy sigh.

'You need some advice?'

'Not advice, Jane, a tutor.'

'What kind of tuition does he require?'

'English. Grammar. How to construct a sentence. No problem with maths and science but you need to pass English or you're not allowed to stay on for your A-levels and he wants to study medicine, follow in his father's footsteps. Quite honestly, Jane, I don't think he's the first idea what a sentence is. I blame computers. No, don't tell me now. Think about it. Obviously, I'd pay the going rate.'

Jane *had* thought about it, but it was never a good idea to sound too keen. Teaching the boy two or three times a week during the summer holidays might be quite amusing. Sentence analysis. Some of the basics of the English language.

'Just one more thing.' Willa's face came rather too close. 'Would you mind not mentioning it to Brian? He and Arthur, not the best of friends. His age. Arthur's age I mean. Fifteen, coming up to sixteen.'

'I won't say a word.'

'So, you'll do it. Oh, thank you.' Willa planted a kiss

on Jane's cheek, most likely leaving a smudge of lipstick? 'You've no idea what a weight off my mind that is.'

'You think Arthur will be agreeable to the idea?' Jane visualised the boy being dragged, quite literally, to her house.

'Won't get a say in the matter. I've told him to jolly well pull up his socks or I'm going to jolly well confiscate his laptop.'

Two split infinitives. The so-called experts said it was now permissible, but Jane disliked the lazy use of language. Eddie had accused her of being pedantic, but Jane had never altered her strongly held belief that correct grammar was the basis of good written work – and clear speech, come to that.

As she walked away, she recalled the rumours, probably untrue, that Willa drank. What gossips people were – not that she herself was immune. Men complained how women gossiped, but surely an interest in people was preferable to a passion for fast cars and football. Listening to groups of men conversing never ceased to amaze her. *All right, mate? New goalie's crap. You can say that again. Nought to sixty in five seconds. Ref needs glasses. See you, mate. Cheers!*

The sun had come out, and Jane felt her spirits lift. Willa's son Arthur was at that difficult age, neither child nor man, but she liked a challenge. Perhaps she should wrap up the handcuffs and push them through Willa's door. She could do it in the dark. No, that might arouse even more suspicion. When the time was right she would dispose of the things in someone else's bin, in a different street, and if anyone saw her she would pretend she was looking for Rousseau.

That weight off *her* mind, she decided to visit the Portuguese café on her own. There might be someone she knew by sight who would welcome a chat and, if not, Mrs Cardozo was always very friendly, and what was so shameful about sitting by yourself? Worry about the handcuffs had been replaced by plans to provide tuition for the Molloy boy. Arthur, an old-fashioned name that was back in fashion. One of her uncles had been called Arthur and, during her childhood, she had heard her father say it was better to draw a veil over his business dealings. Possibly he had ended up in prison. In those days people preferred to sweep black sheep under the carpet. A mixed metaphor, but a rather good one.

Willa was on her way back to her house. She turned to wave and Jane waved back. The day was turning out rather well after all. Eddie for one night was not such a problem and, once she was safely back at The Spruces, she would concentrate on planning the tuition. She wondered what the boy was like. Good at maths, Willa said, so he must be intelligent. A dislike of written work was a common problem with teenage boys but she felt confident she would be able to help.

Arthur Molloy. Little did she know what an important part in her investigations he was going to play. In her search for a culprit.

SEVEN

Tuesday was swimming day. The previous week the pool had been bursting with young women, discussing their hairstyles and fingernails. Half the world lacked the necessities of life and the other half indulged itself in unnecessary adornments. And as for food! Thousands, millions, scraped a living, eating grains of rice – whatever they could find –while the rich nations of the world were glued to their televisions, watching chefs compete to cook prettily arranged platefuls of fig parcels, stuffed with marzipan and pomegranate.

Stepping into the pool, Jane laughed at herself out loud. She was a puritan, and not ashamed of it.

Fortunately, there were only two other people in the water today, a large woman whose features were not flattered by her pink rubber cap, and an elderly man with the boniest shoulders Jane had ever seen. The website for the leisure centre gave the impression the water was blue, but of course it was the tiles that provided the colour.

Twenty-five metres long, with eight lanes, and next to the main pool, a learner one, where a small band of children splashed about, enjoying themselves, all except one little lad who disliked getting water in his eyes.

Swimming was one of Jane's activities. Singing was the other. And today she was combining the two. She could do the crawl, but the butterfly was too much like hard work, and recently she had stuck to backstroke; soothing, although she would prefer to be looking at the sky rather than a white ceiling with brown stains. A three-legged deer? A tortoise or possibly a turtle? As a child, she had lain in bed with measles, and only the cracks in the plaster for entertainment. Eddie had explained it was "art *trouvé*", art found wherever you looked, if only you had the eyes to see it: lichen on red brick walls; the peeling bark of silver birch trees. *You've a closed mind, Jane, you don't think it's art unless it's framed and hanging in a gallery.* Not true, but she had played the ignoramus because art was Eddie's domain, not hers.

Someone blew a whistle and Jane bumped her head on the end of the pool. Two girls, aged about nine or ten, had done dive bombs into the water and it was against the rules. So was swearing, ducking, pushing, and petting.

The whistle blew again. 'Don't run!' And the girls, who had climbed out of the pool, clung together, giggling. Poor things, it was worse than school. Quite recently, the pool had been renovated; no chipped tiles or broken taps, and the attendants were smartly dressed in white T-shirts and green shorts. They sat on chairs, high above the water, waiting to save lives. What did these lithe young men and women think about the odd bods that swam slowly back and forth? Probably never gave them a thought. It was a job, not well paid but reasonably agreeable, and possibly the first rung on a ladder that led to a career as a personal trainer.

As she moved through the water, she sang, leaving out the odd word, either because she had forgotten it or because she was out of breath. 'Row the boat, row the boat, steadily onwards, de dum de de dum dum, submit to the tide. If we keep on rowing and something the something, we'll get where we're going ahead of the tide.'

Choir was on Wednesday afternoon, mostly retired people but a few younger ones. It provided companionship and people claimed it was good for your physical and mental wellbeing. Jane had made a friend of a kind. She was called Yvette and she had a habit of removing specks of fluff from her cardigan, and from other people's clothes too. Fluff. The handcuffs. *Don't think about it*. Eddie home in four days' time. Did she still think of it as home? No, The Spruces was her home now. But she might be pleased to see Rousseau.

'We'll get there, we'll get there by rowing together.' She swam faster, trying not to think about the offending item, hidden behind the herbs and spices. Eddie disliked spicy food so it was fortunate meals at The Spruces appeared to be bland, not to say tasteless. What would she be doing now? Sitting on her bed, staring into space, or down in the day room, watching the flickering images of daytime telly. Jane's throat constricted, and she climbed briskly out of the water, pulling off the red wrist band with the number of her locker.

Getting dried and dressed was the least pleasant part since the changing rooms had slimy floors and it was not uncommon to find the odd sock or even a pair of knickers, and once, a stringy purple thing she supposed must be a thong. She had considered joining a health club, where only an exclusive few would use the pool, but peeing in the water was hardly the preserve of the masses.

Feet dried first, and slipped into sandals. Swimming costume removed. It was made of smooth, synthetic material but still stuck round her middle. Clothes pulled on or up as fast as possible. Her cold fingers always struggled with the hooks on her bra. It was right what they said, that pleasure was relief from pain. Food when hungry, a drink when gasping with thirst, and warmth when your body felt so chilled it had started to ache. Perhaps if she had more fat on her she would feel less cold, but putting on weight would be like the beginning of the end.

Blissfully warm, and pleasantly tired, she opened the door of her cubicle and came face-to-face with a familiar figure.

'Corinne.' She would have to stop and have a few words.

'Jane, what a surprise and how lovely to see you. Do you come here often? Sorry, Noel's always accusing me of talking in clichés. You were an English teacher, weren't you? When I was at school I don't think we did clichés. Metaphors and similes but I never understood the difference. And I was hopeless at spelling. We had a test twice a week and I was nearly always bottom. Corinne's bottom, everyone used to say. It was a huge joke.'

'Children can be cruel.'

'Oh, no, it was the teacher. Are you a good swimmer? I'm not. I like swimming in the sea, but it's such a long way to travel and then you'd have to drive all the way back.'

'I've just completed my ten lengths.' Corinne's swimming costume would have better suited a slenderer figure, but the shade of *eau de Nil* was pleasant enough.

'Oh, you've had your swim. What a shame, we could have had a coffee together. I tell you what, if you wait in the café; I only ever do four lengths. After that I'm shattered. I do it for Noel's sake.'

'He likes you to be fit?' It was a malicious thing to say since it could be taken to mean Noel thought her overweight, but Corinne found it hilarious.

'So I can swing from the chandelier!'

'Yes, I see.' She did, but spoke in the kind of tone that implied she had no idea what Corinne was talking about.

'You and Noel are friends, aren't you?'

'I like to think so.' How did Noel stand the woman? Gus was right: it must be the sex.

'He says you're an expert in English. English Literature, isn't it, Jane? Noel goes running.' Corinne clenched her stomach muscles. 'Lots of people do, don't they, but I get out of breath. It's my metabolism, do you think that's what it is?'

'I doubt it,' Jane said, but a group of school children were hurrying past, little girls, giggling and squealing, and Corinne misheard.

'Yes, I thought you'd know about it. Noel says you're a fount of wisdom. What is a fount? Noel knows everyone in Faraday Road. He's very friendly. Everyone likes him. He introduces me to people but it's so difficult remembering their names. Not yours, Jane. Jane Seymour, she was married to Henry the Eighth. Was she beheaded or divorced?'

'Neither. She died, following complications after the birth of her son.'

'Oh, what a shame. When your parents chose the name —'

'It's not actually my first name. Dora, after my grandmother, but I prefer Jane. You complete your four lengths and I'll find us a table.'

EIGHT

The café turned out to be empty apart from the young woman behind the counter, who could have been Eastern European, possibly Romanian or Estonian.

'Good morning.' The smell of chlorine lingered, but the woman had probably become immune to it. 'I'm waiting for a friend if that's all right. I'll order when she joins me.'

The woman nodded and smiled and Jane felt encouraged to continue the conversation. 'Have you worked here long?'

'I like and the hours are good.'

'Where do you come from?' Always a dodgy question but the woman's accent was strong enough to convince Jane she had not been in the country very long.

'Poland. My husband is carpenter and I have a child. He is five. Oscar – he is called Oscar.'

'Nice name.' It was popular in England, among people who in all likelihood had never read *The Importance of*

Being Earnest, or *The Ballad of Reading Gaol*. Jane had an idea it was spelled with a 'k' in Poland, but she had no wish to sound nosey. Friendliness and being intrusive, it was always a fine line. 'Does he like his school?'

'Oh yes, his teacher, she is very kind.'

'Good. I used to be a teacher, but in a comprehensive school. For older children.'

'I would like.'

'To be a teacher? Perhaps you could be one day.' Could she? Jane had tried hard to help her pupils reach their full potential and sometimes it had slipped over into impossible ambitions. That was what Eddie had said, but surely it was better than accepting their parents' plans for them – to stack shelves at the local supermarket or find some low-level job with the council.

Jane sat down and the woman began stacking cups and saucers. A folded newspaper lay on the table, one of the free ones you could pick up on the bus. The headline made no sense so Jane found her reading glasses and scanned the story, something about a competitor in a reality show who had split up with her fiancé, a pop singer Jane had never heard of.

'What a world we live in.' She had spoken out loud and the Polish woman looked up and Jane felt she had to explain. 'Just a silly story in the newspaper.' She could ask her about Poland – did they have silly reality shows and puffed up celebrities? Surely not, although she had an idea they took part in *Eurovision*.

By the time Corinne joined her, she had grown tired of

speculating about the woman behind the counter. After she retired, she had persuaded herself she enjoyed people-watching. *It was fascinating. People were all so different and had such a variety of mannerisms and facial expressions.* Not true. Normally, it was exceedingly tedious, as were most overheard conversations.

'That was quick.' She pushed out a chair with her foot so Corinne could sit opposite her. Plastic seats with plastic backs. Metal legs. Not particularly comfortable and inclined to skid on the polished floor.

Corinne was short of breath after her brief foray into the water, and the look in her eyes confirmed Jane's suspicion that she wanted to *talk*. About her son perhaps. How old was he? Noel said he was called Barnaby and he never came to see them.

Jane ordered two cappuccinos and Corinne started talking into her phone. 'Yes. No. Yes, of course, darling. I'm at the pool. The swimming pool. The café actually, darling. With Jane. Jane Seymour.' She pulled a face, an apology for the interruption. 'Yes, six lengths.' She pulled another face, this time to let Jane know she was lying. 'Yes, I'm sure she is, much better than me. Yes, all right, my darling. Love you. Bye, sweetheart, bye.

'Noel sends his love. He's at number twelve, talking loft conversions.' She leaned forward, showing ample amounts of breast, something Jane found oddly titillating. 'He likes you, Jane, and admires the way you've … oh, I'm sorry, I never say the right thing. Your friend, the one who got ill. In a home, Noel said, so sad.'

Two young women had come into the café, both wheeling buggies. Their offspring appeared to be asleep, which was a blessing, and Jane hoped Corinne's high-pitched voice would not wake them. Fortunately, when she spoke again it was in a whisper.

'I'd love to have one.'

'A child?'

'Seeing all those babies in Faraday Road has made me broody.' Corinne's shoulders sagged. 'Noel thinks we're too old, but you hear of men in their seventies, even their eighties.'

'You do.' The cappuccino was too hot to drink but lifting froth on her spoon gave one something to do with one's hands.

'Noel's only forty-five. And I'm six years younger.'

'Thirty-nine.' The number had slipped out, as though she had been given some mental arithmetic.

'I try to keep in good shape. On TV it said fitness means you're more likely to conceive. I'm only telling you this, Jane, because you're a woman of the world. And making love is so much more fun if you think you might get pregnant, and if I told Noel I was expecting he'd be pleased as Punch but so far it hasn't worked, if you know what I mean.'

'I do.' An image of Noel and Corinne in bed together made her flinch.

'I'm on a diet,' Corinne said, 'but I never seem to lose any weight. For breakfast, all I eat is two croissants.'

'I believe they're quite high in calories.'

'Are they?'

'It's all a question of delayed gratification. Which do you want more? Food now, or a slim figure later on.' Jane knew she sounded priggish, but Corinne was watching her, as though she was the oracle.

'Yes, you're right. A moment on your lips. A lifetime on your hips.'

'I was talking generally. Not about you, Corinne.'

'Delayed what was it? You're so clever, Jane. You see, I'm worried about my son.'

'Barnaby, isn't it?'

'Noel says there's a book called *Barnaby Rudge* and he's simple.'

'I like the name.'

'Do you?' Corinne's hand covered Jane's in a gesture of gratitude. 'He's seventeen. In the sixth form. The thing is – he and Noel … you're thinking it's because of me and Gerard going our separate ways. Gerard's my ex. Only it's not that. We've plenty of room. He could stay the night, only he won't. Loyalty to his father, you're thinking, but Gerard and I had been drifting apart for years.'

'How did Barnaby feel?'

'He's seventeen. I told you that, didn't I? An adult, almost, spends most of his time in his bedroom. He's like his father, loathes demonstrations of affection, prefers to be left to his own devices. Such a handsome boy, I adore him. Beautiful eyes. And long, silky hair. Looks like a poet.'

'I'll look forward to meeting him.'

'Oh, I do hope you do. If he ever agrees to come and see us. Jane?' Corinne paused, licking the froth off her lips. 'You know Willa Molloy?'

'I do.'

'Brian's my doctor and I've met Willa but she talks so fast it's difficult to hear what she's saying only I know she has a son only I'm not sure how old he is.'

'Fifteen. You're thinking he and Barnaby could be friends? Arthur, he's called Arthur.'

Corinne sat up straight and locked her fingers. 'It's so good to talk, Jane. I mean, you're such a good listener. Your friend – I'm afraid I've forgotten her name.'

'Eddie. Edwina.'

'And Noel says the two of you had planned to travel round the world after you retired. Such a shame. So unfair. Alzheimer's, isn't it, and they say you can catch it when you're still quite young? Noel does crosswords, to exercise his brain. Cryptic ones. Do you do them? Oh, sorry, I'm talking too much. It's because I don't know what to say – about your friend.'

'Nobody does.'

'Don't they?' Did Corinne have tears in her eyes, or was it the chlorine? Jane recalled reading somewhere that tears produce sadness, not the other way round, a theory that, since it was counter-intuitive, rather appealed.

'Eddie's in a home,' Jane told her. 'The Spruces. It's very well run. She's coming back next weekend, just for one night, while they repair a window in her room.'

'Is she? Perhaps I'll meet her. Noel says she's an artist.'

'Used to be. Quite a successful one.'

'Was she?' Corinne giggled. 'Noel and I met in the bedding department at John Lewis. I was buying a duvet cover and some pillow cases for my spare room, and Noel asked me if Egyptian cotton was better than ordinary cotton. And I said it was softer and lasted longer and we took it from there!' She frowned. 'Willa Molloy? I've heard rumours. I expect you have too. Her clothes. Not to my taste but I suppose some men might find her attractive. Not Noel, he's a high heels man. High heels and plenty of sexy underwear.' She was laughing so much she started to cough. 'You're lucky being old, Jane, you don't have to worry.'

Poor gullible Corinne, the laughter would have died on her lips had she known what was to come.

NINE

How many times during her teaching career had Jane been woken by the alarm and wished she could turn over in bed and go back to sleep? Now she woke early, sometimes at five a.m. and the empty hours stretched ahead.

According to the experts, most people had two or three close friends. Jane had innumerable acquaintances but no one she could call close. Her own fault – she had relied on Eddie's company too much. It had been easier, less of an effort. Why had it never crossed her mind Eddie might become ill, or die? Perhaps she had assumed *she* would go first? After all, she was the elder, although only by a couple of years.

The itchy rash on her wrist had subsided so her appointment at the health centre was unnecessary. Still, it was not the first time the rash had appeared, so she had decided to ask Brian's advice. At the very least, there might be some ointment that stopped the itching.

On her way to the health centre, she spotted Gus

coming up the road, carrying a box that turned out to be full of tins of paint. Did that mean he was going to decorate his flat, prior to putting it up for sale? No, he rented, only needed to give a month's notice. The thought made her spirits sink. If he left, she would miss him more than she liked to admit.

'Morning, Jane, why the long face?'

'I've been worrying about Simmy,' she lied. 'She wants me to ask Dave what happened to her mother.'

'Died.'

'Yes, I know that, but she says Dave won't tell her what happened.'

'Cancer.'

'You know that for certain?'

He shifted the weight of the box. 'It's a fair assumption.'

'Simmy's got it into her head she ran off with another man, and she thinks Noel knows about it. Perhaps *you* could talk to Dave. Simmy's thirteen, a teenager, she has a right to know ...'

'I'm the last person Dave's likely to confide in.'

'I thought you were friends.'

'Is *that* what you thought?' Gus smiled to himself. Recently he had become secretive, not to say, evasive. He was up to something. Connected with the closure of his photographic shop? But that had been over a year ago. The previous day she had decided to ask his advice about the handcuffs, then changed her mind because it would mean telling tales about Brian and Willa's sex life. Worse than that, she would have to confess her own unforgiveable behaviour, opening someone else's parcel.

'Right then, I must be off. Appointment at half past.'

He nodded but didn't ask what kind of appointment. Being discreet? No, it was because he had no interest in her uneventful life.

Almost ten to. Jane was always on time for appointments whereas Eddie had had a habit of being late. No concept of time, she used to say, laughing when Jane pointed out that, were that the case, she would sometimes be early.

Sitting in the crowded waiting room, she struggled to rid herself of stupid self-pity. What was the matter with her? Thousands of people were in dire straits whereas she had a comfortable home and enough to eat. Somewhere there must be someone who was worse off than anyone else in the world. It was a thought she had had before, not a cheerful one since it meant making a mental list of all the worst things that could happen.

'Jane.' Brian was standing in the long corridor that adjoined the waiting room, and she stood up, hurrying to join him. 'Come along in.' He welcomed her into his consulting room, gesturing towards a chair close to his own. 'What's bothering you?'

'Something and nothing, Brian.' She pushed up the sleeve of her flowered blouse. 'The redness is mainly the result of scratching it during the night. I wouldn't have bothered you, but I've had it before.'

'Ah.' He studied the rash with interest. 'Has it

56

appeared on any other part of your body?'

'No, that's the odd thing about it.'

'And you say you've had it before. When would that be? During the last few weeks or months?'

'Yes. Yes, I think so. I forget the first time. Weeks rather than months.

He leaned back, hands locked behind his neck. 'Skin. Where would we be without it, and frequently an outward expression of our inner lives. Fascinating. The loss of your close friend and companion. Not a death as such, but a bereavement nevertheless. Eddie's condition developed slowly, gave you time to adjust, prepare, but the loss is no less painful.'

'Eddie going into The Spruces could give me a rash on my wrist?'

He smiled but said nothing. A kind man but also excessively aggravating.

'I thought it might be something I'd eaten.'

'An allergy? I doubt it. Have you added something to your diet recently?'

'I don't think so.'

He smiled again. 'If you're agreeable, I'd like to fix up a longer appointment. Next week, at the end of my surgery, so I can extend the consultation.'

Extend the consultation? For counselling? Was Brian trained in such matters? Had he been on a course? Unlikely. An old joke sprang to mind. *What's the difference between a doctor and God? God doesn't think he's a doctor.*

Poor Brian, he was doing his best and she ought to be grateful. Was she alone in feeling like two separate individuals – one cynical, critical, with a somewhat sour outlook on life, and another, thin-skinned and sympathising too much with other people's pain.

'I'll think about it. I'll go home and give it some thought.' The usual escape line. 'The rash recurs but usually clears up in a day or two.' An involuntary smile crossed her face, and Brian responded warmly, leaning across to pat her on the arm, blissfully oblivious to the fact that she was picturing him dressed as a schoolboy. Willa was wearing the teacher's outfit, and ordering him to bend over so she could beat him on the bottom. Who wore the handcuffs? Perhaps they were attached to the bed in order to keep Willa, or possibly Brian, a prisoner.

'To express your feelings, Jane, get them out in the open.' He was still talking about the counselling. 'Help you come to terms.'

'Yes, as I said ...' If he was right and the rash *was* psychosomatic, guilt about the handcuffs was a more likely explanation than missing Eddie. 'I thought there might be some ointment.'

'Ah. Treating the symptom rather than the underlying cause.' He stood up and she noticed how a button had come off his shirt, allowing his hairy stomach to bulge through the gap. Jane doubted if sewing was one of Willa's interests but attaching a button only required a stitch or two. Come to think of it, Brian could do it himself. Did men do mending these days or was it just washing up and putting out the bins?

'Good to see you, Jane.' Her response to the offer of counselling was something he was familiar with, something he understood. 'Some people tend to somatise their symptoms, present them as physical complaints, but I've always been impressed with how open-minded you are.'

'You mean for my age.'

'Not at all, not at all. We're two of a kind, lacking the interest in home improvements favoured by many of the residents of Faraday Road, more inclined to intellectual pursuits, matters of the mind. You know Noel's new partner, I expect.'

'Corinne? I do.' Was he going to betray a confidence? She sincerely hoped not. Unless it was something revealing about her background.

'Noel's a friend of yours, I believe.'

'I like to think so.'

Their eyes met but neither of them spoke. Later, she would recall their brief conversation about their neighbours, and wonder where Brian had been when the tragedy happened.

TEN

Rousseau was missing, had been for several hours. A punishment from the gods because she had been foolish enough to open Willa's parcel? If she had not known better, she would have assumed Rousseau had a lady-love. Impossible, so someone in the vicinity must be feeding him. How stupid people were. If whoever it was wanted a cat they should adopt one from the dogs and cats home, instead of "stealing" their neighbour's pet.

Another parcel had been left with her – this time for Mr Owen. At one time, he had been a leading light in the field of educational tests. Retired now, Jane had no idea how he spent his time, but the parcel was a book, a large one. She rang his bell and the door opened immediately, as though he had been watching out for her.

'Parcel for you.'

'Ah. Yes. The man knocked earlier but I was in the lavatory. They don't wait, you know.'

'I believe they're paid per delivery.'

'Even so.' He turned to call up his stairs. 'A parcel, Judith. Miss Seymour's been kind enough to bring it round.'

'Goodbye then.' Jane was not sure if pity or irritation was her primary emotion. As everyone in Faraday Road knew, or almost everyone, Judith had moved out two years ago and was living with her tennis coach in another part of the town. Living in sin. A silly expression but Jane often thought the "anything goes" culture had made life that little bit duller. After all, who would still remember *Brief Encounter* if Celia Johnson and Trevor Howard had left their respective spouses and settled into domesticity?

No sign of Rousseau in Faraday Road so she would have to scour the nearby streets – Vernon Road and Elm Close, then on towards the allotments, where people pretended they had returned to nature, and past the garage where she took her car for its annual service and MOT. It was run by two old men, Maurice and Wally, who she trusted implicitly not to overcharge her, or tell her she needed a new part when the old one was perfectly satisfactory. What a gullible old fool she was.

Past the rough ground that had been bought by a builder who intended to erect four "executive homes", and on towards Church Road, then The Pines, a circular route that would take her back home. A car with a "Baby on Board" sticker had been parked on the pavement. Baby on Board? What were you supposed to do about it? Desist from ramming the back? But the real reason for the stickers was obvious. Look, everybody, we've successfully bred!

Back in Faraday Road, she decided to check the lane behind the houses on the opposite side from her own. Some cats were couch potatoes but Rousseau was a prowler, an adventurer, although she had no knowledge of how far he explored. Pausing at Brian and Willa's garden gate – it was ajar and coming off its hinges – she peered through the greenery, more out of curiosity than because she expected to see Rousseau, who could well have returned home in her absence.

When she gave the gate a push it creaked open, revealing long grass and a collection of overgrown shrubs. Clearly, the Molloys were not keen gardeners. Two apple trees and a plum were in serious need of pruning, and aquilegia had multiplied over what might once have been an herbaceous border. And, in the distance, the wretched cat was crouching on a patch of earth, digging away. And she knew what that meant.

People complained about dogs, but at least they relieved themselves in places where their offerings were clearly visible and could be disposed of in a bag. Cats disliked fouling their own nests and made a point of visiting other people's gardens, a favoured place being a neighbour's vegetable patch. Not that any vegetable could have flourished in Brian and Willa's garden, but that was hardly the point.

'Rousseau!' His ear twitched and he prepared to run. 'No, wait!' Jane moved swiftly through the long grass, hoping to make a grab for him. Glancing at the house, she noted that a conservatory had been built onto the back, quite out of keeping with the rest of the building since it was redbrick with plastic window frames. Through the glass, she thought she could see a sofa and two chairs, flowery ones, the kind people bought for garden rooms. If Willa and Brian spent time in the room, one would have thought they would have taken more trouble with the garden. Open spaces that were left to run wild were a godsend for birds and insects but Jane doubted that was the reason for the negligence.

Did they have a loft conversion? Probably not, since they only had Arthur – not that having one child put off homeowners set on raising the value of their properties. Property was one of Jane's bugbears. Houses were supposed to be homes, not investments, and the fact that her own house was now worth an exorbitant amount only served to make her think she should down-size. One day perhaps. Not yet. The thought of solicitors and surveys, and removal vans was more than she could bear. Never mind the lack of the familiar as she struggled to settle into new accommodation.

No one was about. No sounds of life. Brian would be at work and Willa was likely to be at Pilates or Mindfulness, or her latest passion: Zumba dancing. Jane pictured her in a swirling skirt, her wiry hair flying in all directions. What *was* Zumba dancing? She had an idea it included singing and hand-clapping, something Willa would enjoy.

'Come here, you beastly creature.' She reached out for

Rousseau but he sprang onto the roof of a dilapidated shed, sat down, stuck out a leg and began licking his private parts. If she crept round behind him she might be able to cut off his escape route. On the other hand, it made it more likely she would be spotted, trespassing. The house had an air of silence – she and Rousseau were the only ones about – but Willa could have had a lie-in and be about to come downstairs for a hearty brunch.

Something was going on in the road. One of the delivery people asking for help with an address? It never ceased to amaze her how many of them had arrived in the country, with a smattering of English, and, in no time at all, had mastered the language, sufficient to drive round at lightning speed, making deliveries. Or the sounds could be scaffolders – they delighted in making the maximum noise – or Tricia Tidewell and her noisy brood.

Out of the corner of her eye she saw movement in the conservatory. And froze. Willa, but not alone. Her lips were moving and, by the look of her, she was not in the best of moods. Brian must have come home after morning surgery and said, or done, something that had upset or enraged her.

Hidden behind one of the gnarled fruit trees, Jane had a clear view and, provided she kept still, should be invisible to the occupants of the conservatory.

Even from a distance, it was clear Willa was in a highly-agitated state, gesticulating, wiping her eyes, gesticulating again. The object of her agitation was out of sight. Brian had found out about Arthur's planned tuition?

Jane had not inquired why he was not to know about it, which was not to say she had not speculated. Brian thought Arthur was doing well at school, had never had any doubts he would gain the right grades to be accepted at a training hospital? If he had discovered the truth would he really be so angry? Willa was the volatile one. Brian was dim, but peaceable. The attraction of opposites, she had thought, yin and yang – if you believed in that kind of thing.

As she edged towards the gate, keeping close to the wall, she kept her head down, hoping the two of them were too absorbed in their argument to notice her, but was unable to resist a final peep. And the scene that met her eyes would be imprinted on her memory forever. Willa in floods of tears, and the object of her distress, wearing a mortar board and holding aloft the patent leather knickers. And laughing so much he lost his balance and almost fell against the glass. It was Noel.

ELEVEN

'The loft conversion,' Mrs Garcia, explained unnecessarily, 'I've come to see how it's progressing.' Her jet-black hair was scraped into a bun at the back of her neck and reminded Jane of her old geography teacher, who had humiliated her when she pronounced Chicago as chick-a-go.

'How much longer will it take?' Jane addressed her question to the builder. She thought his name was Martin, or was it Mark?

'Hard to say.' His cigarette bobbed about between his lips. 'Depends.'

'Is there going to be a balcony at the back?' Jane asked.

'There's always a balcony.' Mrs Garcia stared at her with her cold, businesswoman's eyes. 'You saw a copy of the architect's drawings. If you had any objections, then was the time to voice them.'

Since Jane could think of no adequate retort, she was

obliged to keep quiet. The woman should be placating the victims of her noisy building work, not looking down her nose at them. Was her hair dyed? Must be. She looked well into her fifties, possibly more, and not a hint of grey. Jane was not prone to bitchiness but in Mrs Garcia's case she would make an exception.

Noel was approaching and when he spotted Mrs Garcia he gave a skip and a hop. 'Life in the old dog yet.' He winked at Jane. 'All going according to plan, Mrs G?'

'I'm here to check, Mr McNeill. Fitting in the shower has proved problematic but I think we've found a solution. Then there's the doors leading to the balcony. One of them was sticking but I'm hoping it's been fixed. I'm going up there to check.'

'Good-o.' Noel moved closer to Jane and whispered in her ear. 'Owns two more properties she lets out. Got an invalid husband, disabled, fell off some scaffolding.' He raised his voice. 'I could do with your advice, Jane, one large room or two smaller ones, what d'you think? There's still time for a partition.'

'It depends who's going to live there.'

'Fair point. Studio apartment always sounds good.' He jumped up and swung on the scaffolding, and his white T-shirt rode up, revealing firm, lightly-tanned stomach muscles.

'Be careful,' Jane said, but he laughed, letting go too quickly and almost losing his balance when he landed.

'Not as fit as I used to be. Soon be losing my pulling power.'

'That I would doubt.'

It was the first time Jane had seen him since the incident in Willa's conservatory. What would he think if he knew how she had been hiding in the garden? Not her fault – she *had* been trying to retrieve Rousseau – but Noel would accuse her of prying, although perhaps not. After all, he had been mocking Willa, not having sex with her. Poor Willa must have been ousted by Corinne. Was that what had happened? Could Noel really have been having an affair with her, or was it wishful thinking? *O beware, my lord, of jealousy. It is the green-eyed monster which doth mock.* Othello. Act Three, Scene Three, as she recalled. Envy, jealousy – such strong emotions – but ones that would be superseded by the coming disaster.

An unshaven Gus had appeared, rubbing his eyes with large reddened hands that had nails that needed cutting. 'If you want the truth, Noel, I'm pissed off with all these loft conversions. Is it right the people at number thirteen are having one?'

'Seems like it.'

'What d'you mean, "seems like it"? Either they are or they aren't. Started a fashion that's got out of hand. If the houses in Faraday Road had been left alone they'd be listed by now, of architectural interest. Not that anyone cares. Only interested in "adding value to their properties." I blame Mrs Thatcher.'

'Going back a bit, aren't you?' Noel gave him a friendly punch. 'Times move on. All right for you, mate, living off the sale of your shop? How much did it go for?

A fair bit, I imagine even though it's off the beaten track. See, we're both in property, one way and another.'

Gus gave a snort so Noel tried again. 'Not the picnic you think it is, my old mate. Bloke in Vernon Road keeps demanding I go round so he can show me tiny marks on the floor or wall. Needed a magnifying glass to find them. Talk about obsessional, you'd think he'd have something better to worry about. Work was completed five months ago. Probably made the marks himself.'

'Deliberately?'

'Wear and tear, Jane, wear and tear. Just one of those people who make a virtue out of never being satisfied. Think if their living quarters are perfect, their life will be too. Doesn't work like that.'

'No, it doesn't.' Jane would have liked a new carpet in her sitting room but it would mean moving all the furniture. Did she want one that much? Probably not.

Noel was warming to the subject of his loft conversions. 'As you'll know, if you've been up to see, they're finished to the highest standard.'

Jane had not been up to see. Would not have dreamed of doing such a thing unless invited. 'Mine was there when we bought the house. Definitely not up to your standard, Noel. Not even a balcony, never mind a shower room. Eddie used it as her studio.'

'Good old Eddie.' Noel lifted Jane's hand and planted a theatrical kiss on the back of it. 'Not many people can boast they got a picture into the Summer Exhibition. Is it true creativity and madness are closely aligned?'

'Eddie's not mad.'

'Of course not. Just interested in the subject. They say Einstein was autistic. Isaac Newton too. No good at small talk but —'

'Lacking social skills but highly intelligent and obsessed with complex problems.'

'Mine of information, isn't she, Gus? Don't know what Faraday Road would do without her.'

Simmy had come out of the ground floor flat with her hands over her ears. 'I'm trying to read a book about mothers that fail to bond with their babies, but the builders are so noisy I can't concentrate.'

'Hard at it, Sim, keeping Mrs G happy.' Noel smiled at her, turning on the charm. 'Where d'you buy that T-shirt? Wouldn't mind one myself. Character from a computer game, is it? Looks like he's up to no good.' And he bounced up the stairs.

'Dad shouts four-letter words at them.' Simmy had sidled up to Gus and was sucking the cord on her hoodie. 'Anyway, it's not Mark and Lee's fault. Lee likes cats, Miss Seymour. He calls Rousseau "Tiger" and he gives him bits of sausage roll. Gus, do *you* know what happened to my mother? My dad won't tell me so I think she must have run off with another man; only I could have brothers and sisters, half ones I mean. I saw this programme about long lost people and …'

'Couldn't say, I'm afraid.' Gus glanced at Jane, hoping she would help him out, and she opened her mouth to tell Simmy she would speak to her father, then spotted him on

70

his way back from his workshop.

He must have heard what Simmy's high-pitched voice was saying, but he chose to ignore it. With his slight build and deep-set eyes, he reminded Jane of a gnome, the evil one in her book of fairy stories, and the way he talked about the loft conversion, through fiercely clenched teeth, could be a little alarming.

'That landlady woman here, is she?' he said. 'Thought I saw her BMW.'

'She's up in the loft, with Noel.'

Dave fingered his beard. Unlike Gus, he had small, rather beautiful hands, and probably small feet, Jane guessed, although he always wore heavy boots so it was impossible to tell. His beard was flecked with grey, as was the light-brown hair that trailed over his collar. 'Did she say when it would be finished?'

'Mrs Garcia? No.'

Dave licked his lips. They were narrow and very pink, a bit like Rousseau's. 'Expect she'll let it to students? Have you thought of that, Gus? Coming back at all hours, talking at the top of their voices, playing loud music, throwing up on the doorstep.'

'You play loud music, Dad.' Simmy turned to Jane. 'I expect you've heard it, Miss Seymour, through your wall. Jazz. I hate jazz. I've told him he ought to save it for in the workshop where it won't disturb people.'

'See what I'm up against?' Dave took out his tin of tobacco. 'Do this, don't do that. Right, I'm off to the hardware shop. When they come down again, you can tell the Garcia woman I'm not paying any more rent until the building work stops.'

Gus gave one of his snorts. 'You'll get an eviction notice.'

'Thought you were on my side. If we both withheld the cash ...'

'Only have to pay it later. Where else are we going to find? Anyway, the worst of the building work's over, just putting finishing touches.'

'Your friend Noel been softening you up?'

'No.'

'Thought he might have compensated you for the disruption.'

'Why would he do that?' Gus looked distinctly annoyed.

'I spend my time in my workshop. You're in most of the day. Besides, he knows I can see through his smarmy act.'

You're another who's jealous of Noel, Jane thought, because he's tall and good-looking, and women are drawn to him like wasps to a picnic. Listening to Dave's exchange of words with Gus, she had been a little surprised. Because they lived in the same house, she had assumed they were on good terms. Had something happened? It was true Gus had a habit of walking up and down, but his flat was carpeted and she doubted he disturbed Dave and Simmy very much. Perhaps Gus knew how Simmy's mother had died and was threatening to tell Simmy? But why would he do that, and how *had* she died?

It was possible Eddie knew, although she had never mentioned it and, even if she did, she was unlikely to remember now. Looking back, Jane could see that the first signs of her illness had manifested themselves in mood changes and an inability to make decisions. As the condition progressed, Jane had downloaded an article with a list of symptoms and their likely progression, although it varied from person to person. Vascular dementia, the second most common kind after Alzheimer's, beginning suddenly after a stroke. *Had* Eddie's symptoms been sudden? Not as far as Jane recalled, although the fact that she already had a streak of eccentricity could have disguised them. Her powers of concentration had never been good, except when she was painting, and liking rather too many tots of whisky could have explained her unsteadiness on her pins.

Jane had given up alcohol, a decision based on superstition rather than reason. If I deprive myself of something I enjoy, the gods will reward me. Like hell they would! Sometimes, Eddie had accused her of taking life too seriously, worrying over things she could do nothing about. But there had been plenty of laughter and merriment, like when they decided to go camping, bought all the gear, and ended up in a sea of mud, returning home the following day and donating the tent to a local charity shop. *Your idea, Jane.* Had it been? *You're a masochist, think suffering's good for the soul!*

Simmy had disappeared but Dave and Gus were still

arguing about Mrs Garcia and the prospect of new tenants in the loft conversion at the top of their house. Jane wondered why Gus still rented. Surely if he had sold his shop he could afford to buy. He preferred the freedom of renting? If he took the fancy, he could move up north to be nearer his daughter and granddaughter? But rents were high and felt like money down the drain. She wanted to ask him if that was what he had in mind. If he moved she would miss him more than she liked to admit. Would he miss her? But she was not prepared to risk such a question. They were friends, nothing more, and that was how it would remain.

'Ironmonger,' Dave said, 'need some linseed oil. French polishing. Lucky we've still got a shop around the corner.'

'What *is* French polish?' Jane asked, 'I've often wondered.'

'It's a process, not a material. Have to apply lots of thin coats – shellac dissolved in alcohol – and use a pad lubricated with oil. Come to the workshop sometime and I'll give you a demonstration.'

Jane smiled. 'Thank you, Dave, I might take you up on the offer.' He was a bit of a mystery – she would welcome a chance to get to know him better – and it would mean she had an opportunity to ask a few tactful questions about his dead wife. For Simmy's sake, not her own.

TWELVE

Yet another parcel had been left with her, but since it was for Noel, Jane was happy to oblige. He must be out, and so must Corinne, so she would wait a bit, and spend the intervening time preparing for Eddie's visit. It preyed on her mind, kept her awake at night. What would Eddie want to do? If the weather remained warm would she be prepared to sit in the garden? Seeing her old surroundings might trigger off memories and Jane could point out how Rousseau's bed of catmint had spread and he enjoyed rolling in it and came in, smelling delicious. What would she want to eat? No use agonising about it. If she refused what Jane had prepared, she could always fill up with the biscuits she liked so much. After all, it was only for two days and one night.

The fact that she was relieved the visit was short ought to have made her feel guilty. Or sad. She felt neither, felt nothing, apart from apprehension that if things went badly, it might convince the matron at The Spruces that

Eddie needed more care than The Spruces was able to offer.

What was she thinking? It was not as though Eddie would provide an account of her brief weekend at Faraday Road. Even if she did, her words would be incomprehensible. Sometimes Jane tried to picture her own brain. The links between cells becoming weak, blurred, the cells dying off at the rate of knots. Oh, for heaven's sake! Make up Eddie's bed, have a quick flick round with a duster, and deliver the parcel.

With it tucked under her arm – it was something in a small, flat box, possibly a tablet or an e-reader – Jane walked the short distance up the road, stopping on the way to put two beer cans in the nearest wheelie bin, and knocked on Noel's door.

'Jane!' Corinne clasped her hands in delight. 'What a lovely surprise. Oh, is this for us? I was upstairs, doing my nails and the bell doesn't always work. Come in. No, please do. Noel was out but he's back now, working in his office, planning a new loft conversion. They're wonderful, aren't they? Have you been up in one? Noel shows me the plans and we've got one ourselves, of course, but it was here before ... before me! I hate thinking about Noel's life before *me*. No, that's silly, isn't it? It's best to live in the present, isn't it? How are you?'

'I'm well, thank you.' Jane stepped inside.

Heavily made-up eyes shining, Corinne was squeezing the parcel. 'Something hard. A surprise. Noel's always giving me presents. Last time, it was a vanity case. Come through.' She led Jane into a large, airy room with a cream carpet, and Jane wondered if she should remove her shoes. The sofa, like the rest of the room, looked new. Upholstered in a linen fabric – pink roses and grey leaves on an off-white background – it had been placed at an angle, providing a good view of a television set with a screen that was even larger than the one in Gus' flat.

'Lovely room, Corinne, you have very good taste.'

'Do you think so? Oh, thank you, Jane. Noel had let the house become a little shabby but he gave me a free hand and it's such fun choosing furniture and fittings, isn't it? And they have such useful hints on those TV programmes. I don't expect you watch them. I expect you're reading books. I read them too. Maeve something – she's a wonderful writer, Irish.'

A glass-topped coffee table held an assortment of up-market magazines – *Better Homes, Vogue,* and something called *Islands.* 'Puts my place to shame,' Jane said, 'but unfortunately Rousseau has a habit of sharpening his claws on the furniture.'

'Your cat? I'd love one. Or a dog. If I had a dog, it would be one of those small, fluffy ones that sit on your lap.'

As usual, Corinne was smartly dressed. Today it was a navy-blue, body-hugging dress and a short matching jacket. Red high heels with the ankle straps that always reminded Jane of prostitutes, but they could be the fashion these days. Were her eyelashes her own? They were exceptionally thick and dark. Still, so was her hair.

'Noel had to sort out a problem with a conversion,' she was saying, 'the one next to your house actually, something to do with the balcony. People love balconies, don't they? Opening the doors and pretending you're on the French Riviera.'

'My loft doesn't have one.'

'Oh, what a shame.' Corinne had misinterpreted her remark. 'I'm sure Noel could arrange for you to have one added.'

'Our loft had been converted before we bought the house. Quite a modest affair. Eddie used it as her studio.'

'Did she?' Corinne bit her lip. 'How is she? You must miss her terribly. I didn't know she was an artist. I'd love to learn to paint. You can go to classes but I'm not sure I've any talent. I must tell you, Jane, I think I may ... you know, what I told you – at the swimming pool ... early days yet but if I'm right Noel will be thrilled. He loves children.'

'Jane!' It was Noel, dressed in jeans and a bright red sweater. 'To what do we owe the pleasure?'

'A parcel.'

'Left at your house? What would Faraday Road do without you?'

'What indeed?' The slight tension between her and Corinne had evaporated. Noel was an expert at putting people at their ease. One of the reasons everyone in Faraday Road, or almost everyone, liked him.

Corinne was locking and unlocking her fingers. The way her hands kept moving was something she had in common with Noel. But, as far as Jane could tell, it was the only thing. Shocked at her malice, Jane said the opposite to what she was thinking. 'Corinne seems to have a flair for interior décor. Your house is looking very smart.'

Noel laughed. 'Come and see the rest of it.' He steered her back into the hall and through another door.

'The dining room,' Corinne explained, 'but we only use it for visitors, don't we, darling? Dave found the paintings at an auction.'

'Oh, I thought they must be your ancestors, Noel.'

'No, just some portraits,' Corinne said.

Noel winked at Jane, and she was afraid Corinne had noticed. 'We've had a new kitchen put in. I was perfectly happy with the old one but —'

'But it was so old-fashioned, darling. Not even a Belfast sink. Come and see, Jane.'

The pristine décor was making Jane increasingly aware of how the rooms in her own house needed what people called a "make-over". Would she bother? Almost certainly not. Like the proverbial well-loved jacket, thrown out, amid protests from its owner, her worn carpets, shabby furniture, and aged kitchen units felt comfortably familiar.

In Corinne's kitchen, a row of stainless steel implements hung on the wall behind a catering-size range. The worktops were granite and Jane thought she could spot three different coffee-makers. Even the bowl of fruit on the scrubbed pine table was tasteful – two avocado pears, four shiny apples, and a handful of nuts.

'Faraday Road dates back to the turn of the century.' Corinne ran a finger over a chopping board with a picture of a cow. 'The last century, I mean.'

Noel gave her a friendly slap on the bottom and she bumped him with her shoulder and began describing the blender that made smoothies and all kinds of other delicious drinks. 'Yoghurt, grated ginger and green tea. And it crushes up the ice too, doesn't it, darling?'

The other women in the road exchanged glances when Corinne's name was mentioned. Perhaps they envied her, living with the glamorous Noel, who was charming to everyone, women and men alike. How much did anyone know about his earlier life? Not much, Jane guessed, whereas Corinne was unable to resist baring her soul, and people, who are both irritating and vulnerable, are bound to get hurt.

Now she was talking about babies. 'Have you seen him, Noel, the latest addition at the Emersons? So cute and such a lovely name. Gethin. I think it's Scottish, or is it Welsh?'

Noel gave a snort. 'If you want my opinion, one sprog's much like another.'

'No, they're not, darling!'

Jane glanced at Noel, trying to assess if he knew Corinne was trying to get pregnant, but his face gave away nothing. They had left the kitchen and were climbing the stairs so she could inspect the bedrooms.

'Need some more windows open.' Noel pulled his

sweater over his head, and Corinne hung it over her arm. It smelled of something musky and Jane suppressed a fantasy, herself and Noel, had she been several years younger, although there *were* men who had a penchant for older women.

'How's Eddie?' he asked, and she felt herself blush, and he would think she disliked talking about The Spruces.

'She threw another resident's belongings down the loo.'

'Oh dear.' His hand covered a grin.

'It's all right, I feel the same. Don't know whether to laugh or cry.'

'That's the spirit.'

'Do you like the duvet cover, Jane?' Corinne patted the king-size bed. "Duvet" is French for cover. I think that's right. Noel thinks it's too pretty, don't you, darling? It's almost the same as the one they had in that TV series about the serial killer. No, I don't mean it was on his bed. The detective, a woman. She was promiscuous but it was because of her childhood.'

'I'd better be off.' Jane took her keys from her pocket. 'Thank you for the guided tour.' Her comments about the bedrooms had been a bit perfunctory, but she was running out of adjectives that would adequately describe the fluffy rugs and fitted cupboards, filled with Corinne's suits and dresses and jogging outfits. Did she jog? Perhaps they were what the marketing men called "leisurewear".

A large photograph in an ornate frame hung on the

landing wall, a striking-looking woman with hooded eyes, reminiscent of Margaret Leighton or Lauren Bacall.

'My mother,' Noel said. 'She died three years ago.' A shadow crossed his face and Jane guessed the two of them had been close. For all his jolly demeanour, he was quite a sensitive soul. Corinne opened her mouth but thought better of it, and they made their way down the stairs with Jane smoothing the back of her skirt, with that silly irrational fear all woman have that it might have caught in their knickers.

'You must come round for a meal next time,' Noel said. 'Incidentally, Corinne went to see Brian Molloy about her ear and he told her infections were the unconscious result of not wanting to hear what people were saying. The man's an idiot.'

'Oh, but he's so kind – and helpful.' Corinne had come in fast. 'Wax, but they don't like to syringe these days. Married to that Willa woman, the one with the hair. Do you know her, Jane? Looks like the mad woman in the attic. *Jane Eyre* – did you see it? We missed the last episode but Noel said she married Mr Rochester, even though he'd been blinded in a fire.'

'Jane was an English teacher, my darling, I expect she's familiar with the works of the Brontë sisters.'

'Are you, Jane?' She gazed at Noel adoringly. In her eyes, he could do no wrong.

When he opened the front door to let Jane out, a boy with a shaved head and a nose-piercing that looked like two bogeys was standing in the front garden.

'Ah.' Noel winked at her. 'Just in time to meet Miss Seymour, one of our neighbours. I see you have a new hairstyle, Barnaby.'

'How do you do?' Jane held out a hand but the boy ignored it, hanging on to the handlebars of his cycle.

'You'll have to wheel it through the house. No, wait, the carpets.' Noel called over his shoulder. 'Corinne, your son's here. What shall we do with his bike?'

'Darling!' Corinne appeared, looking less thrilled than Jane had expected. 'Can't he leave it out here?'

'Likely to get nicked.' Noel hoisted it onto his shoulder. 'Bye for now, Jane, and we'll fix a time for you to come and eat with us. Out of the way, Barnaby, I'll carry it through to the back.'

Barnaby was silent, but the look he gave Noel was something Jane would recall, something that was to give her serious pause for thought.

THIRTEEN

Their first encounter was not encouraging. When Jane opened her front door, he had his back turned, tapping his foot and whistling through his teeth.

'Arthur?'

His head moved but his body remained in the same position. He had a pleasant profile, small nose, slightly jutting chin, and hair, tousled on top but short at the sides. Definitely an improvement on Barnaby's latest style. And no piercings or, if he had, they were not visible; although, come to think of it, he was probably too young.

'Come in then,' Jane said, the "then" to express her mild irritation that he was ten minutes late.

'I'm Arthur.'

'Thought you might be. Follow me. I thought we could work up in the loft. I don't use it very often but there's a table and two chairs so we should be all right.'

His footsteps behind her were a little intimidating and she found herself wondering what size shoes he took.

Large, she imagined; elevens or twelves. How did he feel about the tuition? Not too thrilled by the look of him, but he had turned up, that was a start.

The loft had been the reason they bought the house. A studio for Eddie. Her main source of income had been her teaching, but she sold the occasional painting when she exhibited locally and when her landscape was accepted for the Summer Exhibition, to add to the excitement, it had been bought by a member of the Royal Family. The children at the comprehensive loved her. She was good fun, disorganised, unconventional, and entertaining. Jane had never been "good fun".

Arthur was peering up at the dormer window. Nothing to see, except bright blue sky, but he appeared to have spotted something of interest, a passing bird perhaps. His feet and hands were, in fact, average for someone of his height. Shoelaces undone but Jane had a vague recollection that was the fashion among his generation, although Simmy, who wore white plimsolls, never had trailing laces.

'Come and sit down.' The table was a small one but the correct height for writing. She had placed her own chair opposite his but would take care their knees never met. 'How did you feel when your mother suggested you come here?'

'Sorry?'

'I wondered how you felt about having extra tuition.' It was the kind of question counsellors asked and did not come naturally to her. 'Your mother discussed it with you,

I expect.'

He raised a hand to his mouth, too late to contain a yawn. 'Simmy lives next door.'

'She does indeed. You know her?'

'We play computer games.'

'Really?' Jane was surprised, but presumably computer games transcended an age gap even of two years.

'We're planning a new one, based on Greek myths. Noel will be a rapist and pillager – there were plenty of those – and my mum's the Gorgon.' He was struggling not to laugh. 'The rapist and The Gorgon. The Gorgon had hair made of poisonous snakes.'

Better not to ask. Definitely better. But curiosity got the better of her. 'Why is poor Mr McNeill a rapist?'

'Hades.' Arthur tipped back his chair. 'That's the underworld. Most of the gods lived on Mount Olympus, and Pythia – I think that was her name – was infallible and gave prophecies on the seventh day of the month. My dad'll be Orestes. He killed his mother, who'd killed his father. Agamemnon. I think that's right.'

'So you and Simmy are basing your characters from Greek mythology on the residents of Faraday Road?'

'Apollo taught Cassandra how to use prophecies but she refused to give him her body, but he had it anyway, and put a curse on her so she could still see into the future but no one believed her. That Noel makes me laugh.'

'Yes, well enough of all that.' Jane was a little shocked, not that she was going to show it. Shocked, but also intrigued. 'We need to get started.'

In spite of the sun streaming through the windows, the room felt bleak, alien, as though it knew Eddie was safely ensconced at The Spruces and no longer had need of a studio. It was a room Jane tended to avoid and the decision to use it for teaching Arthur had been taken in one of those defiant moods. *Don't be such a coward. Face up to it. Life moves on.*

'I thought it best to start with a short comprehension. It will give me an idea of your written work and any problems you may have.' She paused, hoping her suggestion would meet with Arthur's approval, but his face was expressionless. 'I've selected a passage about Heathrow Airport. You've been there, I expect.'

He nodded.

'When you were going on holiday?'

'Are you an artist?'

'No. No, my friend. Did you bring a pen or would you like one of these?' She had placed a collection of ballpoint pens and newly sharpened pencils in a glass jar on the table.

Arthur reached out for one of the pens. 'I'm no good at English.'

'What about your other subjects?'

'Maths is OK, and IT, but you have to pass English.'

'Yes, you do.' The powers-that-be insisted on a specified level of Maths and English before pupils were allowed to stay on at school and study for their A-levels, but there must be some who were brilliant at numbers but would never gain the required grade in English grammar. And *vice versa* of course.

Arthur was staring at her. 'Have you got a computer?'

'A tablet. My old one broke but I've bought another.'

A faint smile crossed his face. 'If you need any help ...'

'You're my man. Thank you, I'll bear that in mind.'

She expected him to say "no problem" or "no worries", but he was silent, looking all about him as though he had never seen a loft conversion before. His eyes were red-rimmed, probably from lack of sleep. Was he allowed to play games on his computer until all hours? Jane imagined Brian was the kind of father who issued dictates but failed to follow them through. Willa would be inconsistent. Strict one day, negligent the next.

'You say you like maths and IT, Arthur. What about history and geography?'

'They make us learn this stuff by heart. What's the point when you can look it up online?'

'Yes, I'm inclined to agree. Have you heard of Socrates?'

'Played for Brazil.'

'I was thinking more of the Greek philosopher. He believed in asking his pupils questions rather than telling them facts.'

'The one I'm thinking of died of food poisoning. Beef stroganoff.'

'Really?' She almost added, you learn something new every day, but she was growing impatient and suspected the boy knew perfectly well she had not been referring to a South American footballer. He was wearing black jeans, with rips across both knees, and a blue T-shirt with a picture of a cartoon character, a monster of some sort. Her own clothes were not dissimilar. Determined not to dress like a teacher, she had decided on dark blue trousers and a pale blue T-shirt with three-quarter length sleeves.

'The comprehension.' She passed him a pad. 'Do you normally use lined or plain?'

'Absolutely.' He tore off a sheet. She had meant him to leave it in the pad so she could save it in a hard-backed file, in order to monitor his progress, but he had ripped off the corner, along with one of the holes. He had a faint moustache, faint because his colouring was fair, and he smelled of soap.

Footsteps padded up the stairs and Rousseau's head came round the door. Arthur grinned and reached out an arm. 'Hello, puss. I like tabbies. What's his name?'

'Rousseau.'

'Rousseau.' He leaned across to scratch the cat's ear.

'He lived in the eighteenth century, wrote a book about a boy called Emile.'

'Emil and the detectives.'

'No, I think that came later.'

The day was a warm one. Jane stood up and struggled with the catch on the dormer window. 'Heathrow then. It shouldn't take you more than ten minutes.'

'Absolutely.' Head down, he began scribbling away, holding his pen much as Jane imagined a parrot might hold a stick of celery.

Closing her eyes, Jane attempted to relax. Arthur appeared perfectly at ease, almost enjoying himself. Would he tell Simmy about the lessons? Or if his father was not to know, had Willa sworn him to secrecy. Not easy in a place like Faraday Road where gossip was rife.

The previous evening, on her way to a talk about the global economy, she had bumped into Brian, coming out of a local supermarket with two litres of semi-skimmed milk and a harassed expression. Sent to the shop by Willa no doubt, even though he had been at work all day and Willa was a lady of leisure. The thought made Jane smile, but it was not an amused smile. If something was going on between Willa and Noel all hell would be let loose.

If Eddie had been *compos mentis* they could have attended the talk on the global economy together. Not true. Eddie had no interest in politics, and would have refused, regardless of the fact that Jane always accompanied her to art exhibitions. The talk had not been enlightening but you had to give these things a go. An elderly – very elderly – acquaintance had advised her not to give up any of her interests or activities. *If you do, you'll never take them up again.* How true.

'Finished.' Arthur handed her his sheet of paper.

"Some people at heathrow lost there luggage. If you lose you're luggage you go to lost property. A girl saw it in the café and told them were it was. Heathrow is very crowded. The boy likes airports."

'Your answers are correct, Arthur, but some of the

spelling …'

'I'm not good at spelling.'

'And the word "your" doesn't need an apostrophe. The "your" you want is when something belongs to you, your coat for instance, your luggage. "You're" with an apostrophe is an abbreviation of "you are".'

'You're only allowed one bag, unless you put the other in the hold.'

'You're a seasoned traveller?'

'Absolutely.' He fingered a spot on his chin. 'If you send a text there aren't any apostrophes.'

So he had been listening. 'No, I'm sure.' Jane used her cell phone now and again but never to send texts. It was too fiddly and, besides, if she wanted to tell someone something she rang up. Actually, she disliked the telephone, landline as well as mobile, although on occasion it came in useful. 'Texts are that way because they need to be brief and use as few letters as possible.'

'Absolutely.' He stood up and she thought he was going to leave, but it was only to make it easier to take something from his pocket. 'The money,' he said.

'Oh, thank you. I was going to send an invoice to your mother. No, that's fine if she prefers it that way.' Should she have charged more? Memories of the school, ones she normally pushed away, flooded back. During the last year, she had taught mainly older pupils. They had studied *A Winter's Tale* and *Bleak House*, and the poetry of John Donne, and two of the girls, and one of the boys, had gained places at Oxford colleges. Her final year should have been particularly enjoyable but had been marred by worry about Eddie.

Arthur was searching in his pocket again and this time he pulled out a tissue that had turned into a long grey string. 'You know Gus?'

'I do. Like Simmy, he's one of my neighbours.'

'Yeah, lives above her and her dad. Gus has got this friend and I reckon the two of them are planning something. The first time I saw her I thought she was a man. Moved into number twenty-two. She and Gus were in the café, the Portuguese one. I'd like to learn Portuguese so I could visit Brazil. The other South American countries speak Spanish – I think that's right.'

'It is.' Jane felt shaky. 'You've met the woman who's bought number twenty-two?'

'I reckon Simmy's mother's living in Cornwall. I heard my mum talking to Noel about it. They used to be friends.'

'Your mother and Mr McNeill?' She had to be careful.

'Then that Corinne moved in. In the computer game, she's going to be Aphrodite. Have you heard of Aphrodite?'

'I have.'

He laughed, pushing the grey tissue back into his pocket. 'She was crazy, that's what it said in the book. Aphrodite – a tormented woman!'

FOURTEEN

One cup of coffee a day was Jane's rule, something Eddie
had found ridiculous. *Rules are to be broken, Jane, you're
such a stickler, must be the way you were brought up.* As
though Eddie was immune to irrational habits, although in
her case she called them "sensible precautions". Jane had
looked it up online and "rules are made to be broken" was
first said by Arthur C. Clarke, the science-fiction writer,
although someone else had attributed it to Richard Nixon.

Most of the time, she and Eddie had got on pretty well,
even though the way Eddie had insisted on cutting her
food into small pieces had been a little trying. An only
child and, in Jane's experience, only children tended to
fuss, Eddie had lived with her parents until she was in her
thirties and when they both died, within a few months of
each other, Jane had befriended her. More than thirty
years of friendship, but no friendships are without their
problems. The cinema was one. Jane liked foreign films,
slightly gloomy ones, if she were honest, whereas Eddie

loved musicals and romances. They could have gone their separate ways, in terms of visits to the cinema, but they never had. Eddie had endured dark, Italian pieces, with peasants dressed in black, and Jane had sat through Eddie's choices, pretending to enjoy schmaltzy American stories about people who overcame insuperable odds to achieve their ambition and win, or win back, the love of their life. Not that the pretence had been very convincing. *I don't understand you, Jane. Going to the movies is a way of losing yourself in a different world.*

What an irony that sentiment had turned out to be.

The noise from the loft conversion next door was deafening. Jane closed the window and fetched herself a slice of fruit cake. She only allowed herself one slice a day, but today might be an exception. In fact, the vibration from the electric drill called for a stiff gin and tonic, although, as usual, Rousseau appeared unconcerned.

He was Eddie's cat, not hers, but familiarity had a way of making you fond of things. People talked endlessly about lost love, but more often than not it was the familiarity they missed. Shared experiences. A shared routine. Had she loved Eddie? She disliked putting the question in the past tense but one had to be realistic. They were close friends, knew almost everything there was to know about each other, but was that love?

Some people had thought they were an item. An item – what a silly expression. In any case, it was not true, although she had wondered what it would be like to lie

94

naked next to another female. But not Eddie. The house was in both their names and, sooner or later, she would have to consult a solicitor and arrange power of attorney. Would there be a problem? They had made wills a few years back, leaving all their worldly goods to one another, but if someone was still alive, but not in their right mind, it would be more complicated.

Out of the corner of her eye, she thought she spotted someone walking past, then Noel's face appeared at the window, pressed against the glass so he looked like a criminal with a stocking mask. Jane hurried to let him in.

'Noel. How can I help?'

He gave a sheepish grin. 'In need of a spot of advice.'

'The complaints about next door's loft conversion?'

He shook his head, 'Barnaby. Corinne's boy. You saw him when you were leaving our house. What did you think?'

'Come along in. Coffee? Tea?'

He shook his head, entering the sitting room ahead of her and choosing the sofa where she would like to have joined him. Instead she decided on the armchair Eddie had found in a sale and made an effort to push the memory of the scene in Willa's conservatory out of her head.

'Open house as far as I'm concerned,' Noel said. 'The boy could stay the night if he wanted to.'

'But he never does. Corinne misses him, I expect.'

He nodded vaguely. 'The thing is, Jane, he asked for a loan.'

'I see.'

'Corinne doesn't know. You won't tell her. No, of course you won't.' He leaned forward, hands on the knees of his designer jeans. *Were* they designer ones? People paid well over the odds, but they all looked the same to her.

'Laptop playing up. That was the boy's story but obviously I didn't believe him. Gave him a hundred quid. Only now I'm wondering if it was drug money. Yes, I can see the same thought's crossed your mind. At the time it never occurred to me. See what a trusting soul I am. Thing is, I'm afraid he may ask for more.'

'You think that likely?' Outside in the road, two men were shouting at each other. Something to do with a parked van, the usual. Jane was enjoying having Noel in her sitting room, just the two of them, having a confidential chat, and she willed him not to go and sort out the argument.

No need – he was still worrying about the "drug money". 'It's not so much the cash, Jane. Making me promise not to tell Corinne. Yes, you're right, refuse to give him any more unless I can talk to her first. He knows the Molloy lad.'

'Arthur?'

'Play badminton together. I think it's badminton.'

'If it's any help, I know Arthur quite well.' She would like to have told Noel about the tuition, mainly because it would demonstrate how she was still an active teacher, not simply a retired person. Still an active teacher? How superficial she was and, in any case, she was sworn to secrecy.

Noel had returned to Barnaby and the loan. 'Corinne's besotted with the boy but I'm afraid ...'

'I wouldn't worry too much. The loan may have been a one-off, to test you – or punish you, I suppose.'

'For stealing his mother? Never thought of that, but you could be right. Although moving in with me was Corinne's idea. She left her phone lying about and her husband found some texts and threw her out.'

'I see.' *So, you're feeling trapped. Your own fault, Noel. Is that why you're here? You want my sympathy, or possibly advice on a way out? What were you doing in Willa's conservatory? Are the two of you having an affair or, more to point, were you having one and now it's over is she trying to resurrect it with the help of a ridiculous teacher's outfit?* All questions she could never ask.

He reached out an arm to stroke Rousseau. 'You chose the name, I expect. I gather his namesake had high principles and several illegitimate children.'

'Not guilty, are you, Rousseau? Been done.'

Adjusting the cushion behind his head, Noel leaned back and closed his eyes. Then, clearing his throat so loudly, he made both Rousseau and Jane jump, he clapped his hands and sat up straight. 'Enough of all that, how are you, Jane?'

'I'm well.'

'I admire you. Admire your determination, your strength of character.'

'I don't know about that.' His white shirt, unbuttoned

almost to his waist, revealed a hairless chest. She wanted to ask if he had ever been married, but it would break the spell.

He smiled at her. 'Tough-going on your own.'

'It has its advantages.'

'It does indeed.' He sighed and she wondered what was coming next. Letting Corinne move in had been a mistake? Things had not turned out as he'd hoped and he was wondering if he ought to tell her to return to her husband and son. But her wishful thoughts – if that was what they were – were running on ahead of her.

'She's easily hurt.'

'Corinne is? In my limited experience, all human beings are sensitive to criticism. It's simply that some are better at hiding it.'

The grandmother clock struck the hour. Noel consulted his watch, and Jane was afraid he was going to leave. 'She worries in case people don't like her. Tries too hard, if you know what I mean.'

'I do.'

'It was good of you to have a coffee with her at the leisure centre. She came home full of it. She needs female friends. No, I didn't mean ...'

'I have a swim every week, normally on a Tuesday, but I'd never been in the café before. Nothing to write home about but run by a rather pleasant Polish woman with a young son.'

'You see, you have this knack for drawing people out of themselves.'

'Nosey and in need of human contact. No, don't look like that. If you live alone you're at risk of talking to yourself, or the cat. Swimming's good for you, Noel. You should give it a try.'

He laughed, standing up and kissing her on the cheek. 'Eddie all right?'

'Coming back on Saturday, just for one night. Repairs being done to the window in her room at The Spruces.'

He gave her a sympathetic smile and she resisted an impulse to throw herself into his arms. People made light of physical attraction, insisting it was personality that mattered, but human beings had evolved to respond to what the biologists called "releasers" – she had listened to a programme on Radio Four – a gull chick to the red spot on its mother's beak, or, in her case, it was Noel's thick, glossy hair, or his blue eyes. Of course, it was always flattering if someone asked for advice, not that she had given him much, but sometimes the asking was sufficient since one already knew the answer.

'You're a good listener, Jane.'

And if I was twenty years younger. Or you were twenty years older. 'My advice, for what it's worth, is to assume it was a one-off loan. And I'd stay well clear of the lad unless Corinne is there too.'

'So you think it best not to tell her about it?'

'I do.' He was right: the loan might be blood money, literally forcing him to pay for his parents splitting up. After all, it could well be wishful thinking on Corinne's part when she said her son had taken her departure in his stride.

Noel was tracing a pattern on the palm of his hand. *Round and round the garden, like a teddy bear.* The only children's rhyme Jane's father had known.

'Is there something else?' she asked, regretting her words as soon as she had spoken them.

'I'm outstaying my welcome.'

'No, no, not at all. I'll make some coffee?'

He smiled to himself. 'You saw the portrait of my mother?'

'I did.'

'She used to call me her little prince. No, don't laugh.'

'I wasn't going to. Everything changes when your parents die, particularly your mother. You become the older generation.'

'My father walked out on us when I was eight years old. I can't remember much about him, just the smell of pipe tobacco. And he had a book with facts about cricket. Funny, the things that come back to you.'

'Yes. Eddie sometimes recalls events from the past in surprising detail. I believe it's not uncommon with dementia.' Should she ask if he knew what had happened to Simmy's mother?

'You never wanted children,' he said. 'No, why would you, spending all your working life with the blighters.'

Jane caught her breath, hoped it had gone unnoticed. 'Oh, by the way, Noel, you don't happen to know why Simmy's mother died?'

'Ah.' He pressed his lips together.

'You do but you're not going to tell me.'

'No, it's just – Dave's touchy about the subject. Something traumatic, I imagine, although any death's traumatic, particularly if it's someone so young.'

'Simmy can't remember her mother but …'

'Pretty little thing.'

'Simmy? Yes.'

'Anyway, I'd better be going. Expecting a phone call. Left my phone at home and if Corinne answers it she's likely to muddle up the message. No, don't look like that, she has her good points, means well.'

'One of them being that she adores you.'

He grinned. 'Yes, well that too. So you think it best I keep quiet about the loan and hope the lad doesn't ask for more.'

'I don't think he will.'

'No, well let's hope you're right. You usually are. Good to talk to you, Jane. If I have a problem, you're my first port of call.' He turned towards the window. 'That's an umbrella plant? Am I right?'

'Needs its top lopped off. Now it's reached the ceiling it's growing at an angle.'

'Our garden could do with someone with green fingers. Not as overgrown as Brian and Willa's.' He blinked several times, almost as though he knew she had witnessed the scene in the Molloy's conservatory. 'Good.' Clapping his hands together, he crossed the room, pausing to kiss her on the cheek again. 'Love you and leave you, Jane, and thanks again for your eminently sensible advice.'

Later, looking back, Jane could remember every detail of their conversation, as if it had taken place the previous day.

Probably because it had been their last.

FIFTEEN

Arthur was coming down the road and Jane managed to turn what she feared was a dour expression into a cheerful smile.

'Hello, where are you off to?' He had a sports bag in one hand and his phone in the other. He was wearing royal blue shorts and a matching T-shirt. Chelsea, she thought.

'Basketball at the leisure centre.'

'You play in a team?'

He nodded, putting away his phone, something that pleased Jane, since children, and many adults too, normally kept their eyes glued.

'I go there for a swim,' she said. 'Once a week.'

'Cool.' His phone beeped – a text – but he ignored it. 'You know the computer game me and Simmy are planning.'

'I do. A story based on Greek myths and the inhabitants of Faraday Road.'

'You know Gus.'

'I do.'

'We thought he could be the hermit that made a makeshift home on the cliffs overlooking the sea.'

'Really? Did you study Greek mythology at school? No, I believe I asked you that before.'

'My dad gave me a book for my tenth birthday. He always gives me books.'

'Good. I mean, I'm glad he takes the trouble to choose something for you. Not all fathers are so conscientious.'

'That means "painstaking and scrupulous."'

'It does. Your character, the one assigned to Gus, is not one with whom I'm familiar.'

'We looked it up online.'

'You and Simmy.' The boy was full of surprises. Well up on Greek mythology but unable to differentiate between "were" and "where", or "there" and "their". 'A hermit. I'm not sure Gus is a hermit. It's true he spends time in his flat – he watches sport on television – but when you're retired you tend to have less energy.'

'You've got energy.'

'I'll take that as a compliment, Arthur. Right, well, I mustn't hold you up. Enjoy your game.'

'Cheers.'

'Oh, by the way, I believe you know Barnaby, Corinne's son.'

'He plays badminton.'

'Yes, Noel said.' She wanted to ask what Arthur thought of Barnaby but that would be inappropriate, and he might tell the boy she was making inquiries. 'I'll see you on Monday then – for your lesson.'

'Cheers.'

'And we'll talk about subsidiary clauses.'

'Cheers.' He had seen Simmy and was hurrying to catch up with her. How she envied them their youth. Their whole lives ahead of them. Another cliché. But clichés had a way of expressing universal truths. That was why they were clichés!

During her last visit to the leisure centre, Jane had completed ten lengths while reviewing her life. She missed the pupils at her old school, no denying it, but surely there must be other ways she could put her people skills – dreadful expression – to good use. Voluntary work was an option, although possibly she was too old. No, that couldn't be right. She could visit the lonely – the blind leading the blind – or help out in a school, listening to infants like Liam practising their reading. No, definitely not that. Not something to be proud of, but she knew she would resent being given her instructions by a young, inexperienced teacher.

Swimming and choir – surely that was enough. Eddie – the old Eddie – had not joined the choir, preferring to stay at home and watch a film on Channel Five, usually about a stolen baby, or two sisters who hated each other, or a long-lost brother who turned out not to be a brother at all. The ads that punctuated the movies were mostly for indigestion tablets, or proprietary products that prevented your false teeth from falling out, or orthopaedic chairs.

Did Eddie miss the films? At The Spruces, the television was always switched to ITV. When she came for the weekend would she expect the television to be switched on all day? How would she spend her time? Sitting passively on the sofa or scurrying about like a toddler, grabbing whatever she could get her hands on.

Simmy was approaching and Jane steeled herself for the usual question. *Have you spoken to my dad?*

'Hello, Miss Seymour.' The child was looking in good spirits. Something Arthur had said to her? Something about their computer game?

'Hello, dear, Arthur told me he was off to the leisure centre. Do you go there, for sports or swimming, and I think they have dancing, don't they?'

'I don't like dancing. We have it at school when it rains and we can't play hockey or netball.'

'I haven't forgotten, Simmy, about talking to your father.'

'Oh, that.' She chewed a strand of hair. 'He won't tell you. Won't tell anyone. I asked Corinne. Noel knows, I can tell, but I don't think he's said anything to her. Most people confide in their partners, don't they?'

'I don't imagine they tell them everything.'

'No.' Simmy smiled to herself. 'I'm never going to get married, or live with someone. It's not worth the trouble.'

'Oh, I don't think you should think like that, dear. Eddie – Miss Knox – is coming home on Saturday and I know she'll be pleased to see you.'

Simmy's face expressed doubt, as well it might, although it turned out she was thinking about something quite different. 'Dad's denim jacket smelled of sweat so I put it in the wash. Only he said I'd ruined it.'

'Did he?' And did the poor child have to do all the household chores?

'I don't mind doing the washing 'cos he's really good at cooking, and not just ready meals, he buys all the ingredients. Yesterday we had Moroccan meatballs. He found the recipe on the BBC website.'

'Really? Sounds delicious.' This was a new and pleasing side of Dave. 'What happened to the denim jacket? If it needs repairing I'd be happy to help.'

Simmy shook her head. 'No, it wasn't that. It was because of the fabric conditioner. It was supposed to have the scent of a meadow of flowers but Dad said it smelled like a brothel. Cats wash far more than dogs do, don't they? And they do whatever they want. They don't care what humans think. Not like dogs. That's why I like them.'

'Yes, I know what you mean.' She felt a twinge of concern for the child, but as Simmy continued up the road, Jane's thoughts returned to Eddie and whether she would be pleased to see Rousseau, or would she ignore him? If the weather held, a drive out into the country might be a possibility, provided Eddie agreed to have her seat belt fastened. They could have a short walk, and possibly afternoon tea at the café Eddie liked. No, not a good idea. What might she get up to in public, particularly if someone stared at her, or the cakes were not to her liking. Best to stay at home and, provided the weather was good, spend time in the garden, cutting back some of the sprawling plants while Eddie watched from the safety of the basket chair.

The best laid plans of mice and men ... or, to put it another way: the futility of thinking you had any control over your own or other people's destiny.

SIXTEEN

Without his fisherman's cap, Gus looked vulnerable, rather as people do when they remove their spectacles. He sat down, rubbing his forehead with a hairy-backed hand, and Jane recalled how Simmy had described him as a brown bear, and how she had assumed Simmy was referring to his habit of shutting himself away in his flat, hibernating.

'I'm sorry to disturb you, Gus, but Rousseau's gone missing again. He often stays out all night but normally he's back for his breakfast. I thought he might be in your garden.' It was a lie, and she felt ashamed, but not that much, since knocking on Gus' door always meant taking your life in your hands.

'Not my garden, Jane, belongs to Dave and Simmy.'

'Yes, I know, but you might have spotted him through your window.'

'Poster on a tree at the top of the road. Ginger tom been missing since April. That's the trouble with cats. No road sense.'

'I know.' Gus was never one for helpful remarks. A gender thing perhaps. Women were more tactful than men. No, not true. When Eddie went into The Spruces, Willa Molloy had asked if it was a home for people who had gone off their heads. 'Eddie's coming home, Gus. Only for one night.'

'Is that wise?'

'I didn't have a say in the matter. Repairs to her room, that's what the matron said, but I'm afraid it may be an excuse. She threw another resident's valuables down the loo.'

He rolled his eyes. 'What's it like at The Spruces?'

'I can't really fault it.'

'Had a friend who suffered the same fate. Killed himself. DIY. Sliced through an artery.'

'How horrible. You mean because he suffered from dementia?'

'Made him careless. I expect that's what happened. Or he might have had enough. Ralph, he was called Ralph. Had an interest in old cameras. Liked to drop in for a chat.'

'You must miss your shop.'

'Still take the odd photo.' He pointed to a camera, lying on a low table, along with the free newspaper, a packet of painkillers, and a slice of cold pizza. 'Hardly worth the effort.'

'You need to get out more.'

He was silent, so she had another try. 'Just a thought,

but since we both need cheering up perhaps we should treat ourselves to lunch at the Portuguese café.'

Gus gave a loud sniff. 'I'm on your list of people who need taking in hand.'

'Why do you say that?' People wrapped up hurtful remarks in a joke, rather as mothers hid a nasty-tasting tablet in a spoonful of strawberry jam. It rarely worked since children were not so easily deceived. Either the tablet was spat out – Rousseau did the same – or the child was put off jam for life.

Regretting his remark, or perhaps not, Gus opened a drawer and took out a small album. 'As I said, I still take the odd picture, mainly insects and birds. Need a special lens.' Flicking through until he found the one he was searching for, he held it out for Jane to inspect. '*Acherontia atropos*, otherwise known as the African death's head hawkmoth. I was watching some butterflies and this fellow landed on a leaf.'

Jane gave an involuntary shudder. 'Skull-like pattern on its back. Is it true they make a squeaking noise? How large are they? Looking at your photo, it's hard to tell.'

'Size of a small bat. I was lucky to spot it.' He turned the page. '*Metellina segmentata*, the lesser garden spider. Slimmer than the typical one and with longer legs.'

'Eddie liked spiders.'

'I remember. Showed me a particularly fine one on that prickly plant of yours at the front.'

'Did she?' When was that?'

More silence.

'Your daughter, Gus – Sarah, isn't it?'

'Lives up north. Outer reaches of Greater Manchester. Got a kid of her own now. Little girl.'

'Your granddaughter.' Gus' eyebrows needed trimming. Nothing wrong with bushy eyebrows but his were starting to look like a hanuman monkey, commonly called a langur. 'You should visit them.'

'They live with my ex.'

'What's her name, your granddaughter? Have you got a picture?'

He held out a photograph of a bright green beetle.

'Oh, yes.' Jane took off her glasses and cleaned them with the ends of her blouse. 'I had some of those on my cotoneaster. Iridescent. Beautiful.'

Above them, the builders were hammering so hard it felt as though the ceiling might collapse. When a cascade of stones and pieces of mortar fell down the chimney onto her gas fire, Jane had called up next door's stairs to tell them, and the younger man had offered to come down with a brush and pan. As if that was the point. They could hammer hard for a short time, he said, or not so hard for a longer time. Big deal, as Simmy liked to say. Jane had chosen the longer, gentler time, but rubbish had continued to fall.

Gus yawned. 'No one else involved in the break-up with Margery. I was impossible to live with.'

'Margery's your ex? Not necessarily.'

'That's what you think, is it?'

'I do.' He was turning the pages of his album in what

she hoped was a companionable silence. He had kicked off his shoes, trainers that had once been white with black stripes on the sides. His socks had holes in the big toes. 'People grow apart.'

He stared at her, as if to say, what would you know about it, but she was not so easily put off.

'So when the marriage ended you moved here. Did you have a particular reason for choosing this area and Faraday Road in particular? Don't talk about it if you don't want to.'

He didn't.

'Formula One on soon.'

'At this time of day?'

'Not this time of day all over the world.'

'No, I suppose not.' The mantelpiece had a layer of dust. So did a round table next to where Jane was sitting. Did he own a vacuum cleaner? She would have enjoyed having a quick flick round, but it was not something Gus would appreciate. 'That new person in number twenty-two,' she said, 'You've met her, haven't you?'

'Not moving in for a week or two. Place needs doing up.'

'Oh, she's told you about it. Is she local? Where has she come from?'

He ignored her question, taking a jacket from the back of a chair, a new one, grey wool, quite smart. 'Expect it's the workmen, Rousseau doing a bunk. Blame Noel, he encourages people in the road to have his conversions, pretends he's offering special rates. Hang on, I'm coming down. Need some milk. Oh by the way, "whom" – no one uses the word any more, am I right?'

'It can sound a little formal. Why do you ask?'

'You know me, Jane, left school at sixteen.'

'And studied photography.'

'Sorry to disappoint you, I'm self-taught.'

'Nothing wrong with that.' Was asking about the word "whom" a way of getting at her? It was true she regretted the fact so many people avoided using words of more than two syllables. Tricia Tidewell had once referred to her as a "walking dictionary", one of those remarks that, on the face of it, sound like a compliment. But only on the face of it. 'Oh, I must tell you, Gus, Eddie quoted from W.H. Auden and the odd thing is, she never liked poetry when she was …'

'You were going to say "when she was alive". In life we are in death. Shakespeare, is it?' He tightened the belt on his cord trousers. 'It's a bad business.'

'Yes.' Did he mean Eddie, or Noel's loft conversion? 'I'll walk down to the shops with you if that's where you're going.'

Down in the street, the driver of a truck, containing large sheets of plasterboard, was attempting to reverse into a parking space between a white van and a people carrier. 'Actually, I'd better have another look for Rousseau,' Jane said, but Gus had moved out of earshot. He raised a hand, but didn't turn his head, and a moment later she saw him knock on the door of number twenty-two, and the new owner, dressed in an unbecoming boiler suit and a thick woolly hat, invited him in.

Setting off in the opposite direction, Jane felt her face and neck grow hot. Gus and the woman from number twenty-two? Was that the reason for his new jacket? In the past Jane had prided herself on her lack of self-pity. When Eddie began to act oddly she had been sorry, but not for herself. Poor Eddie had had such a wide knowledge of art, both contemporary and historical, and she was a skilful painter in several different media and a fine draughtsman. And her sense of humour had been second to none.

Gus and the woman from number twenty-two. Stupid tears filled her eyes. Life was so unfair, so full of pain. But, had she but known, her jealousy was soon to be eclipsed by a genuine tragedy.

SEVENTEEN

Saturday. Would sleeping in her old bedroom please Eddie, or alarm her? *Was* it a test, a precursor to saying they were unable to keep her at The Spruces? *You say you managed, Miss Seymour, so it may be that Miss Knox is unsuited to residential care.* Putting pressure on her. Making her feel guilty for forcing her friend into a home.

Eddie was wearing her best dress, her only dress. Not a good choice, but Jane assumed it had been selected by one of the staff. It had a belt, and belts were fiddly and likely to lead to a loss of temper. What was wrong with her usual trousers, blouse, and cardigan?

When they left The Spruces, she had been reluctant to climb into the car. It was quite a struggle, and Jane had come off worse, damaging her hand on the seat belt catch, but making light of it. Not that Eddie cared. Now she was scurrying about, inspecting the house as though she had never seen it before, and ignoring poor Rousseau, who was letting out loud yowls that could be pleasure or, more likely, the possibility of extra food.

Jane had made some tea but Eddie had swept hers aside, almost literally, crouching down to peer into the cupboard where the pans were kept. She had found a lid, inspected it closely, and dropped it on the floor, hurrying back to the sitting room and picking up the remote control then Jane's reading glasses, which she had been stupid enough to leave on the table by the window. Another tussle had ensued, ending in the glasses being trodden underfoot. Fortunately, Jane had a spare pair.

The matron had explained, as if Jane needed warning, that returning home might be confusing. *You can give her one of her tablets, Miss Seymour, but not until after lunch.* Now it *was* after lunch. Ten to two, a time that was to run through Jane's mind, like a mantra, when she tried to work out who had been doing what, and where, that dreadful afternoon.

During lunch, Eddie had refused the quiche and salad, pushing it aside and asking for jelly babies, but the summer pudding, with the vanilla ice cream Jane had rushed down to the shops to buy, had been more acceptable. Jane rarely ate puddings, but Eddie's liking for them had remained intact. Gobbling it down, she had pushed back her chair and hurried out into the garden – to look at the flowers perhaps – although it had turned out she was more interested in a broken flowerpot and had not reacted well when Jane attempted to take the sharp pieces out of her hand.

Upstairs now, she was crashing about, opening and

closing drawers, and Jane decided to leave her to it. Seeing her in her familiar surroundings, rather than at The Spruces, had resurrected painful feelings of sadness and loss. Also, guilt, and anger. Obviously, the anger was not directed at Eddie herself, and there was no point in blaming God, so she was stuck with rage that life was so unfair, hardly a new observation, but one never quite grew out of those child-like feelings. *It's not fair. It's not fair.*

Someone was ringing the doorbell. A neighbour's order from an online business? The way Jane was feeling today, she might refuse to take it in. *Do you know Miss Seymour? Oh, you mean the woman who takes in all the parcels.* The previous day, a so-called expert on the radio had bemoaned the fact that old people were invisible. Not true. Many were only too visible, with their walking aids and those alarming mobility scooters. During Eddie's last year in Faraday Road, she had been particularly visible and once, at four in the morning, a group of kindly students from number nineteen, returning from a boozy evening out, had found her walking about in her vest and knickers and brought her back home. Subsequently, Jane had formed quite a bond with them, until they finished their courses and were replaced by a new bunch, who gave her cold, uninterested stares. *Uninterested, disinterested.* No, now was definitely not the time to get worked up about the use of language on the media.

'Just answering the door, Eddie,' she called. 'Is Rousseau asleep on my bed?'

Since it was Saturday, the men were not working on

next door's loft conversion so the road was relatively quiet. Ready to do battle over yet another parcel, she wrenched open the door – it stuck on the draught excluder she had inexpertly attached the previous winter – and was obliged to make a quick adjustment when she found Simmy, standing there in tears.

'What is it, dear, what's happened?'

'My dad,' she sobbed. 'I asked him again – about my mother – and he told me to go away.'

'Come along in.' How would Eddie react to seeing the child?

'He said someone had been gossiping.' Simmy sat on the edge of the armchair with her hands tucked under her legs. 'And it was my fault because I must have been talking to people, and he asked if I'd spoken to Mr McNeill and I said I hadn't and he said he didn't believe me.'

'Why did he think you might have spoken to Mr McNeill?'

'Arthur says Mr McNeill used to be an actor. He had a chequered career. I didn't know what it meant but Arthur says —'

'It means doing a variety of things.'

'Bad things?'

'Not necessarily.' What had Arthur heard? Something from his mother, no doubt, angry when Noel rejected her advances. 'I don't think you should take notice of remarks like that, Simmy. I believe Mr McNeill was once a male model, but that was a long time ago and it's a perfectly respectable job.'

Eddie had appeared, holding a jar of marmalade and a fork.

'Look, it's Simmy.' Jane took the fork, noting that Eddie smelled faintly of onions. 'You remember Simmy. She lives next door.'

At the sight of Eddie, Simmy had brightened. 'Hello.' She turned to Jane. 'Has she come back to live with you?'

'Just for the weekend.'

'Simmy,' Eddie said.

'Yes, that's right.' Jane held her breath, afraid Eddie might come out with one of her expletives, but to her surprise she shook Simmy by the hand.

'What did you do with the Cézanne?' she murmured, and Jane was torn between wanting to weep, and fearing Simmy might think she was being criticised in some way.

'Nothing to do with you, dear. She gets confused. Did you find Rousseau, Eddie? Was he on my bed?'

'Bed.' Eddie shuffled away, and Jane hoped she was going up to check.

Simmy screwed up her nose. 'Has she got bad legs?'

'They wear slippers at The Spruces but I suggested she put on her shoes. I mean, I put them on for her. Now, this business with your father. I expect he was tired, or stressed. His work. He's always very busy which means his business must be doing well, but I expect it can be hard for —'

'In our computer game he's going to be Cronus. He was a very, very bad father. He ate his children.'

'Oh, Simmy. I tell you what, why not go and see Arthur? I expect he'll be at home.'

'You know Barnaby.'

'Corinne's son?'

'He was outside Mr McNeill's house and they were shouting.'

'When? Was Corinne there?'

Simmy shook her head. 'Arthur reckons Barnaby fancies himself because he goes to a private school.' Jane was relieved to see Simmy's face had broken into a grin. 'He told Mr McNeill to fuck off. It was something to do with his bike.'

What was Eddie up to? She needed to check.

'Arthur's having lessons.' Simmy was holding her amulet.

'He told you about them? He has exams next year and —'

'I asked Mrs Tidewell but she's always in a hurry.'

'About your mother? I doubt if she would know anything.'

'Ada's nose was running.'

'Was it?' Ada's nose nearly always needed wiping. Television ads made babies look like pristine creatures that never regurgitated their milk or filled their nappies. Older ones, dressed in designer outfits, burst with joy at the sight of a plate of fish fingers, or waited for the washing-up liquid to be finished so they could do something creative with the empty bottle. Babies and small children had become fashion accessories. No, perhaps that was a little unkind. All the same, it was clear they took priority over everyone else, since it was not uncommon to find a car door wide open, blocking the pavement for passers-by so innumerable children could be fastened into car seats.

Simmy was staring at her, willing her to speak to her father. 'Dad would listen to you. He wouldn't dare shout.'

'Yes, well I haven't forgotten. Just waiting for the right time. Leave it with me, dear. I think I'd better see what Miss Knox is doing. She remembered you, Simmy, I was pleased about that.'

No sign of Eddie. Jane checked the bedrooms, the bathroom, under the beds, inside the wardrobes. Some drawers had been emptied – but she could have done that earlier – and Jane's pillow had been moved to the other end of the bed, where Rousseau had made it into a warm nest. Talcum powder had been sprinkled on the carpet, but that could have been before Simmy turned up too.

The garden. Eddie had been out there twice before, searching for something in a flowerbed, and had probably returned. 'Are you there, Eddie? Eddie?' Nothing, and it was not the kind of garden that provided hiding places.

After they came back from The Spruces, Jane had locked the front door but when Simmy rang the bell she had unlocked it, and left it that way, and while she was talking to the child, Eddie must have escaped. How long ago? Ten minutes, less, but quite long enough for her to be well on her way to the shops.

EIGHTEEN

Leaving the house, half walking, half running, and all the while listening for the sound of screeching brakes, Jane reached the main road only to find the traffic was at a standstill. Nothing to do with Eddie. A large truck was doing a U-turn and in the process holding up a bus that had pulled out, blocking the road.

Eddie had no money, not that lack of cash would prevent her from pocketing something that took her fancy. First stop, the sweet shop, where she asked if anyone had spotted an elderly woman, wearing a grey dress with a red belt.

'She's not well.' But now was not the time for euphemisms. 'Her memory. She may have lost her bearings.'

No luck, so on to the mini-market, the greengrocer's, the shop that repaired computers, the Portuguese café, the cycle shop. Did Eddie know her way back to The Spruces? If she turned up there, the matron would think

Jane incapable of keeping tabs on her for half a day. She had no coat, but the rain that had poured down in the night had been replaced by a cool, clear day and, in any case, Eddie had never felt the cold. In that respect, she had been like the teenage boys, many of whom arrived at school coatless, even in midwinter.

A light breeze shook the branches of the chestnut trees in the park. Could she have gone there? Unlikely. Shops would have a greater appeal. Food shops. Eddie was not above helping herself. The fast food place. Yes, that was the best bet.

Nothing, just an exhausted lad, who probably had a Ph.D. in astrophysics, taking the orders while simultaneously checking chips frying in boiling fat. Five past two. She would have to call the police. Fear that Eddie had fallen under a bus had been replaced by fury that she had taken advantage of Simmy's visit to disappear. She knew what she was doing. Cunning was one of the attributes of dementia. Not true, but Eddie had always had a devious streak, saying one thing and doing another, like the time she had told her she had a low opinion of Tricia Tidewell, and her foolish remarks, and later Jane had discovered the two of them in the Portuguese café. A few years ago, when Liam was still a baby, and Eddie was still her old self.

Walking, half running towards The Spruces, Jane stopped, changed her mind. Eddie had never walked there from Faraday Road and if she was not at the shops she was more likely to have returned to the house. Yes, that must be it. She had set off for the shops then lost her nerve, and instinct had carried her back home.

Retracing her steps, Jane looked all about her for a glimpse of the grey dress with its red belt. She could ask passers-by but they were unlikely to have noticed an elderly woman hurrying along. They had better things to think about and, besides, most of them had their heads down, studying their phones. Round the corner she spotted Gus talking to the wretched woman from number twenty-two. No use asking them, they were far too absorbed in whatever they were discussing. She thought she heard Gus laugh. He was enjoying himself with his new friend, had no interest in Eddie. Had probably forgotten she was coming home for two days.

Back home the house was deathly quiet. Nothing to indicate Eddie had returned then gone out again, no cupboard doors thrown open or beds stripped or taps running. How long had Jane been searching? Fifteen minutes, twenty? Later, it would be important to remember. No, not just important: a matter of life and death.

Out in the garden, she was joined by Rousseau who rolled in the catmint then climbed the magnolia and sat on a branch, preparing to jump down on the other side of the fence.

'No, Rousseau.' Dave was not fond of cats, although the Burmese one from number thirty-one was a frequent visitor. Jane had seen it from her window. Needless to say, Rousseau took no notice of her, pausing a few seconds to lick his paw then leaping down and disappearing out of sight.

Out in the street again, but still no sign of Eddie, although she saw that the door to Dave and Gus' house had been left open. The builders working an extra shift, or possibly Mrs Garcia. She had better check. Stepping inside, she called Simmy's name. Then Dave's. The door to their flat was closed and when she knocked nobody answered. Simmy must have gone to look for Arthur. Jane started up the stairs then changed her mind and decided to try and retrieve Rousseau.

The garden door at the end of the passage had a key in it but was not locked. She stepped onto the patio and was met by a forest of dandelions, some still in flower, others turned into fluffy seed heads. When Simmy was younger, she had shown her how to blow the seeds off the stalks. Five blows and they were gone meant it was five o'clock although some of them always seemed to remain. Not a sign of Rousseau, who must have continued on to the next garden, but out of the corner of her eye, she caught a glimpse of a dark shape on the patio – and reached out to steady herself against the wall.

He was lying face down, with his head turned to one side. Blue jeans and a red T-shirt. White trainers, bright blue socks. No blood. But it could be hidden from sight. No movement and, when she spoke his name, no response. But he could be unconscious.

'Noel, it's me, Jane. Noel? Can you hear me? What happened? Can you speak? Noel?'

What was she doing? An ambulance. Her phone. It was in her pocket. Because of Eddie. With trembling fingers, she dialled 999 and a flat voice asked if she wanted police, fire or ambulance, and in order to tell them she had to draw in a big gasp of air.

'Ambulance.' She stammered out the address. 'A neighbour. He's fallen. From high up, I think. A loft conversion, the balcony. Breathing? I'll check.' Crouching, close to his head, she repeated her words. 'It's me, Noel. Jane. Noel, it's Jane.' It was hopeless. He could have been lying there for ages. If it had just happened she would have heard him shout. 'I think he's breathing. I'm not sure.'

'An ambulance is on its way.'

'Thank you.' She searched for a pulse. Was sure she felt one. Then not sure she could find it again. 'It's all right, Noel. You fell, but an ambulance is coming. You're going to be all right.'

Where was Eddie? If someone found her, shop-lifting or doing something inappropriate, they would call the police. Did she have her name and address on her? Unlikely. She had no bank card or diary, or any other means of identification. She should have hung a label round her neck but how was she to know she would slip through the front door. It was Simmy's fault. No, it was her own. Don't think about all that. Concentrate on Noel. He was as still as a ... as still as ... how had he fallen? Leaning over to check something. Standing on the balcony, one of those wretched balconies. Why couldn't he have been more careful? He was never careful. She touched his neck, searching for a pulse. Nothing. But she might not be pressing the right place. Was Gus at home or still chatting with the woman from number twenty-two? He couldn't be back or he would have heard Noel shout. Surely he would have shouted, except there might not have been time. And even if Gus looked through his window, he would be unable to see the body. The body. No, he was still alive. He must be.

'The ambulance will be here soon.' But would it? She had heard stories about people waiting up to forty minutes. And it was the weekend. No, surely that made no difference, they worked in shifts, it was the same as a weekday.

Somewhere close by, a bee was buzzing about, and far off she could hear music, a pop song with its ubiquitous drumbeat. One of his arms was under his body and the other was flung out and she saw black paint on his fingers, or it could be varnish. Why couldn't he have left it to the builders? Why had he been so reckless? Would the ambulance men call the police? Was that what happened when there was an accident? Would they tell Corinne or would she have to break the news? *It's about Noel, Corinne, I'm so sorry but ...*

'Noel, can you hear me? It's Jane.'

A small sound, a whisper. He *was* alive. 'It's all right, Noel. No, don't try to talk.' Should she go and look for Gus? No, better to stay. She felt cold, shaky. Should she try CPR? No, if he could speak it was not necessary. Had he spoken or had she imagined it? No, the single word had been unmistakable.

Footsteps heralded the arrival of two paramedics, a man and a woman, dressed in green overalls, the woman taller than the man. Both young.

'We were in the area.' The woman's voice was calm, matter of fact. 'Are you a relative?'

'No, a friend, a neighbour. I live next door.'

The woman was kneeling by Noel. 'Did you see him fall?'

'No. No, I didn't. I came round to look for my cat and ... Noel. He's called Noel. He has a business. Loft conversions. This one's still under construction. He must have been checking the balcony.'

'Noel? Can you hear me, Noel?' The paramedic had started pumping his chest.

Jane brushed earth off a metal chair and sat down. Through a small gap in the fence, she could see the bright colours of her Californian poppies. Their real name was eschscholzia and she had told Eddie how her mother had taught her to spell the word, and ever after Eddie had stumped round the garden repeating the letters. Es-ch-sch-olz-ia.

The paramedic had stopped pumping and was shaking her head. Jane could smell fungi, and something else. Lavender? Rosemary? All her senses were magnified, smells, sounds. The pop music had been replaced by *Nessun Dorma*, sung by one of those fat Italian opera singers.

'I'm sorry.' The male paramedic was standing next to her. 'Is there someone we can phone? Someone who could stay with you?'

'No thank you.'

'The police will have to be informed.'

'Yes.' And when she saw them, what would she say? That Noel had spoken to her, a single word that might simply have been breath escaping from his lungs. Better not to mention it. Not for now. She could be wrong. Could have misheard.

The crossword clue, that had been keeping her awake at night, came back to her. Of course. How could she have been so dense? *Conceal round old amplifier for crime.* Conceal. Hide. Old was o and amplifier was microphone. Mic. "Hide" round "o-mic". *Homicide.* When she returned home, she could fill it in and the crossword would be complete.

NINETEEN

Conflicting feelings of guilt and fear tormented her. In her head, she ran and re-ran the day, from the time she collected Eddie from The Spruces to the moment she saw Noel lying motionless on the patio. The whispered word. She could so easily have imagined it. Because she had desperately wanted him to speak – to prove he was still alive. If he had landed in a flower bed he might have survived but Dave had no flower beds, just hard patio slabs and, beyond them, knee-high grass, full of daisies and dandelions.

The hot tears that had poured from her eyes when she woke in the night, and remembered Noel was dead, had left her exhausted, wrung out. Their last conversation played out like a film, together with regret that she had never told him how much she valued his friendship. He had known – there was no need to tell him – but it was a mistake to believe people instinctively knew how you felt. Most people were far too concerned with their own thoughts and feelings.

It was Mrs Cardozo, from the Portuguese café, who had brought Eddie back. Worried she was crossing the road without looking, she had taken her arm and persuaded her to return to Faraday Road. The fact that she believed she was Jane's sister was neither here nor there. Eddie was safe.

In the circumstances, it had seemed best to take her straight back to The Spruces. Better for Eddie and certainly better for Jane who was too shocked to cope with her demands. Instead of offering sympathy, the matron was only concerned Eddie might have seen Noel's body. *Very unfortunate, Miss Seymour. I think we should leave it for the time being.* What had she meant? Until Eddie had another weekend at home? Passing Eddie on to another member of staff, she had accompanied Jane to her car and the hand on her arm had offered little comfort.

As with any sudden death, the police had been involved and some of the residents of Faraday Road had been interviewed – briefly, since no one had anything useful to tell them. Jane had described her part in the affair, but not mentioned Eddie because what was the point? Did that count as a lie of omission? Possibly, but she was too tired to agonise over her decision. There would be a post-mortem – accidental death due to a fall, resulting in a fatal injury – and that would be the end of it.

After breakfast, she strolled round the garden, hoping to calm herself. The potentilla could always be relied on, and had been flowering since May, and the hollyhocks thrived in their sheltered spot. Even though she lived in the middle of a city, she would have liked a cottage garden, full of scarlet pimpernels, lady's mantle, purple toadflax, and vetch. She and Eddie had different tastes in plants and a few years back Eddie had planted a yucca. Jane disliked its stiff leaves and waxy flowers, but pulling it up would be like removing the last trace, and the thought that Eddie would be indifferent made her weep.

When she discovered Eddie was missing, *Any Questions* had been close to finishing and someone had been holding forth on today's teenagers. Jane preferred *Any Answers* – the opinions of so-called ordinary people tended to be more sensible, and frequently better informed – and experts were rapidly becoming one of her *bêtes noires*. Pundits. Originally the word had meant "a learned person, a teacher". Now it was applied to talk show hosts and football commentators. The last question on *Any Answers*, the light-hearted one, was about teenagers. How irrelevant it seemed.

By the time Mrs Cardozo brought Eddie back it was well after three. The ambulance had left but two police officers were still making house-to-house inquiries and Jane had explained to Mrs Cardozo what had happened, while simultaneously thanking her profusely. Eddie, oblivious of the tragedy, had made a beeline for the biscuit tin and Jane had left her to it, waiting until Mrs Cardozo had gone before questioning her, but receiving nothing in terms of a sensible reply. *Be quiet. Go away. Bugger off ...*

Someone was ringing her bell. Please God, not Simmy complaining about her father. Or poor Corinne needing a shoulder to cry on. It was Gus.

'Feeling any better?' For once, he was quite smartly dressed – grey trousers and a sports jacket, open-neck shirt. A sop to the seriousness of the last few days or was he on the way to meet the woman at number twenty-two? Touched by his concern, Jane's spirits rose a little, then sank when he wanted her to go over again how she had found Noel. 'You're thinking I should have tried harder to revive him. I thought I found a pulse, but I couldn't be certain. Then the paramedics arrived – they were already in the area – and I …'

'I imagine he'd have been killed on impact.'

'Yes. Yes, I hope so. I mean …'

'Going to invite me in then?'

'Yes, of course. I was out in the garden but you can hear the bell. It's a new one, wi-fi, and after reading the instructions I managed to turn up the volume.' Why was she burbling on about a bell? Gus was being kind. He had no other reason to call by.

Rousseau was in the sitting room, sniffing the book she had left on the floor, a thriller set in North Devon. The house was not as tidy as she would have liked, but she had not been expecting visitors, had not even cleared away the breakfast things. Gus had interrupted her routine. Good for Gus. She was becoming far too set in her ways. Normally, on Mondays, she put her washing in the machine. She would like to have included Gus' shirt.

He reached out a hand to Rousseau. 'What do you think then, you old hedonist?'

'Wouldn't mind being a cat, would you?'

His silence put her on her guard.

'Coffee?'

'Not for me.' He felt inside his jacket and scratched his armpit. 'Must have shaken you up.'

'At least Eddie knew nothing about it. Mrs Cardozo brought her back. She escaped while I was talking to Simmy. I'd locked the front door, but when Simmy ...'

'How long was she gone?'

Why was he asking? 'About half an hour. No, more. That was how long I looked for her. Then I came back and while I was checking the garden in case she'd managed to open the door to the alleyway, Rousseau jumped down from the magnolia tree into yours, I mean Dave's, and your front door was open so I thought the builders must —'

'Think I might have that coffee. Milk and two sugars.' He followed her to the kitchen. 'Perhaps you should get something from the old doc.'

'I'm fine, just sad for poor Noel. And Corinne.' Against her better judgement, an image sprang to mind. Noel, wearing a mortar board and holding up the ridiculous knickers. She could tell Gus – it would amuse him – but it no longer seemed funny. 'What do you suppose will happen to her? To Corinne?'

'Not our problem.' Gus took the kettle from her hand and filled it at the tap. 'You go and sit down. No, don't look like that. I can make a cup of coffee as long as it's instant. As a matter of fact, my cooking's improved too. Been watching some of those programmes with celebrity chefs. Have you noticed how their kitchens never get in a mess. Spotless. Not a thing out of place. Off you go then. Milk and sugar?'

'Just milk.' She felt weak with gratitude. Someone who wanted to look after her. And Gus, of all people.

By the time he rejoined her, she had decided to tell him what Noel had whispered. She wanted to, needed to, but when he sat down and waited patiently for her to speak, something held her back. Supposing Eddie had gone up to the loft conversion while she was talking to Simmy. Ten minutes, that's all it would have taken, then off to the shops without bothering to mention what she had done.

Gus was telling her how he had spent Saturday morning taking photos for a competition. No mention was made of his conversation with the woman from number twenty-two. Had he been on his way home? Was she interested in photography? A shared interest that had brought them together?

'Were you pleased with them? A local competition, is it, or a national one? I always buy that calendar you can order. Wildlife. Wonderful pictures of animals and birds. And insects, I expect. Does it have insects?'

'Noel enjoyed taking risks.'

'Yes, yes he did. You think he leaned over the balcony and lost his balance?'

'Seems the most likely explanation.' He placed a table in front of her and put her cup on it, splashing coffee in the saucer. 'How are you going to spend the rest of the day?'

'I haven't thought.' Was it an invitation? They could go to the Portuguese café together. She might tell him then. See if he thought she could have heard correctly. It would be such a relief.

'I should rest,' he said, 'read a book. Watch the telly.'

'I ought to visit Eddie.'

He picked up his coffee and took a sip. 'Made it too strong. Sorry.'

'No, it's fine.'

'Did she know what had happened?'

Jane shook her head. 'Hadn't a clue. Have you seen anyone else? Everyone in the road must be so shocked. People were fond of him.'

Gus gave a snort. '*You* were.'

'I know you don't like the loft conversions but most people … the Emersons had theirs converted a few months ago and they're delighted with it. Where did you go – to take your photos?'

'Travelled on the bus.'

'Oh,'

'Not far. A few miles out of the city. Wooded area.'

'Oh.' He thought she was asking too many questions. 'I'll go round to Corinne's later. See if there's anything I can do. I didn't tell the police Eddie had been staying here. And I didn't tell the matron at The Spruces about her going missing.'

'Very wise.'

The silence between them made her swallow several times. Had he guessed she was keeping something from him? How could he? 'Eddie had been looking round the shops. That's where Mrs Cardozo found her. Outside the pet shop, holding a bag of hay.'

Gus was watching her half-closed eyes. 'She likes shopping. Used to.'

'She still has a passion for sweets. The kind small children like. Jelly babies are her favourite. Oh, and ice cream. I should have thought of it, stocked up before she came. As it was I had to make a dash – to that Polish shop. They keep all the usual brands. I was quite surprised.'

Gus stood up, abandoning his "too strong" coffee. 'Right, I'd better be off.'

'A business meeting?'

He smiled to himself. 'A good long rest, Jane. Get you back on your feet. Got to keep your strength up.'

As she let him out, her mouth trembled. Delayed shock? 'Oh, just before you go, Gus, your friend at number twenty-two didn't notice anything, did she?'

'How d'you mean?'

'On Saturday. I thought she might have seen Noel going up to the loft conversion. Did the police speak to her?'

'Don't think so.' He was frowning. He had taken the trouble to call round and she was being nosey, interfering.

Or had the reason for his unexpected visit been to convince her he had been miles away from Faraday Road when Noel fell?

TWENTY

'Last Saturday, Eddie, you remember? You came back to Faraday Road, back to the house. And you saw Simmy. Simmy from next door. And you had a look round the shops. Is that what you did? Did you go anywhere else? Eddie?'

'I'm cold.'

'They've almost finished the loft conversion next door.'

Eddie nodded as though she understood.

'Such a disruption for poor Dave and Simmy. And Gus. You remember Gus who wears a fisherman's cap.'

'I'm cold.'

'Poor Simmy hasn't got a mother. She died when Simmy was very young. Cancer, I expect. Dave won't tell her what happened. I've no idea why.'

Eddie looked up with interest but it was only because the old man, sitting opposite, was fiddling with the zip on his trousers. 'The new loft conversion, Eddie, all those vans and skips and scaffolders. And it's going to stick out at the back and throw shade onto part of our garden. You remember Noel?' Jane's eyes filled with tears. Of sadness, or was it fear? 'You liked Noel, he made you laugh.'

'Is it time?'

'Those balconies are dangerous. I dislike the things. No planning permission required, or if there is it's minimal. And the builders make such a racket. Radio One – or it could be some local station, I suppose. Love, love, love, I loved her and she left. And I'm bereft.' Jane laughed out loud, a nervous reaction since there was nothing amusing about love and loss. Earlier in the day she had bumped into Willa in floods of tears. *Oh, Jane, I can't bear it. He was so young. I mean, he wasn't old. It's so awful, such a shock.*

'Is it time?' Eddie was struggling to fit her foot into one of her slippers. They were the kind that have no left or right foot but she looked as if she was checking which was which. And working herself up into a state.

'You remember Arthur? No, I don't think you knew him. Brian and Willa's son. He's fifteen, coming up to sixteen, and I'm giving him some extra tuition in English grammar.'

'Gramma Moses.' Eddie kicked away her slippers, and farted.

Where *had* she been that afternoon? Not shoplifting – she had nothing in her pockets – although she could have stolen food and eaten it. When Mrs Cardozo spotted her, she had been outside the pet shop, sniffing some bundles of hay. Then she stepped into the road. Where had she been before that?

Sometimes it was as though she was deliberately being obtuse. She had always had a streak of obstinacy and, despite the devastating effect of her illness, some of her personality remained intact. Now and again, when she was still living at home, she had remembered something from long ago with an accuracy Jane found incredible. *We had a puncture and a boy with red hair changed the wheel and we gave him ten pounds.* That was long-term memory. Short-term was a different matter, but short-term meant literally a few minutes ago. What about last weekend?

A woman Jane had never seen before had entered the room. Jane said hello and the woman, who had white hair, so thin her scalp showed through, nodded and smiled.

'Eddie and I worked together, at a local comprehensive school.'

'Yes, I know.'

Did she mean Eddie had told her? Perhaps the weekend at home had jogged her memory. The woman looked more "with it" than Eddie who was muttering something about cadmium yellow.

'Yes, we looked at your paintings. In the loft. Your studio. You came back for the weekend and on the Saturday you went for a little walk and Mrs Cardozo from the café brought you home.'

A shrug of annoyance, like a child who has been told off.

The other woman stood up, smoothed her skirt, and sat down again.

'Eddie used to teach art,' Jane said.

'Yes, I know.'

The Spruces encouraged creativity and there had been an incident when Eddie had been offered some crayons and a sheet of paper and had thrown them on the ground and stamped the crayons into the carpet. Jane had some sympathy with her although the member of staff, who had no knowledge she had been an artist, would have meant well.

One of the helpers – Jane had never seen her before – wheeled in a tray of tea things. Visitors were offered a cup of tea and a rich tea biscuit but Jane rarely accepted. There was something about the smell of the place that took away her already meagre appetite.

'Hello.' The helpers probably welcomed a brief, comprehensible conversation. 'I'm a friend of Miss Knox, Eddie. We used to live together. My name's Jane.'

'Clara,' the woman said. 'I come yesterday.'

To work at The Spruces or from her native country? No, surely no one could obtain a job that quickly. Although you never knew. A builder from Latvia, who was working in Faraday Road had come to live with relatives, speaking no English, and now spoke fluently and worked from seven in the morning to nine o'clock at night.

Declining the offer of tea, Jane turned back to Eddie. 'You remember Simmy who lives next door? They're converting the loft in her house. The usual upheaval and noise and I wondered … I thought you might have gone up there to have a look.'

'Loft,' Eddie said.

'Yes, that's right. Did you see Noel? You remember Noel. Dark hair and very bright blue eyes.' Jane turned to the white-haired woman. 'Eddie came home last weekend.'

'Yes, I know.'

Mercifully, the sound on the television had been turned down low. Jane recognised an actor from *Eastenders* – the one who had been murdered the previous week. *Eastenders* was Jane's guilty secret. Mondays, Tuesdays, Thursdays and Fridays. Half an hour of non-stop conflict and misery. Why guilty? Human beings loved stories. Dickens' novels had been serialised in the newspaper. *Smoke lowering down from chimney-pots, making a soft, black drizzle.* It would have taken a whole episode of *Bleak House* to get beyond the London smog. Jane was attached to the book – she had studied it for A-level – and when she tried to sort out Eddie's bank and building society accounts, following her admission to The Spruces, she had discovered nothing much had changed, with regard to the legal profession. Frustrated by delays and loss of paperwork, she had made a light-hearted remark about Jarndyce and Jarndyce. It had not gone down well.

'Teatime, Eddie.' No point asking any more questions. Her prompts about Saturday afternoon only irritated. She would have to be patient and hope Eddie inadvertently let slip where she had been.

Somewhere in the building, she could hear Matron's booming voice complaining about a ladder. Eddie's window, a wooden one, had been replaced by double-glazed PVC – but the builders were still hard at work – although, by the sound of it, not as hard as Matron would have liked.

'Eddie?' Jane decided to have one final try. 'You remember how you came back to the house last weekend? Back to Faraday Road. And you saw Simmy and after that you walked down to the shops. Did you go anywhere else? They're having the loft converted next door. In Dave and Gus' house. And sometimes the front door is left open although not normally on Saturdays.' She had said too much, made it too complicated. 'Did you go up the loft in Dave and Simmy's house?'

'Loft,' Eddie said.

'Yes, that's right. You might have wanted to see it. If you did, it doesn't matter, but can you remember – was Noel there?'

'Is it time?'

'Time for what?' Jane's voice had been too sharp. 'Noel, Eddie, you remember Noel.'

'Go away.'

Jane felt hot with frustration. Was there a keyword that would make the cells in Eddie's brain wake up? 'I'll have to go home in a minute, Eddie. I just wanted to make sure nothing was worrying you.'

'Is it time?'

Matron's head came round the door. 'Ah, you're still here, Miss Seymour. Good. I wondered if Edwina left her hairbrush at your house. Naturally, we found her a new one, but she rejected it, insisting it didn't belong to her.'

'I'll check when I return home.' Surely they could have ignored Eddie's demands and the wretched brush would have been forgotten in a matter of days. Where was it? Had it been packed in her overnight bag? Had she taken it up to next door's half-finished loft conversion?

'If you would.' Matron was smiling too much. She suspected something? How could she? And if she did, surely she would have come straight out with it. Jane took a grip on herself, accepting a rich tea biscuit and a cup of tepid tea.

'As I think I told you before,' she lied, 'once she'd looked round the house, and greeted the cat, she had a sleep. No, first she had her lunch, then a sleep. She was tired. Not surprising really when she hadn't been back to the house for some time.' She was talking too fast, stumbling over her words. 'The hairbrush. Don't worry, I'm sure it will turn up.'

'Oh, we're not worried, Miss Seymour.' Matron straightened a rug. 'We just like to keep the residents as calm as possible, I'm sure you understand. When you brought her back on Saturday evening she did appear particularly agitated. Nothing happened to alarm her, did it?'

'No, I told you. I made sure of that.'

'Perhaps she picked up on how upset you were feeling.

146

Do you suppose that was it? The new tablets doctor prescribed seem to be having the required effect.'

'I gave her one, like you said.' Had she, or had there been no chance? Matron had insisted it must not be taken until after lunch, and then Simmy had turned up. Or had she given it to Eddie before that? Did it matter? Would it have made any difference?

Matron's tall, angular body was receding into the distance. As Jane watched, she turned, catching at a thick lock of hair that had blown across her face. She suspected something, Jane was sure of it, but what? Or did she simply want to underline how difficult Eddie had been since her one night at home? *Your idea, Matron, arranged to suit the carpenter or whoever it was that repaired the bedroom window. And your choice of a weekend.* No, probably the only weekend the window man could come. And the weekend Noel decided to check the balcony in his wretched loft conversion. And she let Eddie slip through her fingers because she was too busy being nice to Simmy.

Thus conscience does make cowards of us all. Poor old Hamlet, someone else who didn't know whether he was coming or going.

TWENTY-ONE

Corinne answered the door with a pink chiffon scarf clutched to her face. 'Oh, Jane, oh, thank you. I'm so glad to see you. I don't know what to do.'

'I wondered if you'd like to accompany me to the Portuguese café? It would do you good to get out of the house. Have you had lunch?'

'No. Nothing,' Corinne was wearing a black dress that stopped just above her knees, and her silk scarf was a subdued lavender and grey. 'The police think I must have been the last person to see him ...' She broke off, unable to say the word "alive".

'Come along then. Do you need a jacket? It's overcast but not cold.'

'Do you think I do?'

'We're not going far.' It was like a conversation with a child. 'Have you been in touch with your ex-husband?'

'Gerard?' She twisted the ring on her left hand. 'We're still married. He wouldn't agree to a divorce. I mean, he would have done in the end. The house. What will happen to the house? It's always about money, isn't it?'

'Tends to be. Come on, we can talk over lunch.'

'Oh, Jane.' Her hand shot up to her mouth. 'It's your swimming day.'

'I'm having a rest from swimming.'

'Because of Noel.'

'Come on.' Jane took her arm. 'Fish pie. Mrs Cardozo makes an excellent fish pie. A Portuguese recipe. She says they eat a lot of fish in Portugal, something to do with having such a long coastline I expect.'

Corinne swayed on her high heels, almost falling against the wall, and Jane reached out to steady her. On the opposite side of the road, Willa was shouting at Tricia Tidewell.

'Why do you let them? Don't you know what's happened? A death in the street and they're still shouting and pulling at each other. Leave the honeysuckle alone!'

'I'm sorry.' Tricia took hold of Pippa, but there was no need since she and Liam were staring, open-mouthed, at the "mad woman".

'Wait there, Corinne.' Jane crossed the road. 'Hello, Liam. Pippa. Where are you off to?'

'The playground.' Tricia raised a hand to Corinne and whispered to Jane. 'Is she all right? I don't know what to say. We'd gone out for the day and when we came back … Ian thinks the balcony must have given way.'

'I'll explain later.'

'You'll come round.'

'Yes, if you like.' There was a faint possibility Tricia might have seen something.

Liam was trying to stamp on a beetle and Pippa was pulling leaves off a shrub. Tricia came closer and lowered her voice. 'It *was* an accident, wasn't it? Only someone said …'

'Who?'

'That man who lives by himself. I don't know his name.'

'Mr. Owen?'

'His wife took an overdose.'

'No, she went to live with her tennis coach.'

'Did she?' Tricia's expression brightened. 'Anyway, he said the police had been asking questions. Liam wants to be a policeman when he's grown up. He said he'd seen someone going into your neighbour's house.'

'Mr Owen did.' Jane glanced at Corinne but she was waiting patiently, pushing up her hair with both hands and holding it in a bunch on top of her head.

'No, Liam. Liam said he saw … I don't know what he saw. He loves cats. Your cat, the one with a funny name. Willa shouted at him.'

'Yes, I heard. What did he see, Tricia? I mean, who did he see?'

'I don't know. He didn't know. I think it was her.' She jerked her head in the direction of Willa.

'What makes you think that? We should all make an effort not to gossip, it doesn't help. Poor Noel's death was an accident. He must have leaned too far over the balcony.

150

It's a tragedy. Everyone's upset. Especially for poor Corinne.'

Willa had walked away. Jane returned to Corinne and took her arm. 'Take no notice of all that. Everyone's upset.'

'What are they called?'

'Tricia's children? Liam and Pippa, and the baby in the buggy is called Ada.'

'Ada? I had a cleaner called Ada but she cut corners. Gerard gave her the sack and I wished he hadn't because we used to have coffee together in the kitchen.' Corinne's voice had reached a pitch of near hysteria. 'We were friends but she never moved the furniture when she vacuumed. She's so lucky.'

'Lucky?' Jane had lost the thread. If there had been one.

'Mrs … I've forgotten her name. Liam and Poppy. I'd give anything for a baby.'

'Pippa,' Jane corrected.

'I saw her car. It had a sticker – "Little Princess on board".'

'I don't think it was Tricia's car. I don't think she drives, but I know what you mean about the sticker. One hopes the "little princess" will be a tomboy, fond of model railways and toy guns.'

'I'd love a little girl.' And the tears streamed down her face.

Jane handed her a tissue. 'Tricia's finding it difficult to cope, especially now it's the school holidays. Come along then. I hope the café's not too crowded.'

It was, but Jane managed to find a table for two, and hoped they still had fish pie on the menu, something Jane liked but rarely bothered to cook for herself. All those exotic meals she and Eddie had planned to sample. Together they had looked up Senegal online and discovered rice was the staple food, cooked in a peanut sauce or baked in a thick sauce of fish and vegetables. Côte d'Ivoire sounded mildly alarming, something that had appealed to Eddie, but less so to Jane. It had expensive hotels and glitzy high rise buildings, but strolling down the street you were likely to meet soldiers with guns. West Africa was only to be the start of their journey. After that they were to visit Australia, and New Zealand and …

'People used to say he was a sensation seeker.' Corinne dabbed her eyes, being careful not to smudge her pearly eye-shadow. 'They enjoy activities like skydiving and scuba diving. He never sat about doing nothing, he was always on the move, making plans. Sometimes I could hardly keep up with him.'

'He was very happy with you, Corinne.'

'Do you think so? Oh, thank you, Jane, except that makes it even worse, doesn't it? He told me he had something he needed to check.' She closed her eyes and rocked backwards and forwards. 'They'd put the bathroom in but the balcony in the main room wasn't finished and he was afraid the men had skimped on the paint. I'd gone to Yvonne's house.'

'Yvonne?' Jane beckoned to Mr Cardozo.

'She sells lingerie. You can try things on. I was choosing something special and all the time ... a negligée, I was buying a negligée.' Her last words had come out as a wail and Mr Cardozo, who was handing each of them a menu, took a step back.

'The fish pie, Corinne?' Jane stared at the photograph on the wall, a picture of the Castelo de Almourol, a castle on an island in the middle of the River Tagus. Mrs Cardozo had told her about the history of it. No point telling Corinne. At the best of times she would have had no interest. Just now, she was studying her nail varnish, bright pink with one silver nail.

'I'll have whatever you're having, Jane.'

'Very well. Two fish pies, please.' She smiled at Mr Cardozo. His first name was Andre and he had an interesting face but liked to keep himself to himself. 'Now.' She turned back to Corinne. 'Do you know if Noel made a will? I'm sorry, but at a time like this one has to be practical. And if you need anyone to help with the arrangements for the funeral ...'

'I saw that Mrs Emerson in the distance and she crossed the road so she wouldn't have to speak to me.'

'She didn't know what to say. No, that's no excuse. It's the same with Eddie. People use all kinds of euphemisms. A bit forgetful. Feeling her age. She has vascular dementia but people dislike the word.'

'Do you think I should phone Barnaby again?'

'He hasn't been to see you yet?'

'Something to do with his bike. He likes cycling. He's very fit.'

'I'm sure.' These days "fit" was synonymous with attractive, but not in Jane's world, or Corrine's. 'You must be proud of him.'

'Do you think he's glad?'

'Glad?' Jane felt obliged to look puzzled. 'Oh, you mean … no, of course not. He must be worried about you.'

'He didn't say much. When I phoned.'

'That's because he's a teenage boy. When I was at the school, the girls used to come to us with their problems, but the boys hardly ever.'

The new owner of number twenty-two had come into the café. She was still wearing her woolly hat, and had a friend with her, a small, blonde woman in her late thirties or early forties – it was hard to tell these days. Jane would have liked to introduce herself but they were talking animatedly and gave no indication they had recognised her. And it would mean she had to introduce Corinne too and that might be awkward. *Hello, I believe you're moving into Faraday Road. My name's Jane Seymour and I live next door to Gus. And this is Corinne. You probably heard how her partner …*

Corinne was studying the back of the menu. The café was not licensed but sold soft drinks and bottled water. Was Corinne hoping for something stronger? She looked up and there were tears in her eyes. 'He never cried.'

'Noel didn't?'

'It wasn't because he didn't care. His mother died before I met him. Sometimes he told funny stories about her – she called the loo "the lavatory" and she didn't like talking about that kind of thing. It was because he wanted to remember her as she really was, if you know what I mean.'

'I do.' The woman from number twenty-two had asked for six pastries and Mrs Cardozo was putting them in a box.

'I wish I'd met her.' Corinne was still talking about Noel's mother. 'Do you think she'd have liked me? You saw that portrait of her upstairs. She looks a bit fierce, doesn't she, but Noel said she adored him. Once we visited her grave. Not near here – we had to go in the car. It was my idea and Noel laughed when I suggested it. He thought I was being sentimental but he was quite sentimental himself, only not about his mother, about poor animals in other countries that are taught to do tricks. Things like that.'

Let her talk. Some people thought mentioning the dead person upset the bereaved. As if he or she was not on their mind twenty-four hours a day. Eddie wasn't dead, but she might as well be.

Mrs Cardozo had arrived with the fish pie. Her dark, wavy hair was held back by two metal clips and she was wearing a jumper with a picture of a Scottie dog on the front. Jane said '*Bom-dia*' and Mrs Cardozo smiled, but avoided her eyes. No doubt the pronunciation had been incorrect, but she had tried. *Bom-dia* in the morning and

155

boa-tarde in the afternoon and evening. Jane wanted to thank her again for bringing Eddie back but now was not the time.

The two women had left and were collecting a black Labrador that had been tied up outside. Would it be coming to live in the road or did it belong to "number twenty-two's" friend? When Jane left home, Gus had been out in the street, listening to the noise coming from his house. Not the builders this time, it was Simmy, shouting. Dave had come out, on his way to his workshop, and in no mood to pass the time of day. Had Simmy been having another go at finding out how her mother had died? Or was she still upset about Noel, and Dave was disinclined to talk about it?

To Jane's relief, Corinne was tucking into her fish pie with gusto. Gusto – where did the word come from? Gostar was the Portuguese word for "to like". Probably no connection, but Jane's interest in language was as keen as it had ever been. Fish pie was *bacalhau com natas* and it was made with salted cod, onions and cream, and, according to Mrs Cardozo, in the fourteenth century cured fish had been kept in ships' holds for years. This explained why the cod had to be soaked overnight, a throwback to the days when fish needed to be dried because there was no refrigeration.

'Jane?'

'Yes?' Something about Corinne's tone of voice made her pull in her chair and sit up straight.

'Eddie was with you, wasn't she?'

Did she mean when she found Noel's body? 'Only for a short visit.' Had Mrs Cardozo told people how she had found Eddie trying to cross the road?

'Does she know?'

'I took her back to The Spruces. She'd been having a rest.' Lies came so easily. Some people were more convincing liars than others but even small children could make quite a good job of it, although some were more adept than others. 'She's not very strong.' Once she had started she was unable to stop. 'Quite shaky on her feet.' Another lie. During her visit, Eddie had given her a hefty push and she had fallen against the sharp corner of the table and still had a purple bruise on her hip.

Corinne's finger was in her mouth. 'I've swallowed a bone.'

'It'll only be a tiny one.'

'I think it's stuck!'

Heads turned and people stopped eating. 'Here.' Jane broke off a corner from one of the soft rolls in a basket in the middle of the table. 'That usually does the trick.'

'Noel says I fuss.' Fresh tears filled her eyes. She had spoken about him as though he was still alive. 'The love of my life, Jane. We were made for each other. I wanted a baby – I told you that, didn't I? If I was pregnant I'd have something to remember him by. I thought I might be but it was a false alarm. What can I do? I don't know what to do.'

Jane waited. Ever since she arrived at Corinne's house there had been one question she needed to ask. 'Corinne?'

'Yes.' She had taken a small mirror from her handbag and was checking her hair.

'Can you remember what time Noel left your house?'

'Just after two o'clock. Later, we were going to buy some paint. For the bathroom. It's rather dark. You probably noticed. Noel wanted ...'

'You're sure about the time?' She sounded like a police officer, and no doubt the police had asked the same thing.

'He had one of those watches that make a pinging noise. It always made me jump. It pinged at two and he told me he had to check the balcony. Then we discussed what colour the bathroom should be. Noel wanted white but I thought chameleon sounded attractive and we laughed because paints have such silly names.'

'Chameleons change colour.'

'Do they? What are they?'

'Lizards. They adapt according to the foliage they're sitting on.' In the circumstances, a pointless piece of information, and even Corinne was looking a little mystified.

'They sit on foliage?'

'It's nothing, Corinne, forget I mentioned it.'

'Then I said I wouldn't be long.' She closed her eyes, remembering. 'And Noel said there was no rush and I said ... if the balcony wasn't safe, the workmen should be sued. Do you think they should?'

Jane was thinking about Corinne's "alibi", her lingerie party. Had it taken place somewhere nearby? Had it taken place at all? Supposing Corinne had discovered Noel was having an affair, or several affairs. 'He must have leaned over too far,' she said, 'and lost his footing.'

'Yes, that's what I think.' Corinne's face flushed with anger. 'How could he be so careless? Honestly, Jane, I could kill him!'

TWENTY-TWO

Tricia Tidewell had nothing of interest to tell her. In fact, Jane wondered if she ever noticed anything that was going on in the road. If the badly-behaved children allowed her to. Jane had declined the offer of a cup of tea – the kitchen made Gus' flat seem immaculate – but agreed to sit on a grubby sofa and hold the baby while Tricia found snacks for Pippa and Liam. Jane had tried talking to the boy, hoping he really might have seen someone going into the house next door, but he had stared at her blankly, afraid no doubt that if he said anything he would get into trouble. Either that, and this was far more likely, or Tricia had misunderstood what he said, or put ideas into his head.

The baby was fat and placid, and rather comforting. Jane had lost track of how old she was. About eight months, she thought, a time when they often dislike strangers, but Ada seemed perfectly happy, pulling at a loose thread in Jane's jumper.

'You're a good girl, Ada, putting up with that brother and sister of yours. Not that you have much choice.' Jane realised she had spoken to the child in much the same way she spoke to Eddie. In other words, in the knowledge it was of no importance what she said, simply a way of expressing her interest and good will.

Tricia had returned, but fortunately not Liam or Pippa. 'I agree with you about the gossiping, Jane. Roads like this are a hotbed for that kind of thing.'

'Most residential roads, I imagine.'

'Simmy's a lovely girl. Pity she's too old to play with Pippa. I don't really know her father. Dave, isn't it? Pippa's afraid of him and Liam said he saw him having an argument with Mr McNeill, only that was two weeks ago. Could be more. And he couldn't hear what they were saying. Something about a skip I think. Why do they call them skips?'

Excusing herself, as soon as was polite, Jane had tried to think of a reason for going up to the loft conversion to look for Eddie's hairbrush. Telling the builders about the brush would raise suspicion. *Why did she think the hairbrush would be up there? No, if they had seen it they would remember.* Or worse, *yes, they had found a hairbrush, lying on the floor. Did she know how it could have got there?* More than likely, it had turned up in Eddie's room at The Spruces, or the room of one of the other residents, or down the loo!

When she reached The Spruces, a party was under way. Lulu, one of the residents, was celebrating her hundredth birthday. She had a pink bow in her hair and someone had made a cake with pink icing and not quite a hundred candles, but a considerable number.

Jane had put her head round the day room door then withdrawn again, but Matron was being uncharacteristically welcoming. 'Come in, come in. Have you met Lulu? Isn't she wonderful? And this is Dr Holland. Miss Seymour is Edwina's friend.'

'Ah.' He shook hands, looking her up and down as though he was assessing how long it would be before she moved into a care home. 'Good to meet you.'

Over by the window, Eddie was clutching the neck of her blouse. The party would upset her – she disliked anything unfamiliar – but when Matron announced that it was time to blow out the candles, she looked quite animated.

One, two, three! Matron leaned across and blew, and Lulu looked up at Dr Holland and smiled. 'Have you got a big one, doctor?'

Even Matron was unable to keep a straight face. Had dementia disinhibited Lulu or had she retained her sense of humour? Jane hoped it was the latter. *Happy birthday to you, happy birthday to you, happy birthday, dear Lulu, happy birthday to you.* The singing reached a crescendo and the usual clapping broke out – at least, Matron, Dr Holland, one of the helpers, and Jane clapped. The rest of the assembled band were waiting for a slice of cake.

Once the party was over, things returned to normal. Lulu was wheeled away and Eddie sat back in her chair, gazing at the television where someone was demonstrating how to tart up a piece of haddock with the aid of some tarragon – or was it thyme?

'Lovely cake, Eddie.' But talking about something that had passed was pointless. Jane ought to know that by now. 'They're cooking fish.'

'Fish and chips.'

'Yes, that's right. You know when you came home – to the house – while you were at the shops did you have anything to eat?'

Eddie smiled, then the smile faded and she looked as though she was going to cry, and full of remorse for confusing her with questions she was incapable of answering, Jane reached across to give her a brief hug and for once, Eddie didn't struggle to break free.

The fish in the cooking programme had been replaced by some kind of pie and the chef, whose name Jane had forgotten, was spooning a sticky concoction into the pastry case. The trouble with television, there were too many channels to fill. And a worse problem was that no one looked normal. Even the people in reality shows were made up to look as though they had flawless skin. Another of Jane's dislikes was the way ex-sports stars were given make-overs – and ridiculous clothes – that rendered them barely recognisable. A nice ordinary-looking girl who had excelled at swimming now had a not-very-flattering hairstyle, and false eyelashes.

The sanitized glamour of television. The smell of an old people's home. Jane held out little hope of achieving the purpose of her visit, but felt compelled to have another try.

'You remember Noel, Eddie. He was up in the loft, checking something.'

'Up the hill.'

'Noel, Eddie, in the loft.'

'Round and round the garden.'

'The garden?' But it was no good. If she *had* gone up to next door's loft conversion, she had no recollection of it. Jane stood up to stretch her legs and the handbag she had left by her chair fell open, scattering its contents on the carpet. One of the carers, another new one – or at least she was new to Jane – had appeared in the doorway. Squeezing past her trolley, she hurried to help, surprised no doubt that the handbag held such a hotchpotch of stuff – painkillers and the sticky remains of a throat sweet, a curled-up shopping list and a packet of things called "feminine wipes", that sounded obscene but came in useful on the odd occasion.

'Thank you so much.'

'No worries.'

'I'm Jane Seymour, a friend of Eddie's. Where do you come from?'

'Somalia. Four months.'

'You speak very good English.'

'Thank you.'

Jane glanced at the large, flickering television. Now someone was reading a news bulletin, something to do with a hurricane in the Far East. Then it changed to a simpering woman who Jane assumed must be a celebrity. That was the trouble with "The News", it all merged, the good, the bad and the indifferent, in one ear and out the other, and so-called reality shows blended with real-life tragedies and the ads convinced you your kitchen needed replacing, and normal signs of aging were because you had failed to pay a fortune for a pot of restorative serum. *With mirth and laughter let old wrinkles come. Twelfth Night*? No, *The Merchant of Venice*.

'You like coffee?' The woman from Somalia had a beautiful face, and black hair, held in place by a rather attractive silk scarf.

'Yes, please. No sugar. No, not for Eddie, she's falling asleep.'

The woman smiled, showing perfect white teeth. Jane's were far from perfect – the result of poor dental work when she was younger – and last time she attended the dentist she had been referred to the dental health nurse and, whereas fillings were now relatively painless, dental health had replaced them as a new form of torture.

'Custard cream?'

'No, thank you, I had some cake.'

The woman looked blank.

'The birthday cake. For Lulu.'

'Ah. Yes. Lulu. So good for age.' The woman moved on and Jane began listing suspects in her head. Motive and opportunity. Anyone, absolutely anyone other than Eddie. Dave had worried in case Noel told Simmy the truth about her mother's death. How had Noel known?

Dave was unlikely to have told him so it must have been from some other source. And what was so bad that it had to be kept from Simmy? Had her mother been killed in a road accident? Dave could have been driving, over the limit perhaps, and blamed himself for his wife's death. Noel could have been blackmailing him. No, what was she thinking? The Noel she knew would never have done something like that. Except, had she really known him? She was as guilty as we all are of turning people into what we want them to be.

She had enjoyed her conversations with Noel but they were not on par with her discussions with Moira Winn, head of history. Sadly, she had died in harness. An image of Moira, with a bit and bridle, reared up before her eyes. Too many visual images these days and, between her and Eddie, she was supposed to be the verbal one. Perhaps a part of Eddie's brain had transmogrified into her own. Jane stifled a laugh and Eddie turned her head, smiling.

'Last weekend, Eddie.' She should have let the subject drop but she had to have one last go. 'You saw Simmy and after that you went for a walk. They're converting the loft in Dave and Simmy's house. And Gus lives there too, on the first floor. You remember Gus.'

Eddie pulled at a loose thread in her brown jumper. 'Cat,' she said, and her breathing became slower and deeper.

'Yes, cat. Rousseau.' A gardening expert on television had been joined by a woman with exceptionally large teeth and the two of them were enjoying some merry

166

banter. Why did people on TV laugh so much? They laughed in the ads too. Chicken nuggets, new sofas, even cleaning materials, all produced peals of laughter. Jolly families – mother, father, son, daughter – sat round their dinner table, in fits over the gravy. Don't think about Noel's death, not now. Later, when she was home she would make a few notes, to calm herself.

As she was climbing into her car, she heard running footsteps. Matron. And her heart began to thump. Another interrogation, or had Eddie been doing, or saying, something Matron had been unable to mention in front of everyone else?

'Glad I caught you, Miss Seymour.' She was out of breath, holding her chest. 'I just wanted to tell you we found Edwina's hairbrush. And to say how sorry I was. About your neighbour. Was he a friend?'

'Yes, yes he was.'

'Awful for you, but there's no need to worry about Edwina, I doubt if she can remember a thing.'

Jane opened her mouth to say Eddie had not been there when it happened and, just in time, remembered her previous brief conversation with Matron. 'When I found him, she was having a little sleep.'

'Yes. She mentioned a cat.'

'Did she? She used to be fond of him but when she came back to the house she didn't take any notice.'

'We have a volunteer who does a "memory lane" session with some of the residents. In the past, Edwina has shown no interest but yesterday she was quite

167

enthusiastic, talking about Simmy, the cat.'

'No, Simmy is a child, a teenage girl, the daughter of a neighbour. Eddie saw her briefly when she came home. It must have reminded her.'

'You say she was asleep when you …'

'When I found Mr Mc … yes, yes she was. She'd eaten her lunch and wanted a little rest.' She had spoken emphatically, too emphatically, and Matron's pale, unblinking eyes bore into her.

'I only mentioned it,' she said, 'because she talked about a garden, with dandelions.'

'Dandelions? Was she watching a gardening programme at the time?'

'No, nothing like that and, knowing you as I do, Miss Seymour, I imagine there's not a weed in sight in your own garden.'

Knowing you as I do. She knew nothing about her. Except that was untrue. Unwittingly, one picked up all kinds of ideas about people, some of them from stray remarks, others from body language and such like.

Or was it that, when she was away from The Spruces, when Eddie was free of her inhibiting presence, she became more communicative?

TWENTY-THREE

Jane was not used to one-to-one teaching. In the past, if she had supervised a single pupil it had been because the child was in detention and, while he or she completed whatever they had been instructed to do, she had marked homework or tests. Eddie never gave anyone detention because nobody misbehaved in her art classes, or if they did she failed to notice.

On Monday, Jane had forgotten all about Arthur's lesson and on Tuesday evening Willa had phoned, suggesting the tuition was put off for the time being.

'Until you feel better, Jane.' Willa had sounded tearful. 'Until we all do. How do you ever get over something like that?'

Was she thinking about Corinne or herself? Herself, Jane suspected. Willa would have no sympathy for Corinne. She had stolen Noel from her. 'No, tell Arthur to come on Friday as usual. I find it's best to try to carry on as normal.'

'What could have happened?'

'He must have lost his balance.'

'Yes.' Willa sounded as though she had reason to think otherwise. Was she right? Noel's whispered word, but it could have been air escaping from his lungs. Or Eddie could have been up there, watching him, waiting for her chance. No, that was not how her mind worked. Noel would have been leaning over. Too far, on tiptoe perhaps. And Eddie would have needed little strength, although she was still physically strong enough to tip him over.

Head down, Arthur was scribbling away at the exercise she had given him – a piece of prose that contained several grammatical errors it was his job to spot and correct.

Crossing to a shelf, Jane picked up Eddie's book about Chagall and began flicking through the illustrations. Her back was turned but she sensed Arthur was watching her. It was hot in the loft – heat rose – and lacked sufficient ventilation. The back of her blouse had stuck to her skin and she feared she might smell of sweat. Super-duper antiperspirants were available, as the ads on television informed you nightly, but they brought her out in rash. The one she used was harmless but less effective.

As she turned the pages, she noticed, to her annoyance, that her hands were shaking. With nerves? How absurd. A child on its own rarely behaved badly. Groups of them, yes, since there was safety in numbers, but even the most disruptive of pupils could be charming if he or she had your whole attention. Not that she had ever had any problems with discipline. Eddie claimed it was because the children were afraid of her, but that was nonsense. She had never raised her voice because she had never needed to.

But her shaking hands, and fast-beating heart, had nothing to do with Arthur.

Turning more pages, she came across a handwritten note. Eddie's thoughts on an exhibition. Would she still enjoy looking at paintings? No, it was out of the question. Jane had once seen a man throw one of his shoes at a Monet. Supposing the same thought occurred to Eddie. Sadly, Jane reflected, she was unlikely to go to any more exhibitions herself. She avoided television programmes about art too, and was only studying the Chagall book to give her something to do. *Lovers in the Moonlight. The Blue Violinist.* Two different paintings called *I and the Village.* I and Faraday Road, she thought, and for a split second rather regretted she had never learned to draw. Gus, with his craggy face and slightly protruding eyes, would have made a good subject.

Her thoughts were interrupted by Arthur noisily pushing back his chair.

'Finished?' She replaced Chagall on the shelf.

'Absolutely.'

He had rushed it. Perhaps the exercise was too easy for him. Perhaps he felt insulted. His handwriting was appalling. Deliberately slapdash, a way of telling her he wished he was anywhere else but in her house?

'Does your friend live here, the one that did the

paintings?'

'Not now. She used to.' The question had thrown her. 'They're lovely, aren't they? Do you like art?'

'Gave it up.' He was resting his chin on his knuckles and looked perfectly at ease, almost asleep. Because he had diverted her attention away from his work? On second thoughts, he had been relaxed ever since she let him into the house. She was the tense one.

'I didn't come before,' he said. 'Because of ... you know.'

'Yes. Thank you. That was thoughtful of you.'

'I reckon it was harsh, you finding the body. Must have been a shock.'

'Yes, yes it was.' Jane had no wish to think about it but if it helped the boy come to terms with the tragedy, it was up to her to let him talk.

Taking two pencils from the jar, he lined them up, parallel with the edge of the table. 'I reckon he had it coming.'

'Oh, Arthur, that's an awful thing to say. What makes you ... oh, you mean because he wasn't always as careful as —'

'I reckon the cops should have asked more questions.'

'What kind of questions?' It was wrong to encourage him but she was unable to stop herself.

'Like if someone saw someone following him.' He was smiling to himself. 'You know my dad?'

'I do.'

'Mum was listening to *The Archers*. She loves *The*

Archers.'

Jane did too. Sometimes she listened to it on her tablet, using her finger to move the recording on, past the farming stuff, until it reached another juicy bit.

'Anyway, Dad kept interrupting, saying Noel had enemies, and Mum told him to shut his mouth, and Dad smiled, and she hit him.'

'We're all upset about what happened.'

'I'm not.' He stared at her but Jane remained silent. 'Dave didn't like him either. Simmy heard Noel and her dad having an argument.'

She should be telling him off for listening to gossip. 'When?'

'Yesterday Simmy asked if her mother had done a crime and Dave went to the bog, I mean the toilet, and slammed the door. Simmy thinks Noel knew her mother was in prison and he was going to tell her, and Dave found out and —'

'It was an accident, Arthur. A tragic accident.' She rubbed together her damp palms, picked up his work, and started checking it. 'You missed an error in the first paragraph.' She pointed to a word. 'It should have been an adverb, not an adjective.

'The lad's done good.' He laughed. 'That's wrong, isn't it, but what are they supposed to say? "The lad's done well" doesn't sound right, does it? I used to think I'd be a good football commentator.'

'Perhaps you might.' She was watching him carefully, but his face rarely gave anything away.

'Doctors used to be called quacks. Quacking means boasting. The doctor treated his wife badly. "Badly" is an adverb, right? And the stupid doctor treated his wife badly. Stupid's an adjective because it describes a noun.' He was spluttering with laughter. 'You know that parcel you brought to our house?'

Jane pretended to search for something in a pocket.

'Mum said it was a present for my dad but when it was his birthday she gave him a book about the Lake District. The one you brought round wasn't a book. People like getting parcels.'

'They do.' What was he telling her? That he had found the "patent leather" outfit? Worse, that he had seen his mother trying it on?

'Mum buys a lot of stuff online, to cheer herself up. Mostly clothes so I expect that's what was in the parcel.' He had his tongue in his cheek, literally. 'Another of those tops people wear so you can't see how their stomach sticks out. D'you s'pose that's what it was?'

'I've no idea, Arthur. Now, to get back to the use of adverbs and adjectives …' But just now he had no interest in English grammar. And neither did she.

'Simmy had another idea for a computer game. Murders from the past. Cold cases. I told her there was probably one already but she didn't care. She's making a list of motives. Motive and opportunity.'

'Yes, well why not write two paragraphs on the subject.'

'Now?'

'Yes, now.'

He looked up. 'It's a hard life. That's what my dad thinks. "Hard" is an adjective. And the only way to make it better is to buy stuff excessively. Excessively is an adverb. Right? That's my mum, the buying stuff.'

'Two paragraphs, Arthur.' Jane was losing patience. 'Motive and opportunity, but write it as though it's the opening to a crime novel. Do you think you can do that?'

'Dunno. Yes, all right. The characters can be drug dealers, a man and a woman. I reckon most of the people who drive four-by-fours are drug dealers.'

'That's ridiculous.'

He laughed. 'I know. Noel had a four-by-four. I've never seen Corinne driving it.'

After he left she went in search of Rousseau. If she could persuade him to sit on her knees, she could stroke him and it might have a calming effect. She found him in the airing cupboard – either she had left it open or he had learned how to open it with his paw – sitting on the bedspread from Eddie's bed. Her sheets and duvet cover were in the laundry basket, waiting for Jane's next big wash, but she had put away the blue bedspread as soon as she came back from returning Eddie to The Spruces.

'Come here, you beastly cat. A nice sunny day, you ought to be out in the garden.' She was talking to him as if he was a child. He would pick up that she was near breaking point – animals were sensitive to such things. 'Oh, Rousseau, what are we going do?'

He licked his nose, almost as though preparing to answer her rhetorical question, then sprang from his shelf in the cupboard, and darted down the stairs, and she heard the click of the cat flap.

Now what? Stop thinking the worst. Arthur enjoyed observing the residents of Faraday Road. They were grist to his computer game. He was enjoying speculating about Noel's accident but it had never crossed his mind Eddie could have had any part in it.

Pushed. The word she had barely heard. But she *had* heard it. Finding a pad and a ballpoint pen, she started making a list of suspects, anyone who had even the flimsiest of motives.

TWENTY-FOUR

Dave was returning from his workshop and the expression on his face told her it would not be a good time to mention Simmy's mother. And surely even Simmy would realise her problem had to be put on hold for a day or two. Dave's hands were occupied, rolling a cigarette, and his phone was balanced between his shoulder and ear.

'Too right.' He gave a short, unpleasant laugh. 'No, not a chance.' Then, spotting Jane, 'Ring you back when I've fixed a date.'

'Had a busy day, Dave?'

He lit his roll-up. 'Simmy been bothering you?'

'She's never a bother. I'm fond of her, she's a sweet girl.'

'Depends what mood she's in. How are you? Bad luck you were the one that found him. I was at an auction. Other side of town.'

There was something different about him but she was unable to put her finger on what it was. He looked older, his face more lined. How old *was* he? It was something she had never thought about, along with avoiding examining his expression too closely, for fear it elicited a comment from his sharp tongue. *What are you up to, Jane, checking on the neighbours, making sure we toe the line, don't put our bins out on the wrong day.*

'Saw the Molloy boy leaving your house,' he said. 'He and Sim play computer games, at least that's what she says they do.'

'You're not implying … I'm sure there's nothing like that. I expect Simmy's told you they're devising their own game.' *Cronus, the bad father, who ate his own children.* 'Arthur says she's very good at IT. It will stand her in good stead.'

'You think so?'

'I do.'

On the opposite side of the road, the old man from number twenty-four was drawing a line of chalk round a pile of dog shit. Not the work of Lucky, from number twenty-six – the turds were large, could even be human. Jane shuddered and Dave noticed and gave a gnome-like chuckle.

'Been to India?'

'No, have you?'

'Years ago. They think we're too squeamish. Some parts you have to step your way through shit. Get used to. Can get used to anything.'

'That may be true. Perhaps not *anything*.'

'Once you've got a kid it puts an end to foreign travel.'

'I don't see why. You could take Simmy with you.'
Jane was trying to picture Dave "years ago", a student
perhaps, on holiday with Simmy's mother. 'A holiday
would do you both good. Simmy mentioned a caravan in
Cornwall.'

Dave stared at her. His deep-set eyes were intimidating
and Jane suspected he intended them to be. 'Yes, well,
some of us have work to do.'

'Of course, but you need a break now and again.'

'Away from the scene of the crime you mean.' He
jerked his head towards the loft conversion. 'Mrs Garcia
been back?'

'I haven't seen her.'

'Gus says she's going to let the loft to a band. Two
members of some rock group. One of them plays the
drums.'

'Are you sure?'

He grinned. He was joking. But she would take his
words at face value, call his bluff. 'Oh well, if you're
right, I believe there's something you can do to deaden
the sound. They're called mutes. I think that's the right
name. They had a programme about noise pollution and
disruptive neighbours.'

'Watch a lot of telly, do you?'

'It was on the radio. You have one in your workshop, I
believe, so you can listen to jazz.'

'If I get much more work, I'll have to take on a
partner.'

'Really? You *must* be doing well.'

179

'Not what Simmy thinks. She thinks I should get a proper job. With some big company that paid me a monthly salary. And have some idiot telling me what to do.'

'Is that what she said?'

'I expect someone put the idea in her head.'

'Not guilty, Dave, I wouldn't dream of discussing your work with your daughter.'

He laughed, an unpleasant sound, and drew on his roll-up. Overtly, a harmless conversation but Dave had a way of turning everything into a battle of wits. Jane found it irritating. Her only aim was that poor Simmy should have a holiday by the sea, a break from Faraday Road. But was that really her aim? These days she noticed every tiny sign – a barely perceptible pause, a cough, the interlocking of fingers – but she was the guilty one, interfering in people's lives as she attempted to gather what, in all probability, was irrelevant information. So Dave had been at an auction. What auction? She could look it up on her tablet but finding a date and a venue would not prove Dave had been there.

Tossing his roll-up into the gutter, he ran one of his grubby fingers down the grooves in the lamp post. Was there something he wanted? Was he sounding her out? Perhaps he thought she knew something about Simmy. Simmy and Arthur. Teenagers had sex at an earlier age these days, earlier than in her day, but not earlier than Romeo and Juliet. Had Romeo and Juliet slept together? Was it implied in the text? She thought not.

Tricia Tidewell had joined them, holding the baby, but minus the other two. 'Liam's gone to a holiday club and Pippa's at a friend's house. Hello, Dave, I haven't seen you for ages, not since … Terrible, wasn't it, and poor Jane was the one … Ian and I had gone out for …' She seemed incapable of finishing a sentence. 'We didn't know him well but he was …'

'You're talking about Noel?'

'So it's just you and Ada this morning.' Jane said. 'That'll be nice.'

Tricia gave her a grateful smile. Had she come out of her house, hoping for a friendly chat? If she had, she had chosen the wrong moment. Jane glared at Dave and he grinned back and Tricia brightened visibly.

'I was talking to Simmy, Dave, and she told me you're going to Cornwall. How lovely.'

'We're not.'

'Oh, I must have got it wrong. I love Cornwall, don't you, Jane? Although it does get rather crowded in August. Ian and I had our honeymoon in Mevagissey, do you know it? It was in the spring but it was still quite busy, but I didn't mind, I like lots of people about, I'm not one for empty spaces. Is "Simmy" short for Simone?'

'No.' A shadow crossed Dave's face. 'That's what she was christened. Well, not actually christened.'

Fortunately, Ada put an end to any more, simultaneously pulling her mother's hair and kicking her in the ribs. 'I'd better give her a snack. She's horrible when she's hungry. Nice to see you Dave. And you Jane.'

'Oh, Tricia.' Jane dreaded the reply but she had to ask. 'You know you said Liam saw someone going into Dave and Gus' house.'

'Did he? When?'

'I'm not sure. I just wondered if he noticed who it was.'

'Doubt it. He's only interested in cars. Knows all the different makes. Toyotas, Vauxhalls, Saabs. Ticks them off in a notebook. Good for his writing skill. Is that what you think, Jane? Yes, I thought you would.'

Farther down the road, Gus and the woman from number twenty-two were deep in conversation. Who was she, and why did she have to wear that hideous hat? Not that it had put off Gus. From the look on his face, she could have been his dearest friend.

'Jane?'

'Oh, sorry, Dave, did you say something? Even if *you* don't want a holiday it would be good for Simmy. Noel's death was such a shock, the first death of someone she knew well I imagine.' But even as she spoke, she realised her mistake. 'What I meant ...'

'Don't look like that, I know what you meant. She was only two and a half when her mother died, can't remember a thing.'

Now was her chance, but from the look on his face, eleven years had done little to soften the blow of his wife's death. Jane warmed to him a little. His gruff exterior was a defence from pain. She should have realised, should have felt more well-disposed toward him.

Had Noel known what happened to his wife and threatened to tell Simmy, and a furious Dave had ...

No. Anxiety about Eddie was making her irrational. Noel's death had been an accident. Of course it had. Except would he have been silly enough to lean over the balcony and lose his balance? Why take a risk when there was no audience? His leaps in the air, and swinging from the scaffolding had always produced a gratifying response, mostly laughter. But alone in the new loft conversion ...

Jane pictured the fall from two floors up. Landing on Dave's patio, fatally injured but not quite dead. *Pushed.* A single whispered word. His last utterance – a plea for her to uncover the culprit responsible. Or to tell the police.

TWENTY-FIVE

Jane's anxiety had reached a peak. She hoped it *was* the peak. It was as though her life was on hold, and would be until she discovered the truth. Never a big eater, she had lost her appetite almost entirely but, at lunchtime, had managed to force down a poached egg on toast. Washing up afterwards, and putting her plate and cutlery away, was more satisfying than eating because it provided order, moved things on. During the last few days she had made copious notes – writing things down sometimes had a soothing effect – but any information she had acquired was vague in the extreme, and possibly untrue.

Gus had been taking photographs at some unspecified location. Dave had been at an auction. Corinne had been at a lingerie party, whatever that was supposed to be. And Willa claimed she had been at the shops. Jane's fear that Eddie had pushed Noel over the balcony was growing by the day.

Pursing her lips, she attempted without success to

recreate the sound she had heard. *Whoosh. Sh. Pushed.* Everyone with a motive had an alibi. Not a good one since she had no means of checking. And there was Brian, who could have found out about Noel and Willa, and confronted Noel while he was checking the balcony. Part accident, part foul play. If Jane had managed to open the parcel and re-wrap it, so could Brian.

No opportunity to talk to him at home so she would have to make another appointment at the health centre and that might take several days to arrange, although, as it turned out, the receptionist – the friendly one, who smiled rather than behaving like the keeper at the gate – said Dr Molloy could fit her in at five-fifteen. What would she tell him was the problem? A bad back? Stiff neck? Both symptoms where the doctor had to take the patient's word for it. No, there was no need to lie. She would say she was suffering from insomnia. If he reached for his prescription pad, she would ask if he had any other suggestions, a milky drink at bedtime – guaranteed to get you up to go to the loo – or whale music – how ridiculous – or an audiobook – more sensible. But, knowing Brian, he would say it was another psychosomatic symptom, this time brought on by Noel's death.

The waiting room was full of silent patients, apart from a small girl who had found a copy of *Country Life*, with its pictures of working dogs, and shooting jackets, and was enjoying scribbling on the pictures with a red crayon, while singing *Baa, baa, black sheep*. Jane smiled at her and she put out her tongue, and Jane responded in like manner. People said children were not sufficiently disciplined these days – true in the case of the Tidewells – but as far as Jane could remember they had always put out their tongues, provided their parents were looking in the other direction.

A tall man, with rounded shoulders and ill-fitting trousers, was studying a poster for sexually transmitted diseases. He looked a bit past that kind of thing, but one could never tell. How old was Gus? Older than her or roughly the same? She could ask him and, unlike her, he probably had no objection to divulging his age.

'Jane?' Brian was smiling, but looked done in. Was he suffering from lack of sleep, too? They could commiserate together but, in spite of his wish for her to "get her feelings out in the open", Brian gave little away, either in his personal or professional role. Not that she knew him that well, although Arthur had told her rather more than he should. *Mum shouts at him when he leaves his pants on the bedroom floor and he loses his temper and says if she's nothing better to think about she ought to get a job.*

Jane hurried to join him, rehearsing in her head what she was going to say, but there was no need since Brian spoke first and it was not to ask how he could help, but to say how shocked he had been about Noel.

'Yes, we all are. Such a tragedy.'

'How did it happen, do you suppose?' He drew his lower lip over the ends of his neat moustache. 'Leaning over to check something? Leaned too far and lost his balance?'

'I imagine so.'

'And it was you who called the ambulance.' His fingers were intertwined. 'What a blessing you found him. I mean, what a blessing it wasn't Dave's daughter. How long did the ambulance take? It all depends …'

'They were in the area. Quite close by.'

'Good, good.' His voice shook. Not from grief that Noel was dead. Tiredness, overwork, or was it fear?

'I talked to him – you're not supposed to move people are you – but I think I knew it was hopeless. It's such a long drop from those loft conversions.'

Something was going on in the waiting room, raised voices, shouting, but Brian appeared oblivious. Since the slot only lasted ten minutes he ought to be asking why she was there, but he looked as though he was more in need of a doctor than she was. He had a tic in his left eye, and the hands that fiddled with a pen on his desk trembled.

'I've been sleeping badly, Brian. No, not just since the accident. Before that. I go to sleep quite easily but wake at two or three and it's a time when things prey on your mind. No, I don't want medication, it's addictive and makes you feel drowsy the following day. And I like to keep my wits about me.'

He opened his mouth, possibly to tell her there were newer, better drugs, but she came in quickly again. 'It's because I'm old, isn't it? Old people don't need so much sleep.'

He picked up a large plastic apple that bore the name

of a well-known pharmaceutical company. *An apple a day keeps the doctor at bay.* Or was it "away"? Doctors like Brian no longer sat behind a desk. They sat next to it. To put the patient at his or her ease, no doubt. Jane preferred a clear separation, doctor and patient, not a combined attempt to solve the problem. 'How's the rash?'

'Oh.' The sharpness in his voice had made her jump. 'Gone. Disappeared.'

He nodded.

'The problem is, Brian, when I'm lying awake I start wondering if it really *was* an accident.'

She expected an exclamation of surprise, even if it was feigned, but he sat up straight in his chair and cupped his face in his hands. 'Willa's gone.'

'Gone?'

'To her sister in Devon. No, Cornwall. On the border.'

'I see, I thought … I expect she needed a break, will be back in a day or two?'

He shrugged, picking up his prescription pad and putting it down again. 'That parcel you dropped off at our house. Did she mention what it was?'

'No.'

'Just wondered.' His attempt to sound casual was pitiful. 'She's a very sensitive person, easily upset, up and down. No, I don't mean bi-polar, nothing as extreme as that.'

'She was fond of Noel?'

'Fond of him, why d'you say that?'

'We all were. Well, perhaps not all, but he brightened

up Faraday Road with his anecdotes. And antics,' she added, although saying it made her flinch. Jumping up and swinging on the scaffolding, running down the street, with a hop and a skip. Perhaps it really had been an accident.

Opening a drawer, Brian took out a dog-eared sheet of paper. 'Tips for getting to sleep at night.' He began to read and Jane pretended to listen. *A warm bath before bedtime.* Did he want her to admit she had re-wrapped the parcel? *A good mattress and thick curtains. A milky drink, not coffee or tea.* Not something he was likely to mention, but apparently sex made you sleepy. Or, as the handy hints sheet was unlikely to suggest, if you lacked a partner, masturbation.

'Were you around on Saturday, Brian? I wondered if you'd seen Noel going into the house next to mine. Gus was out, taking photographs and Dave was at an auction.'

'Saturday?' He scratched his chin. 'Ah yes, where was I. I know, I went for a long walk. Good for the lungs.'

'With Willa?'

He shook his head slowly. 'She's not a great walker, says she'd walk more if we had a dog. I needed the exercise.' He patted his stomach. 'Spend all week sitting listening to people. Need time to unwind.'

'Did you go somewhere nice?'

'The woods.' He licked his lips. 'No, come to think of it, Willa did accompany me.'

Willa had told Jane she was down at the shopping centre.

'Or was that the weekend before? One week runs into another. I'm sure it's the same with you.' He glanced at his wall clock, relieved no doubt that her allotted time had overrun. Like Gus, he was not prepared to tell her where his walk had been. 'Relaxation, Jane, not looking at screens immediately before bedtime.'

'Yes. Thank you.' She stood up. So did Brian. 'Oh, dear,' she said, 'you do look tired and all these patients, most of them with silly little problems like mine.' Now he would say, "your problems are never silly, Jane", but he was miles away and the lines between his eyes had deepened. What was he thinking about? She would love to have known.

To her surprise, Gus was in the waiting room, sitting next to one of the builders, the young one she thought was called Lee.

'Cut himself.' Gus pointed to an improvised bandage wrapped round the young man's hand. 'Thought it'd be better than A and E, not such a long wait.'

'Oh dear, how did it happen?'

'Screwdriver slipped. Blood everywhere. I offered to bring him here.'

'That was good of you.'

'Lee shares my interest in photography.'

'Do you, Lee?'

'Just family pictures.' Lee pushed up his quiff of hair with his good hand. 'My sister's kids and that.'

'Lovely.' Blood had seeped through the bandage, a strip of cloth that looked none too clean. 'I'm sure the nurse can help.'

'Not as bad as it looks.' Gus shifted irritably on his seat. He was not someone who liked to wait in a queue. 'Not an artery, like that friend of mine I was telling you about, Jane.'

'Anyway, Lee, you'll feel better when it's been dressed.' Such a nice-looking young man, blond and with a clear skin and eyes that were almost as blue as Noel's. Little did she know the two of them would meet again in a few days' time – under very different circumstances.

TWENTY-SIX

She had to tell someone. She had made a decision to keep quiet, partly because she could have imagined it, and partly because involving the police would not bring Noel back. Of course, Eddie was the real reason. *I thought Noel was dead, but I think he was still alive. His lips moved and he said ... I thought he said ...* It was with her continually, all day and when she woke in the night, startled by what she thought had been sounds in the street, a fox or the students returning from a night out. But there *were* no sounds, just a deathly silence.

However much she tried to put it out of her mind, it refused to go away and after dithering for almost an hour, she left the house, and rang Gus' bell. No reply so, having steeled herself, she would have to do it all over again, later. But halfway down the stairs, his door was flung open.

'Who is it?'

'It's me, Jane. Are you busy?' She was losing her

nerve, would have to concoct a different reason for disturbing him. The rubbish bin that had been pushed over, scattering ready-meal containers across the road? No, someone had swept it up, probably Mr Cardozo, a public-spirited man who kept himself to himself.

'Come in if you're coming.' Gus had disappeared back into his flat but left the front door open.

'It could wait until later, Gus.'

No answer so she stepped inside, removed some photographic magazines from a chair with an orange cushion, and sat down.

'It's about last Saturday.'

Gus looked tired. 'Thought it might be.'

'I'm worried.'

He yawned, covering his mouth with both hands. 'What about? Afraid Eddie may have gone in for a spot of shoplifting?'

'There was nothing in her pockets. I checked. But I suppose she could have eaten whatever she snatched.'

'Need something to calm your nerves.' He was standing by the glass-fronted cupboard that contained a selection of bottles, most of them half empty.

'Nothing for me, thank you.' Then she saw the concerned look on his face and relented. 'All right then, whatever you're having but only a dash.'

'Medicinal.' He poured whisky into a smeary tumbler. 'If you want my advice, you'd do well to ignore the rumours and gossip.'

'What gossip?' Everyone she had spoken to, with the

exception of Arthur, had accepted Noel's death as a tragic accident. 'What have people been saying?'

Gus made an enigmatic noise in his throat. 'How's Corinne?'

'I'm afraid she's not the resilient type. I've done what I can, but she seems in a state of paralysis, unable to make plans and obsessed with the fact that she wanted a baby.' Jane felt down the side of sofa, discovered a pound coin and placed it on the coffee table, along with one of Gus' cameras, an open packet of ginger biscuits, and a screwdriver.

'Not much chance of that.' He gave one of his familiar snorts. 'Noel had the snip.'

'Sorry?'

'Vasectomy.'

'Are you sure?'

'A year or two back. Turned it into one of his funny stories. Had it done at some clinic, he said, and, while they were all recuperating they were given some lunch. Meatballs. Poor old sod, cut off in his prime. I'll miss his —'

'I knew you were fond of him.'

'Don't know about that, Jane. We had our differences, mainly about his loft conversions. Know *you* had a soft spot.' He grinned. 'What you thinking then? I could have done without the loft being turned into a building site but it's hardly grounds for murder.'

Jane drained her glass, flinching as the whisky trickled down her throat. 'Oh, Gus, I'll have to tell you. When I found him … he said something. I thought he did. He did.'

'Go on.'

'He said he'd been pushed.'

'So he was still alive.'

'Yes. I don't know. I was trying to find a pulse. I thought … I may not have done it correctly. I was so shocked, everything I'd learned went out of my head. I called for an ambulance and … I knew I shouldn't move him.'

'He was dead.'

'You don't know that.'

'It was a long way to fall. Yes, all right, people sometimes survive a fall like that, but not onto rock-hard patio stones. So Corinne didn't know about the vasectomy?'

'She can't have done.'

'Unless someone told her.' He put up his hands in mock defence. 'No, not me. Not guilty.'

'Did anyone else know? She'd talked to Brian about the best way to get pregnant, but obviously that was confidential.' An image rose up in Jane's mind. Corinne confronting Noel as he leaned over the balcony to check the paint. *Why did you lie to me? You knew I was longing for a baby.* All in an instant, a moment of fury, a crime of passion.

Gus shrugged. 'Brian knew about it, the vasectomy. He arranged it.'

'But he wouldn't have told Corinne. Although he

might have suggested she talk to Noel, in the hope he would confess, so to speak. It would have put Brian in a dilemma.'

'Doctors must have plenty of those.'

'Yes.' Jane's stomach hurt. The whisky or her lack of breakfast. 'Corinne's not as naïve as she appears. She could have guessed and tricked Brian into telling her.'

'Want my advice, Jane?' He offered her a refill, but she shook her head. 'Leave well alone.'

'Yes, you're right.'

'Shock plays tricks. Shame it was you that found him. Should've been me. Would have been if I'd heard him shout as he lost his balance.'

'I thought you were out, taking photographs.'

'That's why I didn't hear. How's Eddie? Does she know what happened?'

Jane shook her head. 'Hasn't a clue. No short-term memory and not much in terms of a long one.' Not entirely true but Gus was making her feel nervous. 'I'm worried The Spruces might refuse to keep her, although now they've increased her medication she seems calmer, at least I think she is.'

Gus returned the bottle to the glass cabinet. 'Business matter to attend to.'

'Another?'

'Same one.'

And he had no intention of telling her what it was. More than likely he had a rendezvous with the woman from number twenty-two. Who was she? Did she feel the same about Gus as he obviously did about her? The thought that he might have a girlfriend had never occurred to her. He was too old, only a year younger than she was, but it was different for men.

Later, standing in her garden, pulling up weeds, she thought she smelled a bonfire. Large ones were not allowed but even small ones had a habit of getting out of hand. In the old days no one minded, but these days you were supposed to pay an annual charge for a green bin for garden waste. Or put your cuttings in the boot of your car and drive all the way to the tip. The last time she made a trip a spider must have climbed out of the garden waste and spun a web. It stretched from her driving mirror to the knob that turned up the sound on the radio.

Straightening up from her weeding, she saw a plume of dark, acrid smoke that looked like it was coming from Dave's workshop.

Was he there? Where was Simmy? At home or with Arthur? Simmy never went to the workshop, not as far as Jane knew. Was Dave there? He could be at another auction.

Hurrying back through the house, she rang next door's bell. No reply, so she banged on the door. Still no answer, so she set off towards the workshop, reaching it just as Dave appeared with a hand-held extinguisher. 'What happened? Are you all right? How did it start?'

'Burning some rubbish.' The pockets of his denim jacket bulged with papers.

'And a spark set fire to the shed?'

'Never got a hold.'

'You removed that in the nick of time.' She pointed to a gas cylinder. 'It could have burned to the ground.'

'That what you'd have liked?'

'No, of course not. What were you burning?' She peered at the charred remains of a photograph. The top half of a dark-haired young woman, who was holding a baby. Dave's dead wife with baby Simmy? If she was right, why had he chosen today to dispose of it? Had Simmy been poking about in the workshop, looking for clues? Why not let her have a picture of her mother? Perhaps it was a face people would recognise. Perhaps Simmy was right and she had committed a terrible crime. 'I was worried you might not be here, Dave. Do you go to many auctions? Eddie used to like them. She collected pigs. Small ornaments and ... I was afraid it might set the fence alight.'

'You didn't call the fire engine?' Dave glared at her, stamping out the remains of his bonfire.

'No, but somebody else might have done. Where's Simmy?'

'You may well ask.'

'Does she have other friends, as well as Arthur?'

He shrugged. 'She's thirteen.'

'Yes, I know she is.' Why was he determined to present himself as a negligent father? But as she moved away, a thought occurred. Did Dave think Simmy was responsible for the fire? Paying him back for refusing to take her on holiday or, more to the point, to explain what had happened to her mother.

Pausing outside her house, Jane decided to carry on to the shops, to the electrical shop, where she could purchase a smoke alarm. She had one, fixed to the wall in her entrance hall, but it had been there ever since she could remember and she had a feeling they needed replacing quite often.

The man in the shop confirmed her suspicion. 'Every eight years is best.'

'The workshop, just off Faraday Road, caught fire,' she said, 'but there was no serious damage.'

'Dave's place?'

'Yes, that's right.'

'Friend of poor Mr McNeill. Used to come here most weeks, Mr McNeill did. You knew him, I expect.'

Jane nodded.

'What happened, d'you suppose?' He was checking the price of the smoke alarm. 'He'd never have been silly enough to fall off one of his balconies. Something fishy about it, if you want my opinion.'

Waves of nausea travelled through her body and sweat broke out on her face and neck. 'He could be ...' Jane struggled for the right word. 'Impetuous, not to say reckless.'

'Even so, when it came to his loft conversions, he knew what he was doing. How's his wife taken it?'

'She's not actually his wife.'

'Very wise. Second marriages are always a problem where money's concerned.'

So he knew Noel had once been married. Did Corinne know? Probably best not to mention it next time she saw her. Jane paid for the smoke alarm, nodding her thanks when he explained how the battery was included.

'Goodbye then.'

'Bye.' He picked up a sandwich and took a bite. 'Nobody saw anything then? What do the police think? Must have had to make the usual investigations?'

'Yes, I expect so.' The bell rang as she opened the door, then let it swing shut. What *did* the police think? With any luck, they had more important matters to deal with. A tragedy, but an accident. People who thought otherwise were simply trying to make a drama out of it because nothing like that ever happened in Faraday Road or the nice, respectable surrounding area.

TWENTY-SEVEN

Jane had climbed the stairs to the loft – Eddie's loft – and was sitting on Arthur's chair, staring at a large painting on the wall. Instead of an expressionist landscape – large slabs of colour that could be interpreted as hills or fields or the sea – Eddie had painted an acrylic with three cats, none of them a tabby like Rousseau, although she had made sketches of him that Jane still valued. They had given him his name because Jane admired the philosopher and Eddie liked the naïve artist, and he had grown into a fine-looking creature, worthy of both Henri and Jean-Jacques.

Eddie's painted cats sat, or stood, in an overgrown garden, eyeing each other suspiciously, a tortoiseshell, a Siamese, and a black tom with green eyes. Was it a sinister painting, or simply cat-like? Rousseau made short work of seeing off visiting cats, as well as any cats in the neighbouring gardens that he included in his territory. Where had he gone when he jumped down from the magnolia into Dave's garden? He was inclined to inspect anything new, a paper bag, a plastic bottle. The body of a man. But by the time she reached the patio, there had been no sign of him.

The largest of the cats stared out from the painting, daring her to look away. Jane stared back, but it was no good. Just as Rousseau could always out stare her, so could Eddie's imaginary creature.

If Eddie had looked after herself better she might have avoided the series of strokes that damaged her brain. Jane allowed herself a little of her suppressed anger. Fucking dementia. Sod everything. Was it Eddie's fault? More likely to be genetic – she had checked it on her iPad. Never a good idea since most of the medical pages offered links to symptoms and diseases that, as yet, had not given cause for alarm. Both Eddie's parents had died of cancer but that was no reason to rule out circulation problems. People lived too long, had been designed not to last much beyond their fifties. Not for the first time, Jane felt painfully alone. *The wind blows over the lonely heart. And the lonely heart is withered away.* Yeats, she thought. Good old Yeats. But the cathartic tears she hoped for failed to materialise. There was housework that needed doing but she felt unable to apply herself to the tasks.

Her landline started ringing and she hurried down the two flights of stairs, missing a step and only just saving herself from a nasty fall. More than likely a cold call – from someone with a thick Nigerian accent who said his name was Rupert and pronounced her name Say-more.

It was the matron at The Spruces. 'Ah, you're there, Miss Seymour. I just a need a quick word. About Edwina.'

'Yes.' Jane prepared herself for more belongings thrown down the lavatory. Or worse.

'Something seems to be worrying her and I wondered if you could help. Samantha – she's our new helper – says Edwina keeps talking about someone called Russell.'

'Russell?'

'We thought he could be a friend she'd been close to. Earlier today she became quite agitated when she failed to make herself understood. I thought if you talked to …'

'Yes of course, I'll come this afternoon. I don't know anyone called Russell but I'll do my best.'

Russell. A teacher at the school? Or possibly a pupil. Or there was an artist called Russell Flint that Eddie had admired.

It was only when she was on her way to The Spruces that she realised how dense she had been. Not Russell, it must be Rousseau, and Eddie had been unable to explain it was a cat. She should have brought a photograph. No, the last one had been torn in half. In any case, in all likelihood, when she raised the subject, Eddie's thoughts would have moved on and she would say something incomprehensible, or nothing at all.

A nagging doubt remained. Now and again Rousseau took an interest in the builders and their materials, and once, if she had not grabbed hold of him, he would have followed them up the stairs. Where was he? It was time for his dinner and normally he turned up promptly, letting out loud yowls. Unconcerned that Eddie had disappeared out of his life, all he cared about was food and a soft, warm place to curl up and sleep. With cats, and all other species, apart from humans, there was no pretence. Human beings were adept at deception, saying one thing while thinking the precise opposite. Was it a habit that increased with age? Arthur spoke his mind. So did Simmy. Except, for all Jane knew, they had secrets too.

The men were back, working on next door's loft conversion, and the front door had been left wide open, and Rousseau was sitting on the doorstep, washing his foot. She reached out for him but he darted away, disappearing up the stairs.

'Rousseau!' As though he would take a blind bit of notice. The door to Gus' flat would be closed so he would carry on to the top. Had he been up there before? Did he go there often?

The builder called Mark was coming down. 'Your cat, is it?'

'Yes, I'm so sorry.'

'Old friend.'

'Is he? I do apologise. It's difficult to keep tabs on them.'

'Lee gave him some of his bacon sandwich. Expect he's back for more.' He laughed, flattening himself against the wall to allow Jane to squeeze past. 'Got to get the job completed but we're not enjoying it.'

'No, I'm sure.'

'I'd warned him to be careful. Must've been checking the balcony. Not his job.' Mark folded his arms, as though to underline the fact that it had not been his fault. 'You'd think, after all the conversions we've done, he'd have left us to get on with it. Lee's up there. He'll help you catch your cat.'

When she reached the loft, Lee was sitting on the floor, holding a breakfast bar in his bandaged hand, and Rousseau was writhing round him. The boy scrambled to his feet but Jane told him to sit down again and finish his snack. 'I've come to rescue my cat.' She gazed all about her. 'Oh, it was decided to have more than one room, was it?'

'We call him Tiger. Have a look round. It's nearly finished.'

'His real name's Rousseau.' Suddenly the name sounded pretentious. 'But "Tiger" will do.'

'Got one at home. My mum spoils him rotten, feeds him chicken breasts and that.'

'What's his name?'

'Puss. Mum calls him all kinds of soppy names but the rest of us call him Puss.' He laughed, running his hand down Rousseau's back. 'Roo. Short for kangaroo is it?'

'No, Rousseau. He was a painter.'

He nodded. 'Hoping to have my own painting and decorating business one day. See what you think of the bathroom. Wouldn't suit a tall bloke like that Mr McNeill, poor bugger. Sorry, only I felt bad about it, I did.'

'Yes, it was a dreadful thing to happen. But nobody's

fault. A tragic accident.'

The conversion was more elaborate than she had expected and already a few pieces of furniture had been put in place – in the main room, a leather sofa and a bookcase, purchased presumably by Mrs Garcia, or moved from another of her "lets". The other room had a double bed and two bedside tables. The ceiling sloped on either side of the bed and a small window behind it looked out on a patch of sky where clouds were scurrying past.

In the bathroom, a shower with its own door had been fitted in neatly, and the walls were white, but with blue panelling up to the level of the glazed window, and cupboards in the space under the eaves. Lee was right. A child would be able to stand upright at the edges of the room, but an adult would have to bend. Jane opened one of the cupboards. It was empty. Whoever lived in the loft would be glad of the extra storage space. Perhaps she should ask Mrs Garcia if she could rent it. No, it was quite unsuitable for a cat. Although in other ways it rather appealed.

Rousseau had joined her. It was time to leave before Mark returned and found her poking about. 'Very smart, Lee, you've made a good job of it.'

'Wouldn't mind living here myself.'

Jane smiled. 'I was thinking the same myself.' Something had caught her eye. A feather, sticking out from behind one of the leather cushions on the sofa. No, not a feather – it was the wrong colour.

Lee was screwing up the wrapper from his breakfast

bar and putting it in his lunch box. Jane ran her hand over the leather, pretending to test the smoothness, and pushed her fingers between the cushion and the back. The throbbing in her temples increased. Mark was coming up the stairs.

'Is Rousseau still there, Lee?' She spoke too loudly.

'Over by the window.'

'Can you catch him, please? He won't scratch if you hold him firmly.' With one tug, she had the whole thing in her hand and had pushed it deep inside her pocket. Nothing of it must be left behind. Not the tiniest speck of pink fluff.

TWENTY-EIGHT

The funeral took place at the crematorium. Jane had expected Corinne to say a few words, but the occasion was too much for her. Her chosen hymn – *The King of Love My Shepherd is* – was one most people knew, so the singing was enthusiastic. Corinne was not religious, and Noel had been an atheist, but rituals helped a little, and it was believed they allowed the bereaved to "move on".

Would Corinne be able to move on? In all likelihood, she would have to, literally. Where would she go? She and Noel had not been married, and she had only lived with him for six months. As far as Jane knew, that gave her no rights over the house. Perhaps Noel had made a will in her favour. He had no dependants, or if he had, he had kept quiet about them.

Dressed all in black – black suit with skirt that finished a little above the knee, white blouse, black and white hat and patent leather high heels – she stood out from the rest of the congregation.

In contrast, Willa, back from her stay in Cornwall, was wearing a red dress with black swirls, and a purple jacket. No hat, but Jane doubted if one would have fitted over her bush of hair. Recalling the parcel of kinky knickers, she suppressed a nervous laugh. Laughter and tears were so close. *If you have tears prepare to shed them now.* But so far, she had remained dry-eyed.

Looking about her – the crematorium smelled faintly of *Aloe vera* – she began counting the number of residents of Faraday Road. Some would have had the excuse they had to look after their children, and others would be at work. Brian and Willa were sitting in the same pew but slightly apart, and Willa's face was puffy with tears.

As they waited for the service to begin, Jane's neighbour, a petite blonde woman had held forth on what a wonderful person Noel had been, and Jane had nodded and smiled. Who was she? Now the woman had a handkerchief pressed to her mouth and nose. Since she had mentioned how she had travelled a fair distance to attend the funeral, Jane assumed she had once shared Noel's bed. She had wanted to ask, or at least to discover a little about Noel's early life. Instead, she had told the woman how well-liked Noel had been in Faraday Road.

When a young girl was murdered, or died in an accident, close relatives frequently described the deceased as "bubbly". Not a word that was used much in life, but perhaps it brought comfort. Noel had been a live wire but "bubbly" had a feminine ring to it. Poor Noel, but he would have appreciated the turnout. *I long to talk with some old lover's ghost.* John Donne, Jane's favourite. Some old lover? How absurdly fanciful she was. But she liked to think her relationship with Noel had been special. Certainly, life was not going to be the same without him.

In spite of it being a warm day, the crematorium felt chilly, and its modernity gave it a clinical feel. Jane was not a churchgoer but she liked churches – cathedrals even more – where the musty smell brought back memories of childhood: hymns and psalms and candles. If you no longer believed, where did you find spiritual refreshment? What did "spiritual" mean? She had a sneaking suspicion it was simply a way of talking about emotions.

The coffin looked expensive, and had a brass plate, and Jane pictured the funeral director telling Corinne he was sure she wanted the best, and Corinne agreeing, because it was easier, and who could blame her? The vicar was a woman. In principle, Jane agreed with women priests, of course she did, but it was a case of head over heart. Men were not the same as women – obviously – and fathers played a different role from mothers.

Dave arrived late, in time for the second hymn, and slipped in beside her, although Simmy was sitting near the front. It was *The King of Love*, a hymn Jane rather liked. Her other neighbour sang out of tune, so Jane increased the volume of her own voice to drown out the cacophony. She caught Dave's eye and he grinned. It was a long time since she had seen him looking so cheerful and, for some reason, it prompted a thought Jane had often had before. How would you feel if your nearest and dearest died on the same day Princess Diana was killed? All that outpouring of grief and none of it for your loss. It was the same with the television news. Twelve people were killed in a coach accident, but there was no mention of the individuals – there must have been several – who had been killed on the road that same day.

Thoughts that ran through your head at funerals, but, in this instance, they were an attempt to push away the one that never left her. Eddie had been up to the loft and it must have been when Noel was there, before she escaped to the shops. *Hello, Eddie.* She pictured the scene over and over. *Come to see my new loft conversion?* Then what had happened? Eddie had said nothing, or something inappropriate, clutching the handcuffs in the pocket of the cardigan Jane had made her wear. Noel would have left her to nose about and returned to his inspection of the balcony. Then what? She had crept up behind him. No, not crept – she would have noticed he had his back turned, leaning over the balcony – and been unable to resist giving him a push.

Conscience does make cowards of us all. She ought to tell the police. She *would* tell them, but not yet. What good would it do? And she would have to explain how Eddie must have found the handcuffs behind the herbs and spices, and then explain how they had got there. And the matron at The Spruces would be involved, and would definitely refuse to keep Eddie. And it would upset everyone, especially Corinne. At least, now she knew Eddie had been up in there, she could stop thinking about the other residents of Faraday Road, and the motives and opportunities she had assigned to them.

The vicar was speaking about Noel. What a relatively young man he had been, a successful businessman who had once been a male model. Who had passed on the information? It must have been Corinne, who would have been incapable of reading out a eulogy herself. Perhaps Jane should have offered. No, it would have been inappropriate. People already thought she still behaved like a schoolteacher, a head of department. Did they think that, or was she imagining it? *To see oursels as ithers see us.* Robert Burns, a poet who deserved to be quoted. *The best laid schemes o' mice an' men.* And her favourite: *But pleasures are like poppies spread, You seize the flower, its bloom is shed.*

Concentrate. Lately her mind had wandered uncontrollably, flitting from one emotion to another. Listen to the vicar. Female vicars seemed to fall into two categories: the dowdy and the glamorous. This one had dyed hair and a fair amount of make-up. Why not? Jane was often ashamed of her prejudices. She tried not to pass judgement, at least not out loud, but what went on in one's head was another matter. One could hardly censor one's thoughts and feelings.

The coffin slid between red velvet curtains, and Jane's neighbour breathed an audible sigh of relief. 'My name's Harriet.'

'Jane. Jane Seymour.'

Harriet held out a hand and Jane shook it. It was cool

and dry.

'He was quite a character.'

'Yes, he was.' She wanted to find a tissue and wipe the lipstick off Harriet's front teeth.

'Do you know what happened?'

'The balcony in one of his new loft conversions. I expect you know he ran his own company.' Jane was thinking about her last visit to The Spruces and how mentioning Rousseau, and then "Russell", had fallen on deaf ears. 'It's possible he was checking in case it needed another coat of paint.'

'Were the police involved?'

'Yes, but it was a formality. I'm afraid he was inclined to take risks.'

'Yes, indeed.' Harriet closed her eyes, remembering perhaps a time when the two of them had been lovers. 'It's his poor wife I feel sorry for.'

'They weren't actually married.'

'Once bitten, twice shy. I knew him when he was married to Miranda. After they split up, she went to live in South Africa. Sad for poor Noel, being separated from his son. I think they lost touch.'

'Noel had a son?'

'Oh, didn't you know? Andrew, no Angus. He must have been five or six when Noel and Miranda called it a day.'

If only he had told her. A shared experience that would have provided a degree of comfort. She felt annoyed, no hurt, that Harriet knew something he had kept from her.

But she and Noel had not been that close. She was fantasising, something it was easy to do when the object of your fantasy was dead.

'If you'll excuse me.' Jane slid out of the pew. 'I need to make sure Corinne's all right.'

When they came out into the open, the sun was so bright she had to shade her eyes with her hymn sheet. 'It was a lovely service.' She took Corinne's arm. 'And very well attended. Neighbours and friends. He was so popular. Everyone liked him.' Clichés, platitudes, but what else was there?

'You will come back to the house, Jane?'

'Of course.'

'I don't know what to do.'

'Don't worry.' Did she mean now, or was she thinking about the rest of her life? 'We can talk about it. I'll come round tomorrow, shall I, or will Barnaby be there?'

'Barnaby?' she said vaguely. 'He doesn't like funerals. You were fond of him, weren't you, Jane, and he thought the world of you. Oh, how could he be so careless? Those balconies stick out and —'

'Try not to think about it.'

'No, you're right. I just want to know what happened, but I never will, will I? No one will.'

'Probably not.' Unless Jane contacted the police. 'Try to remember the good times. I know everyone says that but —'

'No, you're right, Jane, you always are. I'm so grateful. Has anybody said anything to you?'

'How do you mean?'

'I just thought.' Corinne stared into the distance. 'I was just afraid he might have had an enemy. The loft conversions. Dave seemed awfully angry about the one at the top of his house. Did Gus feel the same? If you knew anything, you *would* tell me, wouldn't you?'

TWENTY-NINE

For the wake, Corinne had employed a firm of caterers, who provided a cold buffet. A whole poached salmon, cold chicken in Little Gem lettuce leaves, melon and Parma ham on toothpicks, and a feta salad. Jane had no appetite.

Gus had not come to the crematorium but he was there at the wake, presumably for the free drinks. He was talking to Dave, and Jane was curious to know what they were discussing. The fire and how it had started? *Had* Simmy had anything to do with it? If she had, it was Dave's fault for not answering her perfectly reasonable questions.

Strange how, at funerals, you heard people talking about their work, or football, or the state of the world, even making jokes. Still, it was no good repeating what a sad loss it was and how wonderful the dead person had been. How many people really cared? For Corinne, it was a life-changing tragedy, but for most it was simply the disappearance of a familiar character who had brightened up Faraday Road, or caused friction with his loft conversions, depending on your point of view. With a twinge, Jane thought again how much she would miss their brief encounters. *Don't tell me I'd be better off moving to a smaller place, Noel. Downsizing, isn't that what they call it?* And Noel's mock terrified responses. *I wouldn't dare, Jane!*

Once, she had attempted to "bleed" a radiator, with disastrous results. The washer had come off the valve – something like that – and Noel had come to her rescue and saved her from a flood. But that was not the reason she was going to miss him. For all his jokes and bonhomie, there had been an underlying sadness that had created a bond between them. He had talked about his childhood and she had told him a little about hers. All childhoods have their good and bad aspects. Noel had adored his mother but had no memory of his father. Jane's had been a workaholic, who understood nothing about small children. Perhaps that was why she objected to women clergy. As a child, God and his deputies had provided the father-figure she lacked.

Mrs Garcia had not attended the funeral, but then she and Noel had had a business arrangement, they were not friends. All the same, one would have thought the woman might have come, out of respect for Corinne. Not that any of it was Jane's responsibility. She must stop feeling responsible for other people's woes.

Gus was scoffing a plateful of vol-au-vents and

appeared to be getting on well with the woman called Harriet. He liked younger women. The woman who had bought number twenty-two was probably in her late-forties, getting on in years by Arthur and Simmy's standards, but in the prime of life by Jane's. Who was she, and why had she moved to Faraday Road? Above all, why was Gus so unwilling to talk about her. There was only one answer to that.

Over by the door, Willa was inspecting a pot plant. Jane had a feeling she was avoiding her. Before she found the fluffy handcuffs, Jane had wondered if Willa and Brian had discussed the afternoon Noel fell and decided on watertight alibis? Not that she had ever thought Brian capable of killing anyone, although, in crime fiction, it normally turned out to be the least likely suspect. Did he suspect Willa? If he did, Jane would have been able to put his mind at rest.

Willa caught Jane's eye and she felt obliged to join her. 'Hello, Willa, did you enjoy your stay in Cornwall?'

'Cornwall?'

'Brian said you were spending a few days with your sister.'

Willa looked away, pretending to be brushing something off the shoulder of her jacket. 'I needed space, Jane, time to grieve. Noel was my soulmate.'

Jane suppressed a sigh. The silly woman sounded like a character in a play. *Time to grieve. My soulmate.* Time to escape awkward questions more like.

'Oh, Jane, I did something so stupid.'

Jane waited while Willa took several deep breaths. Was she going to tell her about the sex outfit?

'I booked into a hotel, Jane, a cheap one, horrible, not even very clean. Have you seen a film called *The Deep Blue Sea*?'

'It was a play originally. Terrence Rattigan.'

'Oh, you know it. She gassed herself. I mean she would have done if that doctor hadn't saved her.'

'Yes, I remember.' Poor Hester Collyer, who gave up everything for love, a woman after Jane's heart.

'Because her boyfriend kept going to the pub with his friends.'

'I think there was a little more to it than that.' So Willa saw herself as a tragic figure, on a par with Hester Collyer, quite apart from the fact that she had missed the point of one of Jane's favourite plays.

'Are *you* feeling any better, Jane?' Willa's lips kept twitching, like Rousseau when Jane was opening one of his super de luxe cat dinners.

'Arthur's making progress with his English grammar.'

'Is he?' Her lack of interest was irritating, although her next words provided an explanation. She had been planning to say something Jane was not going to like. 'I didn't say anything before, Jane, but the day it happened, when I was on my way to the shops I saw Gus. I don't know where he was going – he had a zip-up bag – but all of a sudden, he turned back the way he'd come, back towards his house.'

'When was this? He was on his way to take

photographs – for a competition. Pictures of insects and birds, I think.'

Willa frowned. Not surprising, since Jane's remark had not been relevant.

'When you saw him —'

'I forget the exact time. Only I thought …'

What did you think? There are things I could tell you that would give you something to talk about. *Holla your name to the reverberate hills, and make the babbling gossip of the air cry out …*

'Will you excuse me a moment, Willa, I need to speak to Simmy.'

Simmy was on her own, inspecting the vol-au-vent she was holding, and looking thoroughly fed up. Had she asked Arthur to accompany her and he had refused? There was no need for her to be there but she was a child who liked to do the right thing. Her insistence on telling Tricia Tidewell not to put a dummy in Ada's mouth had been embarrassing, although Tricia had thanked her for being so helpful.

Jane touched her arm. 'It was good of you to come to the service, dear.'

'Dad was late.' Simmy replaced the vol-au-vent on a plate. 'He doesn't like Corinne.'

'Why not?' She should have said "Oh, I'm sure that's not right".

'He thinks she'll tell me about the man my mother ran off with.'

'How would she know something like that?'

'Mr McNeil might have told her.'

Jane could see Gus picking up a new glass of wine. Now was not the time to tell him, but she had to, she couldn't wait. 'Have you had something to eat, Simmy?'

'I don't like the food.'

'A soft drink then. Come round to my house later and we can have a chat.'

'About my mother? Yes, all right.'

'Good.' The child might or might not come, and if she did, what could she suggest, but just now Jane had more important things on her mind. 'Gus?' She caught up with him as he drifted away in the direction of a bowl of strawberries.

'Jane.'

'Can we have a word in private?'

'What now? Where? Can't it wait?'

'Not really.' But Corinne was approaching.

'Barnaby's just sent me a text. He's coming the day after tomorrow. Isn't that lovely?'

So the wretched boy had chosen to text her during the wake. 'Yes, lovely.'

Gus had jumped at the chance and was escaping to another part of the room.

'You look worn out, Corinne,' Jane said. And a little the worse for wear from several glasses of white wine. 'I should put your feet up for the rest of the day.' She reached out to steady her, afraid she was going to fall. 'You know you're welcome to come to my house whenever you like. Tomorrow perhaps if Barnaby's coming the day after.'

'Have you seen the loft? The balcony where he fell? I was the person who decided how the bathroom should be. There's a sloping ceiling but you could still make use of the cupboard if you knelt down. Noel took me up there soon after the conversion began. He said he valued my opinion. Oh, what am I going to do?' She clutched at Jane, bumping into her spectacles as she planted an awkward kiss on her cheek. 'I don't know what I'd do without you. You're wonderful, such a comfort. Is it because you used to be a teacher? Is it pastoral care?'

Unlike poor Eddie, Jane's memory was clear as … as a bell, as daylight. And she distinctly remembered Corinne saying she had never been in one of Noel's loft conversions. A lie, or was it just that she had a tendency to gabble on without thinking about what she was saying? The woman called Harriet was waiting to say goodbye.

'So nice to meet you. I have to catch my train.'

'Do you need a lift to the station?' It would give her an excuse to leave.

'How kind, but a taxi is on its way.'

'Well I hope you have an uneventful journey. There've been hold-ups on the line but I think the worst of it's over. Goodbye then.' And she returned to the plates of half-eaten food and Gus refilling his glass.

'I need to talk to you, Gus. No, not here, can you come round later? And don't say there's a match on television. It's important.'

'Going to see a friend. Might stay the night if we're

out late. I'll see you tomorrow. Or the next day. Remind me if I forget.'

Jane turned away, to hide her stupid tears. 'Actually, it's not that important. Just something I need to discuss – when you can spare the time.'

THIRTY

Arthur was wearing a white T-shirt with blue and orange squiggles that might, or might not, have something to do with martial arts. A child's appearance and demeanour was always contentious. Without intending to, teachers assumed polite, well-dressed children must be intelligent, whereas less was expected of scruffy pupils who arrived late and had mislaid their homework. Arthur was one of the former, but how intelligent was he? Jane would like to have given him a test.

'I thought today you could construct some sentences to demonstrate the difference between "its" and "it's". Arthur?'

'Barnaby hated his guts.'

Jane tried to look puzzled, but failed. 'He told you that?'

'He's all right.'

'All right in what way?' Jane was not so out of touch she was unaware "all right" usually meant pretty good.

How much was Arthur going to tell her? Best to keep quiet and let him expand on his opinion in his own time.

A fly was crawling up the inside of the dormer window. Jane felt sorry for it, wanted to let it out into the fresh air. Earlier, she had used a fly spray and demolished a dozen of the pests but the one on the window was an individual and she had watched its struggle to survive. How irrational she was, how stupidly sentimental, but she felt weak with anxiety, and Gus had been out, or pretending to be out, when she knocked on his door.

'Finished.' Arthur handed her his sheet of paper and Jane skimmed the sentences. *Its raining today. The dog wagged it's tail. Its too late to go to the football match. The cat hurt it's paw.*

By the laws of probability, he should have got at least one of them correct. 'Tell me, Arthur, for reasons best known to yourself ...' Her voice trailed away. She had expected him to produce a slow, tongue in cheek smile, but his expression was deadly serious.

'There's a fly on the window,' he said.

'Yes, I know.'

'Thy summer's play my thoughtless hand has brushed away.'

'You've been studying William Blake at school?'

'I like poetry.' One of his trainers touched her shoe and he apologised. 'My mum watches all the soaps. They're stupid. People talk about the characters as though they're real.'

'Possibly it's a similar phenomenon with your

computer games.'

He thought about this for a moment. 'I reckon that Barnaby's lucky. No mother fussing over him and his dad lets him do whatever he wants. He's got a girlfriend.'

'Barnaby has?'

'No, his dad. Some woman he works with.' Arthur smiled to himself. 'She's called Fiona and she stayed the night at their house, and Barnaby didn't know she was there and he came out of his bedroom with nothing on and she screamed.'

'Oh, dear.'

'Barnaby says Noel dyed his hair.'

'I don't think he did.' But what did she know about it?

'Blokes like Noel always have enemies.'

'The homework I set you, Arthur, did you complete it?'

He took a folded sheet of paper from his pocket. 'I know the difference between "there" and "their" and "were" and "where".'

'I rather thought you did.' Their eyes met. Neither of them looked away. 'What is it you're telling me, Arthur?'

A loud yowl heralded the arrival of Rousseau, and Arthur stretched out a hand to stroke him. 'Rousseau – the philosopher one – believed in the noble savage. Are you a noble savage, Rousseau? You think Noel leaned over too far.'

'Don't you?' The look on his face had shocked her. For all he cared, Noel's death was part of a computer game. No, that was unfair. And he was revealing a part of himself she had not seen before, and more or less admitting he was not the dunce at grammar that Willa thought he was.

'Someone could have crept up behind him.' He put up a hand to hide a grin. 'I reckon the men lots of women fall for are the ones that are no good. None of his conversions are built properly. That's what my dad says. They use cheap materials that won't last.'

'None of his conversions *is* built properly. "None" is short for "not one" so it's singular, although you'll find the rule is not strictly adhered to these days.'

'Did you like him?' This time Arthur was not smiling.

'I'm going to ask you something,' Jane said, 'and I want an honest answer. When you came here I was under the impression you were good at maths but struggled with English.'

He stood up. 'I didn't know "none" meant "not one". Simmy told me about your friend and how you were going to go round the world together. I reckon it's pretty harsh, her getting ill like that.'

Jane was touched, not so much by his comment but because he had been brave enough to raise the subject.

'Have you read *Treasure Island*?' He touched an imaginary parrot on his shoulder. 'Pieces of eight, pieces of eight. Simmy's mother died when she was a baby. I reckon if you've one decent parent you probably turn out OK. Gus is going to be Zeus. Apollo convinced Athena a man is more important than a woman because Athena was born of Zeus, without a mother. How could you be born without a mother?'

'They're myths, Arthur.'

'When we started inventing the game it was a bit of a laugh, but Simmy took it seriously. She's such a crazy kid.'

'What makes you say that?'

'She's clever. Cleverer than you'd think. She says some people are so evil they'd be better dead. Better if they'd never been born.'

'Is there something you want to tell me, Arthur?' She ought to make it clear neither Barnaby nor Simmy was responsible for Noel's death.

He put his hand in the pocket of his jeans and took out the money Willa owed her. 'Did your friend go to art college? I mean, when she was young. I went to an exhibition in London. It was rubbish.'

'In what way?' Did he mean Tate Modern? It was not her job to instruct him in contemporary art, installations and the like, but she enjoyed his company. At least, she did when he was not talking about Noel. Perhaps she should try to arrange more tuition, with other pupils. She could put a card on the board at the supermarket. Or perhaps it was something you had to do online.

'A small one,' Arthur said, 'the exhibition. In a kind of shed. Mum likes to think she's an intellectual. This bloke had made a video of a drunk person. It was on a loop, on and on, and someone else had set up an electric car circuit. Models, I mean, and no different to a kid's toy except there was a card explaining what it meant.' He burst out laughing and, against her better judgement, Jane joined in. 'You know the *The Emperor's New Clothes*?'

'I do.'

'I reckon we're mugs going to their exhibitions. I reckon they're laughing at us.'

'I'm not sure it's quite that simple.' But she was being patronising. 'But I do know what you mean, Arthur. Perhaps it's best to try and keep an open mind.'

'About Noel?'

'No, you know I didn't mean ...'

'I can think of at least four people who are not sorry he's gone. Revenge is sweet. That's a family motto I saw once. It was on the wall in one of those boring old houses open to the public. When I was a kid, my dad thought taking me to places like that was educational.'

'Right then.' She wanted to ask who were the four people. But, whoever he had in mind now, he was wrong. It was Eddie who had committed the crime. 'Back to work.'

He gave a slow smile, hitching up his jeans and sitting down again. 'I'm not much good at writing essays – introduction, middle bit, and conclusion – but I don't see why you can't write the stuff in note form. Dave's one of the guilty four. That's what Simmy thinks.'

'I hope you haven't been gossiping to people.'

'My mum and dad had this big bust-up. Something to do with when she asked Noel to come round to discuss loft conversions. Dad said we didn't need one, but I don't think that's what the row was about. She said she was

229

leaving him, leaving Dad I mean, but she was only gone for two nights. I knew she'd be back. Dad gets on her nerves but she'd be no good on her own.'

'I'd like you to write a short description.'

'Of the people in Faraday Road?'

'No! Not people, a place, somewhere you like. Where you went on holiday perhaps.'

'A place?' He made it sound like she had asked the impossible. 'Would the park be all right? I haven't been there for ages. Simmy saw Noel there, with another woman. Short dark hair, could have been Spanish or Portuguese. No, not Mrs Cardozo. No one from this road. His loft conversions all have sticking out balconies, don't they? What are they for, what's the point? Anyway, there's no way he'd have lost his balance. He may have slept around but he wasn't a complete idiot.'

THIRTY-ONE

In the small hours, the world felt like a place, full of pain and suffering. And fear. *It was the owl that shriek'd.* But waking at half past four was not so bad. Radio Five Live had stopped its phone-ins and "The News" had begun, interspersed with plenty of sport, but that was only to be expected. Some sports were mildly diverting but Jane had an aversion to rugby, and Five Live had a habit of broadcasting sudden deafening bursts of sound, medleys of past commentaries that might have been acceptable during the day, but not in the small hours.

Once she had flinched at "breaking news", but lately the term had been extended to include virtually anything. A member of the royal family had expressed an opinion on comprehensive schools. A football manager had been sacked. This morning it was something to do with the supply of energy. Turning onto her back, being careful not to reactivate the cramp that had plagued her left leg during the night, she stared at the light filtering through her bedroom curtains.

Uppermost in her mind was Arthur and his remark about Noel's death, tossed out nonchalantly enough, but she was getting to know the boy and nothing he said was as casual as it appeared. *I reckon the men women fall for are the ones that are no good.* Wise words from someone so young. Was he thinking about his mother? Willa was hardly the discreet type, and Arthur could well have overheard phone calls between her and Noel. Or returned home early from school and heard suspicious sounds emanating from her bedroom.

Sometimes Jane wondered if Arthur knew something about that dreadful afternoon and was teasing her, tempting her to ask him to tell more. When he talked about the computer game he and Simmy were devising, it was clear he was a believer in violent retribution. But Eddie was the murderer. Not intentionally, perhaps – a court of law would say she was not of sound mind – but at what stage of her illness did responsibility come to an end? *Out, out, brief candle! Life's but a walking shadow.* If the truth came out, Eddie would be none the wiser, but Jane would be the talk of Faraday Road. She might have to move.

Lying in bed was a mistake. Vague worries were exacerbated. Imagination ran riot. Best to get up and face the world. A brisk walk to clear her head.

Leaving the house, she came across Gus, stuffing a bag of rubbish into his black wheelie bin.

'Morning, Miss Marple.' He was wearing his dressing

gown, and the frayed ends of grey cotton trousers hung over a pair of red flip-flops. While his shop was still a going concern, he had left early, returning at seven or even later. Now, like her, he had no routine. Your days are your own, as a crass television presenter had remarked, in good spirits herself since she had an interesting, well-paid job.

'Put too much washing in the machine.' Uncharacteristically, Gus felt the need to explain why he was not fully dressed.

'Do you have a dryer?'

'A what? Oh, one of those things that eats up electricity.'

'I don't expect Dave would mind if you hung your washing in the garden.'

'You don't, don't you? Shows how well you know Dave.'

Jane sighed. 'It's not as though he takes any trouble with it. The dandelion seeds blow over into mine. If he doesn't want the bother of cutting the grass, he should have the whole thing paved.'

Gus sniffed and she realised her mistake. 'More patio stones, you mean. How's Eddie?'

'I've been thinking about the day she went missing.'

'Is that what you call it? The Day Eddie Went Missing. Well, I suppose it's an improvement on The Day Noel Threw Himself Off The Balcony.'

'I'm going for a walk. They say it releases endorphins in the brain.'

'Thought you wanted to ask me something.'

'Did I?' Should she mention how Willa had said she saw him returning to the house, not long after two? Gus would think she was accusing him, and Willa could have made it up. Besides, it was irrelevant now. 'I forget what is was. Can't have been important.'

'If you say so. Need to get changed. Business meeting.'

'Another? Starting a new business, are you?'

He gave a snort. 'What did you think of the funeral?'

'I met an old flame of Noel's.'

'That blonde woman?' But he had no interest in anything she had to say and was going back into his house.

Just as well. She had almost decided to tell him about the handcuffs but he had given no indication he was prepared to listen to her, so he was not the right person to confide in. Except, who else was there? 'Oh, Gus,' she called, and he turned, rubbing his eyes.

'On the day of the accident, Willa saw you coming back up the road. I'm not sure what time it was. A bit after two o'clock I expect when she was on her way to a lingerie party.'

'Aha, the plot thickens. So, Sherlock, you think I was on my way to do the dastardly deed. By the way, is Eddie still able to handle money?'

'No.'

'Doesn't need it. Like the Queen.'

'Her memory's worse. It's impossible to have a

sensible conversation. Except now and again she remembers something from the past. A few weeks ago she started talking about a visit to Greece we made twelve years ago. The airport at Athens, the boat that took us to one of the islands. Little details I'd completely forgotten.'

'Odd thing, the brain.' But he was more interested in his bin. Had he thrown something away and regretted it? Not long ago, foolishly, she had bought a pair of shoes because she liked the colour, but when she tried them on at home discovered they squeezed her toes and would undoubtedly give her corns. Searching for the receipt, she had been reduced to looking in the bin, then found it, screwed up at the bottom of her shopping bag.

Gus was muttering away, something about Sainsbury's. 'Only when I saw her, standing outside ...'

'Eddie? You saw her? When? What time was it?' Jane's sharp intake of breath had given her away but, oblivious, Gus was still busy with his bin.

He straightened up, pointing at a pair of magpies on the roof opposite. 'Evil creatures. Raid nests and eat fledglings. Two-fifteen. Had an appointment at half past.'

'On that Saturday? A quarter past two? When you saw Eddie?'

'Checked my watch and realised I had ten minutes to fill so I might as well do some shopping. Someone had tied up a Jack Russell and Eddie was deep in conversation.'

'You're quite sure it was Eddie?'

'Her memory may not be up to much but she looks the

same as she always did. Never one for bothering about her appearance. Artistic temperament and all that.'

'And it was definitely two-fifteen? A dentist's appointment, was it?'

'Why d'you say that?'

'You mentioned last week you'd felt a twinge. A wisdom tooth you thought.' Weak with relief, Jane had calculated it would have taken Eddie at least twenty minutes to reach Sainsbury's. Simmy had knocked on the door just before two so, in order to have reached the supermarket by two-fifteen, Eddie would have to have slipped through the front door while Jane was showing Simmy into the sitting room. And it made sense she would have made a beeline for the place where they had done their weekly shop.

'I wish you'd told me before, Gus.'

'You knew she'd gone to the shops.'

'Yes, yes I did.' She must have taken the fluffy handcuffs to the loft soon after she brought her back from The Spruces. Following loud demands for ice cream, Jane had left her in front of the television – a programme about cats that did things "that made you laugh" – and hurried, half walking, half running, to the nearest shop and back. Ten minutes, not more, but quite long enough for Eddie to forage about in the kitchen, find the handcuffs behind the herbs and spices, and take them next door. 'I've been thinking, Gus.'

'Never a good idea.'

'I know some people liked Noel's loft conversions, but

others thought them an abomination.'

'And like all good private eyes you need to eliminate suspects.' He slammed down the lid of the wheelie bin. 'Not guilty. As I told you before, out, hoping to get a close-up of a summer visitor. Someone had seen a flock of redstarts in a field. Came back for a lens I'd forgotten.'

'Where did you see the bird? No, it doesn't matter. I just wondered ...'

'Love you and leave you.' He had a foot in his front door. 'Need to check my washing's dry.'

A business matter. Was he hoping to re-open his shop, or perhaps he intended to set up some kind of photographic service? Or "a business matter" could mean another rendezvous with the woman from number twenty-two. But none of that concerned her just now. He had seen Eddie outside Sainsbury's at two-fifteen. She was in the clear.

THIRTY-TWO

Simmy had put in an appearance. 'Oh, Miss Seymour, Arthur likes you and he thinks if *you* ask my dad what happened to my mother ...'

'I'll see what I can do.'

'Will you? Today?'

'Yes, if I can find your father.'

'Oh, thank you.' Simmy's contorted expression changed into a smile. 'Arthur says Mr McNeill was an alpha male. The biggest ape in the herd. The one that mates with all the females.'

'Yes, well you and Arthur ...' A familiar figure was approaching and Jane was afraid she might have overheard. 'Corinne. Are you looking for *me*?'

'So you'll ask him?' Simmy was watching Corinne with narrowed eyes. 'A lady who brought her chair to be repaired said we could stay in her caravan in Cornwall, but Dad won't go.'

'I know. I'm sorry. As I said, I'll talk to him later,

dear.' And she would. He would take it badly but knowing Eddie was innocent had given her new energy. However unpleasant he was, she would stick to her principles, refuse to leave until he had told her the truth. 'Come inside, Corinne. Tea, or I think you prefer coffee.' Jane had taken to drinking prune juice but now was not the time to discuss digestive systems.

'I'm not sleeping, Jane.'

'No, I'm sure.' She could have added "join the club" but it might have sounded callous, and in any case, Gus' revelation had meant that, for the first time for days, she had slept for seven uninterrupted hours.

'It's Barnaby.'

'Didn't he come to see you?' Jane was staring at the woman from number twenty-two who was carrying a heavy box into her house. Something to do with her DIY? Gus would know.

'Oh, he came all right.' Corinne started to explain but a baby's yells heralded the appearance of the Tidewell family.

'Morning Jane.' Tricia Tidewell was trying to force Ada into her buggy while simultaneously attempting to separate Liam and Pippa. She turned to Corinne. 'I'm so sorry, Mrs … about your … it was so awful. Ian and I had been thinking of having our loft converted. Oh, I'm sorry, that didn't come out right. Stop it, Liam, what did I tell you?'

'Do as you're told, Liam.' Jane sounded fiercer than she had meant to, but it worked. 'Stand still, Pippa. And

239

you, Liam, can hold the buggy while your mother straps in Ada.'

'Oh, Jane, it must be because you used to be a headmistress.'

'Head of department. Go inside the house, Corinne, I'll be with you in a second.' School holidays were always too much for Tricia but, instead of buying them more and more toys and games, she should be teaching the two older children how to behave, if necessary, sending them to their respective bedrooms.

'Sorry.' Tricia was making her apologetic face. 'Tell Corinne I didn't mean ... about Ian wanting a loft conversion.'

'Tricia?'

'Yes. Oh, is there something I can do to help? I always feel so useless. Ian is away again; he says working away is less tiring than being at home.'

'He should do his fair share.'

'Except I was the one who wanted another baby. Ian thought two was enough. He said if we had another it would be no good asking him to help.'

'I see.' Jane did, but had no wish to discuss the matter. 'Tricia, I meant to ask you, were you about on the afternoon of Noel's ...'

'I can't remember.' Tricia pulled down her white hair band. 'I could have gone to the park. Saturday, it was a Saturday. I'll have a think. You're wondering if I saw something.' Some of the wisps of hair had been caught. 'If someone went up to the loft with Noel. Only why

240

would they? Is that what you were thinking?'

'Was Ian here? I mean, do you suppose he could have noticed what time Noel went up there?'

'Ian? He never notices anything. And I'm always occupied with the children.'

'It'll be easier when they're all at school.'

'Yes, but …'

Jane waited. Surely the silly woman wasn't planning a fourth child.

'I'll have to find a job and I'm not qualified. I passed art and geography but not maths and you have to pass maths. Why did you want to know – about Noel going up to the loft?'

'No reason. Just to get the facts correct.' Jane lowered her voice. 'For Corinne's sake.'

'Oh yes, of course.' Tricia's face flushed scarlet, and Liam and Pippa were silent, and even Ada was sitting quietly in her buggy. *Did* she know something? Had she been one of Noel's admirers? No, of course not, she wasn't his type, quite apart from the fact she never had any time on her own.

Back in the house, Jane found Corinne lying on the sofa with her eyes closed. In spite of her fragile state, she had still managed to apply ample amounts of eyeshadow and rouge. No, these days it was called "blusher". And there was something called "eyeliner" that made people look like pandas.

'He wanted money, Jane. Barnaby – he only came because he wanted money. For gambling debts. Not horses, football. Only they don't play football in the summer.'

'I believe they do in Australia.' Should she tell Corinne how the boy had forced Noel to give him a "loan"? Not much point now, except Noel had been afraid the boy would ask for more? Was that what had happened – and had Noel refused? And Barnaby had followed him and …

'I'm not like you, Jane.' Corinne hauled herself into a sitting position and fluffed up her hair. 'I've never had a job, not a proper one. I did work in a shop for a few weeks when I was sixteen. Then I met Gerard and solicitors earn such a lot – just for letters and phone calls. It's extortion. Me and Noel weren't actually married. I told you that, didn't I? It was only because Gerard was being silly about a divorce, I mean about the house, Gerard's house. And mine. If you're married even if you didn't pay for the house and —'

'You have no money of your own?'

'I thought … you'll be shocked, Jane, but I thought he might have me back.'

'Gerard might?' Jane *was* shocked but managed not to show it. Still, when it came to the crunch, people were pragmatists, even if they pretended otherwise. Corinne never pretended. Something in her favour, although there was a place for subterfuge. 'Are you sure that's what you want, dear?'

'I'm no good on my own.'

'No, I see.' Jane was thinking about the woman who

had bumped into Barnaby in his birthday suit. Fiona. His father's secretary. 'It might be best if the suggestion came from Gerard.'

'You're so sensible, Jane.'

'Take things slowly, test the water.' Jane took a deep breath. 'I wouldn't be asking you this, Corinne, if it wasn't important. Do you know what happened to Simmy's mother?'

Corinne brightened considerably. 'Oh, didn't you know – she drowned. Noel told me but you must promise not to tell Simmy. It was in Cornwall. Noel was staying nearby at the time. It was in the local paper. The inquest and everything. Simmy thinks she died of natural causes and Dave wants to keep it like that.'

'Yes, I see.' Jane didn't, but it was a start. 'Do you know any more about what happened?'

'No. Sorry. Death's so final, isn't it, so hard to take in. I can't believe … sometimes, for a moment, I forget and —'

'To get back to your financial situation, perhaps you should consult your solicitor, if you have one. Do you have enough to tide you over?'

Corinne stood up. She had spotted one of Eddie's paintings, a small one, not her usual style. Pigs – Old Spots – wallowing in mud. 'Oh, did Eddie do that? Isn't it clever. I'd give anything to be able to paint like that. I'm quite creative but … Noel liked pigs.'

'Did he?' She had spoken about him in the past. Progress, Jane thought, although she could be being overoptimistic. All the same, there was something about Corinne that had made her think the grieving widow – well, not precisely, since they had not been married – was tougher than she thought. And a good solicitor might mean she kept the house, although Harriet, the woman at the funeral, had said he had a son. Did Corinne know about him? Unlikely. 'I tell you what, why don't you have the pig painting, take it home with you?'

'Oh, I couldn't.'

Jane took the picture off the wall – it was not one she liked very much – and ushered Corinne out of the house. 'A solicitor, dear. Doing something practical usually makes one feel a little better.'

'Thank you so much, Jane.'

For the advice or the pig painting? And was she heartbroken or just a very convincing actress? Supposing she had found out the love of her life had rekindled his affair with Willa. Or the woman in the park that Arthur said Simmy had seen. *Heav'n has no rage like love to hatred turn'd.*

Closing the door on Corinne, her thoughts returned to Gus. The previous day, in an effort to return to normality, she had attended her choir. Hoping they would sing something inspiring, she had been disappointed when most of the songs were about unrequited love, apart from the one about a dove. During the tea break, a woman she had never spoken to before approached her with an inquiring look on her face, and asked if she knew Gus. Jane said he was her neighbour, and the woman – she thought her name was Deborah – became quite excited and said she had been a regular at his camera shop and how upset she had been when it closed. *Such a dear, sweet man, so kind when my husband died. When you lose someone, those little contacts are so important.*

Gus, a dear, sweet man? Jane had never visited his shop, but Deborah's description had made her realise how important it had been to him, not just a source of income. Not that he would ever admit it. As Deborah droned on about her dead husband, Jane realised coming to choir practice had been a mistake. Normally a good listener, she had felt too raw, too self-absorbed to empathise with other people's pain.

The phone interrupted her thoughts. Matron from The Spruces. Eddie had been talking about the weekend at home and in the circumstances they had felt obliged to contact the police.

'I phoned a little earlier, Miss Seymour, but you must have been out.'

'Oh, I'm sorry, was it something important?' When she was on the doorstep, talking to Simmy? She would have to turn up the volume on her phone.

'I'm afraid it's bad news. Miss Knox had another stroke.'

'Oh, dear, I'll come at once.'

The pause was probably less than a second, but felt like several minutes. Long enough for Jane to know what was coming next.

'I'm very sorry, Miss Seymour, I'm afraid she passed

away.'

'Thank you.' She should have been prepared. She wasn't. Eddie had been difficult, a worry, a nuisance. The months, if not years had stretched ahead. More nursing care would be necessary, and more money to pay for it. Eddie would become incontinent, possibly violent, and fail to recognise her. 'I'll come anyway, shall I? Yes, of course, I'll come now.'

'Do you have a friend or neighbour? Someone who lives close by?'

'I'll be with you shortly.'

Rousseau wanted his dinner. 'Eddie's dead,' Jane said, and he ran on ahead of her with his tail in the air. *One short sleep past, we wake eternally. And death shall be no more; Death, thou shalt die.*

THIRTY-THREE

Arthur had turned up, and he had a cold. Was she expected to give him a lesson? Had no one told the Molloys about Eddie?

'Sorry I'm late, I overslept.'

'Never mind, come along in.' Her first reaction had been to say he would have to come back another day, but a lesson would take her mind off things. Should she tell him what had happened or would that embarrass him? Did it matter if he was embarrassed? Yes, it did.

Up in the loft, he sat with his legs sprawled, waiting expectantly.

'Before we begin, Arthur, I should tell you that my friend Edwina has died. She was in a home, with dementia. She had a stroke.'

He picked up one of the pens and twirled it round between his fingers. 'Shall I go?'

'No, no need for that. I just thought I ought to tell you. In case you heard about it later.'

'Does my mother know?' He blew his nose and she thought it was because he felt awkward, but he was trying not to laugh. 'She's done something to her hair. Mum has. She looks like a poodle. An old one with a moth-eaten coat.'

Jane joined in the laughter. She couldn't stop herself. It was a release. She could have laughed and laughed. Laughed till she cried. The patch of blue, visible a few minutes ago through the dormer window, had turned grey, almost as though the weather was passing judgement on her inappropriate behaviour. 'Right then, Arthur, I want to talk about pronouns.'

'I brought a screwdriver.' He looked about him for somewhere to dispose of his soggy tissue and Jane pointed to the waste paper basket she had put within reach of his chair. 'For your window,' he said. 'It's difficult to open because the handle's come loose. Shall I fix it?'

'Would you?'

He crossed to the dormer window. He was tall enough to reach it without standing on a chair. A couple of twists and he wrenched the handle up and down to demonstrate how much firmer it was.

'Thank you, dear.'

'A boy from school's training to be a plumber. Plumbers are never short of work and the money's good.'

'I'm sure.'

'Except you have to unblock bogs.' He found a fresh tissue. 'An electrician would be better. Or a bricklayer.'

'But you want to be a doctor like your father. And

you're afraid you may not get the grades.'

His shoulders moved in a weary shrug and Jane decided it was best to continue with the lesson. 'Now, can you give me the definition of a pronoun?'

'It's instead of a noun, like "Our dog's black and Jayden's got a white one". "One" is the pronoun.'

'Good.'

'It's called Lucky. Jayden's dog. It barks when people go past.'

'Yes, I've heard it.' There was something different about him. Because she had told him about Eddie? His fingers kept curling and uncurling, but he was anxious rather than ill at ease. 'Pronouns can be the subject or object of a sentence and some of them distinguish singular and plural, for example, I or we, he or they.'

'Right.'

'Then there are compound pronouns.'

'Someone, something, everyone, everything.'

'Good.' Jane picked up her tablet. 'I thought this might interest you, Arthur. A poem about a cat by a poet called Tessimond. Arthur Tessimond as it happens. Arthur Seymour John Tessimond. Both our namesakes. He's reading the poem himself. It's on YouTube.'

'Right.' He had a puzzled expression, as though he was afraid it was some kind of trick. Then the reading began and he watched with rapt attention.

When it came to an end, he put the tablet on the table.

'*Cats no less liquid than their shadows*. That's why they're good at catching birds. Is Tessimond a friend of yours?'

'No, I'm afraid he's dead. Arthur?' She paused, knowing it would mean she had his full attention. 'Why is it your mother thinks you're going to fail next year's exams?'

He sniffed. 'My report.'

'Your marks were not as good as they used to be?'

'Are you going to tell her?'

'Tell her what?'

He sighed, glancing at her then looking away. 'Simmy and me … Simmy and I, you know how we've been planning this game?'

'The one based on Greek mythology.'

'We'd never be able to do the technical part. It's more the story and how the characters interact. I know a bit about programming but it takes a team of programmers to create a game. Hundreds of them. Thousands. I'm not sure if you can sell an idea to the games industry, but it doesn't really matter. It's good practice, thinking how it would pan out. Did he write a lot of poems?'

'Tessimond? Yes, he did. A good one about advertising men. He called them the trumpeters of nothingness, mental prostitutes.' But mentioning Tessimond had been a diversionary tactic. 'You were telling me about the games industry.'

'Not just games. Movies. Computer-generated images. You can earn good money.'

'I'm sure.'

'Mum thinks games are rubbish, a waste of time, but

they can help kids with problems like autism, and ordinary kids too. They develop spatial skills, if you know what I mean.'

'I do.'

Pushing back his chair, he stood up and began examining one of Eddie's paintings, a landscape peopled with strange characters, half-human, half-animal, a little derivative of a Chagall, but surely all works of art were derivative in one way or another.

'I used to like painting,' he said, 'but if you did maths and IT you had to give it up.'

'How short-sighted of whoever drew up the timetable.'

Fishing in a back pocket in his jeans, he found a piece of paper, unfolded it and handed it to her.

'Let's have a look. Oh, it's good, Arthur. I didn't realise you could draw so well.'

'That's Echidna.' He pointed to a drawing, half-woman, half serpent. 'She ate men raw.'

'Really? Oh, and a centaur, with a horse's body and …' Jane broke off, failing to control a smile. 'Noel's head.'

'He's easy to draw. I mean, he used to be.' He pointed again. 'That's Cronus.'

'The character you assigned to Dave.' The rippling muscles were about as different from Dave as it was possible to imagine, but the face was similar.

'And Athena,' he said, handing her a second sheet of paper with a drawing of a woman with voluptuous breasts and a rather modern hair-do.

'Very good. Thank you for showing me. It's a shame you had to drop art, although that doesn't mean you have to give up on your drawing.'

His back was turned, and she had to strain to hear what he said next.

'"This is my son," like I'm an exhibit in a museum. I don't like blood, or illnesses. I don't want to be a doctor.' He checked to make sure she was listening. 'People call computer scientists geeks because they're good at maths, but it's because of them we've got all the stuff we have now.'

'Very true.'

'Anyway, I thought …' He blushed and Jane felt a rush of affection for him.

'What are you telling me, Arthur, that you've deliberately failed at your school work, apart from maths and IT? Was that really necessary? Couldn't you have talked to your mother? Or your father,' she added.

'He doesn't care what I do.'

'I'm sure that's not true.'

'Some people go to the doctor just because they've got a sore throat, or they hate their husband.' He gave a short, bitter laugh. 'Or their wife. He gets millions of those.'

How could she have been so stupid? She was losing her touch. Still, it was because of the classes that he had summoned up the courage to say what he really wanted to do. Poor boy, she had him down as so "cool" and sophisticated. And she had taken Willa at face value too, swallowed the story about Brian when all the time it had

252

been his mother who was trying to force him into a career in medicine.

'You must tell her, Arthur. If you explain —'

'She'd go crazy.'

'Surely not.' But he could be right. First Noel's death. No, first Noel's rejection when she attempted to seduce him with the silly patent leather outfit. Then his death. And now Arthur, her pride and joy, was going to let her down. 'If you like, I could have a word.'

'She shouts.' He paused to have a good, long blow. 'Loses her temper. Once when Dad … I forget what he'd done but she was so angry she threw a plate of spaghetti Bolognese at him. If she hits him he never retaliates. Well, you know what my dad's like. And if shouting doesn't work, she bursts into tears.'

'The accident upset her.'

'Accident? Oh, you mean Noel. She hated him. She thought he was in love with her but she was just a bit on the side. Noel, the rapist and pillager.' He gave a short, bitter laugh. 'I'm glad he's dead.'

So many questions sprang to mind. How much did Brian know? If Arthur was right, Willa could have followed Noel up to the loft conversion. Or Brian could have. No, Willa was a much more likely culprit.

'Miss Seymour?'

'Yes, dear.' Jane held her breath. Now what was he going to come out with? Please God, not a confession.

'I'm sorry your friend died.'

THIRTY-FOUR

Corinne was back. 'Oh, Jane, he wants a divorce. Gerard wants a divorce. Barnaby says he's got a girlfriend and she's called Fiona. Is it a Scottish name? Barnaby says—'

'Come inside.' Jane was tired, and she wanted to talk to Willa, but it would have to wait. 'Now, start at the beginning. You've been in touch with Gerard, have you?'

'He phoned. He said he was sorry, but he needed to make some arrangements. Some arrangements! He asked what was going to happen to Noel's house. He said ...'

'Slow down, dear, at least it sounds as though he's prepared to help.'

'I don't want his help.' Her voice was steely. 'I hate him. I only married him because ... I can't remember. He's never been any fun. She's welcome to him. I've consulted a solicitor and I'm going to fight to keep the house and Barnaby can move in with me. He'll be going to university but they still need somewhere to come home to, don't they?'

'They do.' Jane wanted to congratulate her, but her newly found resolve was likely to be fragile.

'He's called Nigel. My solicitor. He's about forty and I think he's single – he hasn't got a wedding ring – and he's got such nice fair hair. With fair hair, you can't really tell if there's any grey, can you? Anyway, I'm putting my trust in him. Actually I might invite him to the house for a drink. Are you allowed to invite your solicitor?' She was holding her neck as if it was the only way she could get the words out. 'Do you think I'm doing the right thing?'

'I do.'

'It's not that I'm not still grief-stricken about Noel, but you have to move on, don't you?'

'You do.'

The silence that followed was a little oppressive. Corinne fiddled with a strap on one of her high-heeled shoes. 'Oh, I forgot to tell you, the day it happened, when I was on the way to the lingerie party I saw Dave. He didn't see me but …'

'Are you sure? I think he had to attend an auction. Although I'm not certain what time it was or where it was being held.'

Corinne frowned. 'He didn't like Noel. Partly the loft conversion, but there was something else. When I saw him, he looked quite angry.'

'I'd put it out of your mind and concentrate on … on your arrangements. Your solicitor.'

'If he was married he'd have a ring. Do you think he would? Some men don't like jewellery. Are wedding rings jewellery?'

'Time to phone him and make another appointment. Off you go.' Jane guided her through the front door, waited a few moments, then set off for number thirty-four.

A dog-eared notice said the bell was broken. Jane knocked and a faint voice asked who it was.

'It's me. Jane.'

'Hang on.' The voice was only a few feet away.

Jane waited, gazing all about. A deflated football lay beside some flower pots and a plastic water pistol. No, not a pistol, an AK47, designed to drench its victim to the skin.

'Come in.' Willa's hair was not so much poodle – more scarecrow – and she was wearing an unflattering all-in-one outfit, royal blue with a pattern of white polar bears. 'Is it about the classes? I know, you can't work miracles. I'm just grateful you've continued as long as you have. Oh, no, it's about your friend. Arthur told me. I'm so sorry. If I'd known ...'

'He's a very thoughtful boy.'

'Is he?'

Junk mail, shoes, discarded books, a broken umbrella. Willa led her through to the back, past a sinkful of washing-up, the remains of some cold pasta, and a bunch of bananas with blackened skins. Not very hygienic, particularly for a doctor's house. Jane was surprised none of the family had succumbed to food poisoning but presumably they had built up immunity.

'I do hope Arthur didn't exhaust you. He can be quite

rude, and moody, but …'

'Not the Arthur I know. He's charming. I'm very fond of him.'

'Are you? He likes you too, says you're very perceptive. Perceptive! The words they come out with. We'll sit in the conservatory, it's tidier.'

Jane chose a basket chair, a mistake since it creaked if you moved a muscle. Not that Willa would notice. She was walking up and down, happily oblivious to the fact that Jane had seen the conservatory before, from her view in the garden. Had the teacher's outfit been thrown away? The handcuffs were back behind the jars of herbs and spices while Jane decided how best to dispose of them.

'I still can't believe it, Jane.'

'I'm sorry? Oh, you mean, poor Noel.'

'It *was* an accident, wasn't it? You don't think … no, it can't have been. We were so close. Sometimes … well, you knew him quite well, didn't you … he could be quite … not deliberately hurtful, just tactless. You know how he loved to joke. Anyway, I'd never have harmed a hair on his head.'

The lady doth protest too much, methinks. 'I wanted to talk about Arthur, Willa.'

'Yes, I knew he must have done something. Did he give you the money? If he kept it for himself —'

'He didn't. The reason I'm here, he's convinced you want him to follow in his father's footsteps.' She paused to make sure she had Willa's full attention. 'But he says he has a dislike of blood.'

'Blood?' Willa sat down heavily.

'And illnesses. I said I was sure you'd understand. Teenage boys are traditionally incapable of voicing their worries and sometimes it's easier to talk to a ... to someone outside the family.'

Willa's face flushed scarlet. She thought Jane was interfering, had influenced her son, turned him against his chosen profession. She had a temper and if Jane was not careful she would lose it. In the lane at the back of the houses, someone was calling to a child. Not Tricia Tidewell – the voice was far too reasonable. Then a dog barked and Jane took it as her cue to speak again.

'Talk to him, Willa. He's afraid you and Brian will be angry.'

'I had such high hopes.' Willa sat down. She had slumped in her chair like a popped balloon. 'Not an artist.'

'No, not an artist, although it's a shame he had to give up painting and drawing. Computer science I think. I've looked it up and it's a very reputable subject. He wants to work in the games industry.'

'The what?'

'People who design computer games. And you can work in films too, I believe. Computer-generated images. Arthur's educated me on the subject ... Were you asleep? Did I wake you?'

Willa ran her fingers through her hair, what was left of it. 'Noel's death ... it was such a shock. I was so upset. Was it suicide, Jane? He didn't love that woman. It was all a terrible mistake. If you'd seen how worried he was. I tried to help but … oh, Jane, your friend, was it sudden?'

'Yes.'

'I'm so sorry.'

'Thank you.'

'Her heart, was it?'

'A stroke. Why didn't you want Brian to know about the tuition?'

'Oh that. He thinks I'm too pushy, a pushy parent, that's what they're called, but Arthur would make such a good doctor, a consultant, not a GP, and you have to get three 'A's and he wasn't doing his school work, just playing games on his computer. Brian thinks I did it.'

She should have said "did what?" Instead she was silent.

'Did you hear what I said?'

'I did. This has something to do with your friendship with Noel?'

'I loved him.'

'I see. And Brian thinks you pushed him off the balcony?'

'You'd guessed.'

'No one pushed him, Willa, he lost his balance.' On her way to Willa's, Jane had been wondering why Corinne had only now remembered seeing Dave on the afternoon of the accident. A way of trying to incriminate him? Of protecting herself?

'I expect you think Brian's the easy-going type,' Willa was saying. 'He's jealous, possessive, always been the same. He said he was miles away that afternoon, having a walk but … I blame that Corinne.' Willa's hands were tightly clasped. 'People think she's so … I tell you something, Jane, she's not the air-head she likes to make out. Scheming, that's what she is. She wormed her way into Noel's life and forced him to … classic.' Her face was contorted with fury. 'Made sure her husband found out what was going on so Noel felt obliged to take her in.'

'That doesn't sound like Noel.'

'Oh, you didn't know him like I did. He was kind. And sensitive. He hid that side of himself but the two of us – we confided in each other. He understood, hated hurting people. I don't know what I'll do without him. If you ask me, he'd had enough of Corinne and was planning to kick her out so she …' Willa flopped forward, bumping her head on a bamboo table. 'Oh, Jane, it's all so awful. I loved him and if it hadn't been for Corinne …'

'Arthur, Willa. You must talk to him. About his school work and his plans for the career he wants to follow. There are university courses … Willa?'

'Shall I tell the police – about Corinne?'

'No.'

'But why should she get away with it?'

Jane rose from her creaking chair and stood, looking out at the overgrown garden. No sign of Rousseau. That was something. 'I told Arthur I'd talk to you, Willa, and I also told him I was sure you'd understand. Don't let me down.'

Jane expected an angry response, but Willa was beaten, done in. 'They say grief makes you lose your mind.'

'You haven't lost yours, Willa, but if you knew Noel so well, you must be aware that he liked to take risks, cavorting about, swinging on scaffolding and the like.'

'I was down at the shopping centre when it happened. I bought a pair of shoes, and a swimming costume. Swimming's good for you. And two scarves and a pair of those knickers that hold in your stomach. You're sure that's what happened?'

'Certain.'

'In that case it won't matter if I tell you about Brian's boots. He said he'd been for a long walk, walked across a muddy field, but the mud was from our garden. I saw him stamping about in the flower bed. He was lying, Jane, about his walk, and it's my fault because …'

'Don't give it another thought.' Jane had adopted her head-of-department voice, and Willa responded like a child, glad someone else was going to take responsibility for its ill-advised behaviour.

'No, all right. No, I won't. And I'll talk to Arthur. Oh, I think I owe you some money.'

'Don't worry about that, but if you're agreeable I believe it would be beneficial to continue with the tuition for a week or two, just to make sure he gains grades that allow him to stay on for his A levels.'

'Yes, yes of course, whatever you think best. Thank you so much. For everything. I've got one of my heads so I think I'll go upstairs and lie down for a bit.'

'Good idea.' Jane let herself out of the house with

what would have been a sigh of relief. But for the story about Brian's muddy walking boots.

THIRTY-FIVE

Three parcels for the couple who lived four doors up. According to Gus, they were both estate agents. Say no more! Jane had looked up "shopaholics" online – it was now called "compulsive buying disorder" – and apparently, it was not the goods people wanted, but the frisson or, scientifically speaking, the release of adrenalin they experienced as they approached the till. Or, if shopping from home, when they pressed "buy".

Jane disliked the current craze for defining greedy or irrational behaviour as an illness. Apparently, in the case of shopaholics, excessive buying was the result of an inability to tolerate negative feelings. Fucking nonsense, as Eddie would have said during the period, a few months before she moved into The Spruces, when her conversation was peppered with expletives. One of the advantages of living alone was that you could swear to your heart's content. If Jane's neighbours could hear her they would be shocked to the core. They thought she was a dried-up old spinster – how wrong they were – but "fucking" was not her word of choice. It was over-used. Swearing like a trooper, although these days it was builders. Jane had once heard a builder say, "Move that fucking rubbish, you fucking fucker." On the other hand, Mark and Lee, still working on next door's loft conversion, were extremely well-mannered, and as considerate as their job allowed them to be.

Time to pay a visit to Dave in his workshop. To her shame, she was almost as curious as Simmy to discover what had befallen her mother. Dave was unlikely to tell her the truth but she might be able to persuade him what a bad effect his silence was having on his daughter. If Corinne was right, and she had drowned, why not tell the child? She would understand.

When she found Dave, he was cleaning a copper coal scuttle.

'Sorry to intrude.' Jane pushed open the workshop door. 'Time for a quick word?'

He yawned. 'Take a pew.'

His legs were curled under his metal chair and his feet moved in time to the music. Turned down low, which was a relief. Perhaps he was always relaxed when he was in the workshop. Perhaps there was another reason. He had worried Noel would tell Simmy the truth about her mother's death. Now it would remain a secret.

Jane took a pew, literally. It must have come from a church that had given up the ghost. It was dusty, possibly oily, and she hoped it wouldn't mark her skirt, since it was one she was rather attached to.

The workshop was a stone's throw from the house, almost literally, in a gap between two houses in the adjoining road. Jane had no idea why the ramshackle place had been put up there. Had a bomb dropped during the war? Possibly a row of garages had been turned into one long shed.

'I knew you bought and sold furniture,' she said, 'but I hadn't realised ...' She pointed at the coal scuttle.

'Came across it at an auction.'

'The one you attended the day Noel ... will it fetch a good price?'

He kept his head down, rubbing away. 'How can I help?'

'Oh. Yes. I wondered if you saw Noel go into your house.'

'I left just after one.' He looked up to make sure she had grasped the significance of the time. 'Old couple who died within days of each other. Some other stuff too, but mostly it was a house clearance. Cops asked where I'd been. Asked you too, I expect.'

'I think Corinne may have been the last person who saw him.'

'How's she doing?'

'Much as you'd expect.' She was going to add: "I have a feeling she's tougher than we think," but decided against it. 'Poor Simmy was very shocked. Well, we all were. Gus was out too, taking photographs. Birds and insects. For a competition, I think.' She was talking too fast, swallowing

265

her words. 'You know, the smell of this place could easily become addictive. Wood and varnish, and something else. Methylated spirits, is it?'

'Loft conversion's going to be let to two blokes in a band.'

'Yes, you said. Are you sure? Mrs Garcia told you?'

'Noise is likely to reach your house too.'

Jane sighed. 'I doubt if anything has been fixed up yet. Still finishing touches to be completed, decorating and such.'

Dave gave a hollow laugh. 'Vibration through the floor. When Noel told Gus ...'

'When? When did Noel tell him?'

'Day before the *accident*.'

Jane sat on her hands to stop them shaking. Dave knew why she was there and was going to make it as difficult as possible for her. Blood from a stone. Should she tell him she knew his wife had drowned? That Corinne had told her? 'Simmy talks to me sometimes.'

'So you said.'

'I'm glad she's friendly with Arthur. He's a nice boy, thoughtful.'

'Boys his age are never "nice".' He reached for his tin of tobacco.

'Anyway, I just wanted to say, it would help if you could talk to Simmy about her mother. I've no idea what happened, it's not my business.'

'No, it's not.'

'Yes, well, I'd better go.' She had lost her nerve,

despised herself. 'Rousseau will be wanting his dinner. If he comes into your garden, let me know.'

Dave turned over the coal scuttle, inspecting it for any stains he might have missed. 'Cats have territories. So do human beings, but with human beings they're in their heads. No-go areas and watch out anyone who tries to invade them.'

Was he having a dig at her, or was he dropping another heavy hint about Gus' response to the threat of a pop group practising above his head? Was it even true that Noel had talked to Gus the day before he died? Dave might have a good reason for pinning the crime on his neighbour.

'Just before I go —'

'You put ideas in Sim's head.'

'What makes you say that?' His voice had a mocking tone and Jane reacted angrily. 'Why *can't* you put her mind at rest. She only wants to know what happened. No, it's no good looking like that. I tell her to talk to you but she says you won't listen, won't answer her questions.'

He struck a match.

'It's preying on her mind.' Now she had started she was going to see it through. 'Making her imagine all kind of things.'

'What things?'

'Oh, I don't know.' She sat down, this time on a chair.

The cigarette had gone out. Dave struck another match. 'Pity about Noel. Cliff Accident by Eileen Dover. *I leaned ov*—'

'Yes, I've heard it before.'

'What about this one then? Rusty Bedsprings by I. P. Knightly?'

'Please talk to Simmy. I expect she's mentioned the computer game she and Arthur are planning. Based on Greek myths. Poor Noel is a rapist and pillager although I daresay what happened has put an end to that particular game.'

'What about you? Do you figure in it?' Dave stood up, rubbing his back. Simmy was going to be taller than her father, and where Dave's eyes were deep-set, Simmy's were large and spaced well-apart. Simmy said there were no photographs of her mother in their house and, for the first time, it crossed Jane's mind Dave might not be her biological father. Was that what all the secrecy was about?

'We were on holiday,' he said, 'in Cornwall.'

Jane opened her mouth but he put up a hand to stop her. 'I'd hired a boat.' He held a match to his roll-up. It took a long time to get going. 'Wind got up and it started to rain.' He closed his eyes, remembering. 'We should never have started out, but, as usual, I thought I knew best.' He balanced his roll-up on the edge of a table, an old one, pitted and scratched, a permanent fixture in the workshop. 'Water was rough and there were currents.'

'You were staying in Cornwall, you say?'

He stared at her. 'Do you want to hear or not?'

'Yes, yes, I'm sorry.'

'I thought I could save them. I tried to save Cass. Tried

to save them both.'

'The boat overturned?'

'She could swim but it was cold and … Sim was only two, so I had to … I thought Cass'd be all right, thought she'd be able to make it to the shore.'

'I'm so sorry.' Jane felt shivery. 'But you saved Simmy. Oh, Dave, how dreadful, what a tragedy. If I'd known … I wish I'd known.'

'Moving here was supposed to be a fresh start. Simmy attended a day nursery until she was old enough to start at school. Better than spending time with me.'

'No, don't say that. She's a sweet girl, a credit to you.'

'Now you know why I can't tell her. She'd never forgive me. I suppose I could have made up a story; a traffic accident, fatal illness.' The roll-up fell off the table. He stamped on it, covering his face with his hands.

'It wasn't your fault, Dave. It was no one's fault.' It was the first time she had seen him show any emotion, apart from mild irritation, or once or twice a flash of anger when Noel announced how another loft was going to be converted.

'I told Simmy when she was little, when she was too young to understand, but … since then … it's never seemed the right time … she never asked, not until …'

'Corinne says Noel read about the accident in the local paper, when he was staying in Polperro. I don't know if he said anything to Simmy. Or Corinne did. No, I'm sure it wasn't Corinne.'

'You thought I'd tossed him off the balcony.'

'No, of course not.'

'Didn't shed many tears when I heard what'd happened. He'd promised not to tell Corinne but —'

'And I'm sure he kept his promise. I'm so sorry, Dave, but please talk to Simmy, she's a sweet girl, she'll understand, I know she will. If it had been possible, you would have saved both of them. I'm so sorry. It was just one of those terrible accidents that nobody —'

The workshop door was flung open and Simmy rushed at Dave and wrapped her arms round him, almost knocking him off his chair. She must have been listening outside. How much had she heard? Enough.

'I'm so sorry,' Jane murmured, 'so dreadfully sorry.' But she was not needed anymore. It was time to leave them in peace. Dave hadn't killed Noel – she was almost certain of it – but somebody had.

THIRTY-SIX

Jane sat in the garden, staring at the flowers. Begonias, snapdragons, foxgloves, and a blue morning glory that had wound its way up the drainpipe next to the water butt. The euphorbia – Eddie's choice, not hers – was getting out of hand. Fetching a pair of secateurs, Jane held it back with one hand and snipped with the other.

Rousseau was missing, again, but she had more important things to think about. It was one of those days when the whole world seemed against her. At times like this, she became so self-absorbed she forgot other people had their own troubles, and the nice woman from number fifteen might have failed to smile because she was worrying about her health, or her finances, or any number of other problems.

Before she left for the shops, Eddie must have climbed on a chair while Jane was talking to Simmy, found the offending object in the kitchen cupboard and taken it next door. Since it was Saturday, no one would have been working on the conversion, but the door had been left open. A serious oversight or had Noel unlocked it, prior to a visit? In any case, by the time he fell, Eddie had been almost a mile away, outside Sainsbury's, talking to a dog.

The thud of post dropping through the front door interrupted Jane's thoughts and she hurried to collect it, hoping as she always did that there would be something personal among the junk mail. Charities tried to make you feel guilty, including raffle tickets for you to sell, or a small gift you didn't want, and the only way to reduce the guilt was to decide which charities to support, and stick to them. In Jane's case, they were cancer research and Marie Curie nurses, chosen because she had a phobia about cancer. No, not a phobia, a perfectly rational fear, although, in recent months, her fear of dementia had taken precedence.

Between the junk – she almost missed it – was a handwritten envelope with a foreign stamp. Her great-niece in Australia. When she tore it open a photograph fell out, a picture of a baby with a pink sunhat, and, turning it over, she read the smudged words. *Edwina, aged five months.* Her brother Hugh's great-granddaughter. Should she laugh or cry? The name was a coincidence, must be, but there was something consoling about it. Another Edwina to replace Eddie. A sign, if you believed in such things, that life goes on.

When the doorbell rang, Jane groaned. A delivery man with stuff for the Tidewells. Tricia had warned her there might be a package containing a cricket set.

It was Gus.

'I'm sorry, Jane, it's Rousseau. A car was coming up the road and he —'

'He's dead.' First Eddie, now Rousseau, she couldn't bear it.

'Up near Noel and Corinne's house. Nicky's with him. Nicky from number twenty-two.'

Running on ahead, Jane could see the woman bending over Rousseau's inert body. So she was the one who had knocked him down. Jane shouted at her, but Gus put out a restraining hand.

'It wasn't Nicky. A white car. The driver didn't stop.'

'Stunned, I think.' The woman had taken off her coat and laid it on the ground. Now she was gently placing her hands under Rousseau's shoulders and hindquarters and sliding him onto it. 'There's no bleeding but I need to be careful. As far as I can tell, the car only caught his leg, and I don't think it's broken. Gus and I were walking up the road. You know what cats are like. He darted across and now it's getting dark ...'

'Nicky's a vet.' Gus knelt beside Jane and put an arm round her.

'A vet? I didn't know. You think he's going to be all right?' Jane was tearful with relief. 'Thank you. Thank you so much. Oh, Rousseau, what am I going to do with you?'

'Rousseau. That's a great name.' Nicky stroked his head and he sprang up with a loud yowl, and she caught hold of him to restrain him. 'Seems OK but have him checked out at your vet's to make sure.'

'Yes, I will. Thank you. I'm so grateful, so glad you were here.'

'No worries.' She picked up her coat and slung it over one arm. Without her woolly hat, she looked different. Red hair, cut very short, and a sprinkling of freckles on a face that was not dissimilar to Jane's at that age. How could she have thought she was a sinister character?

'I've seen you about, but we haven't been introduced. Jane Seymour.'

'Nicky Robbins. I live down the bottom, number twenty-two. When I say "live", I've been doing it up, decorating and carrying out minor repairs. I'm moving in properly next week.'

'It will be nice to have you as a neighbour.'

Gus laughed. 'In case the cat tries to use up another of his nine lives.'

'You know I didn't mean that.'

'You need a cup of tea.' Nicky was examining the back of her hand and Jane was afraid Rousseau must have scratched it. 'You've had a shock. You'll do the honours, Gus?'

Jane's body had started to shake. It had been the same when she found Noel. But Rousseau was alive and when she opened her front door he leapt from her arms and raced through to the kitchen. 'Oh Rousseau, no I'm not going to let you into the garden. Not yet.' She turned to Gus. 'You know Nicky quite well?'

'In a manner of speaking. Sit down, look a bit

unsteady on your pins.'

'I'm all right,' Jane turned on a tap and water hit a spoon and splashed her blouse. 'Do you think … oh, Gus, it's been such an awful few days. I feel beleaguered.'

'No long words.'

'What about the names of your spiders?'

'Touché.'

'Why did Nicky wear that knitted hat? I mean, why did she wear it in the summer?'

'Lost her hair. Chemotherapy. In the clear now, thank the Lord.'

'Cancer. Why didn't you tell me? I wish you had. I thought …'

'While she was having the treatment, she preferred to keep herself to herself.'

'Yes, of course. How did you meet her? Have you been helping with her house?'

'Hardly. You know me and DIY. Only have to pick up a hammer and I knock a nail through a water pipe. She's buying my old premises.'

'Your shop? I thought the lease had run out.'

'No, it was the customers ran out.'

'Oh.' Jane leaned against a kitchen unit, the one with the cupboard where she had hidden the fluffy handcuffs. The rash on her wrist had reappeared. No surprise there. Brian must be right for once – it was the result of stress.

'Belonged to my dad,' Gus said. 'Did pretty well in the old days. There's still people who prefer proper cameras but it wasn't a good site for passing trade and when the regulars started dying off.'

'You had trouble finding a buyer?'

He nodded. 'Then Nicky came along. Coincidence she's moving into Faraday Road. She contacted me through the estate agent. Wants to open a new veterinary practice, her and her partner. Nearest one's miles off, as you must know to your cost.'

'Why didn't you tell me? I mean that you were having problems selling the shop?'

'Superstitious. Afraid the deal might fall through. Her partner's called Jude.'

'You've met him? I thought since the two of you seemed so close ...'

His face broke into a broad grin. 'I should be so lucky. Besides, she's not interested in blokes. Jude's her girlfriend.' He dropped a tea bag into the mug he had found on the draining board. 'You were good to me when the shop closed, Jane. Don't think I haven't appreciated your efforts to get me back on my feet.'

'That you successfully resisted. And I wasn't being entirely altruistic. It's lonely on your own.'

'You? Lonely? Always struck me as self-sufficient. Iron self-control. Not like us mere mortals. Even when Eddie died you pretended it was for the best.'

'It was.'

'Except nothing's that simple, is it?'

'No. My "iron self-control", as you put it, is a way of keeping going. Some people – Corinne is one of them – throw themselves on other people's mercy. I was brought

276

up to —'

'Stiff upper lip, I know. Shall I move this bag of potatoes? Rousseau wants to go through the cat flap.'

'Oh. Yes.'

'Can't keep him indoors forever.'

'No.' Jane pulled out a chair and sat down. 'Gus?'

'Now what?'

'It *was* an accident, wasn't it? No, not Rousseau, I meant Noel.'

He took his time replying but Jane thought he was probably still thinking about Rousseau. When he finally spoke, she caught her breath.

'If he told you he'd been pushed, he must have known who did it. Any ideas?'

THIRTY-SEVEN

Once the cupboard had been wiped clean, Jane carried the handcuffs to the garden, placed them in an empty flowerpot and sprinkled them with white spirit. Did white spirit encourage flames? She would soon find out.

The ginger and white cat from number twenty was shitting in the nicotianas. Funny how words you would never dream of speaking out loud were regular visitors to your head. Shit and fuck, and wank. Cock and fanny and arse. After she started to become ill, Eddie had come out with strings of words she had never uttered before. A symptom of dementia, Jane had read, but all it meant was that the illness was disinhibiting. The words had been in her head all along.

Rousseau had been watching the ginger cat from the safety of the magnolia. Now he had decided to see it off and Jane watched the angry scuffle, happy he was none the worse for his collision with a car. She would make it up to Nicky for the unwarranted opinion of her she had formed. She ought to be ashamed of herself. She *was* ashamed, especially since the poor woman had been ill.

'Burning your love letters?' Gus was watching from his window on the first floor.

'That's right.' Jane prodded the ashes.

'When you've finished can I have a look at Eddie's paintings? I could do with something to hang on the wall.'

'One of Eddie's paintings? Yes, of course. I'll leave the front door open and we can go up to the loft together.'

'Make sure your fire's gone out.'

Jane stared down at the charred remains. There was no sign of the pink fluff but the plastic had not even melted. She found a garden fork and lifted it out, depositing it in the centre of the bed of cat mint. She would deal with that later – after Eddie's funeral which was to take place the following Monday. How many people would come? Gus would, and possibly Willa and Brian. Not Corinne – Jane had decided not to tell her about it – and not Tricia Tidewell who had the children to look after. Just the four of them would be fine and after the service they could have lunch somewhere, not in her house, possibly the Portuguese café. Ofelia and Andre Cardozo were such kind, comforting people.

Eddie had been up to the new loft conversion at least fifteen minutes before Noel fell. Why had it been left unlocked? Perhaps the builders had been in earlier – Mrs Garcia putting pressure on Noel to complete the work – and Noel had told them to leave it as it was. Dave and Gus both had their own front doors so, if Noel or the builders were around, the front door to the house was often left ajar.

Up in the loft, Gus studied Eddie's paintings, stopping at a representation of the Dorset coast, big slabs of black and green and blue.

'How much?'

'Take it.'

'Are you sure? There must be a going rate. All right then, if you insist. I'll just have another look.'

'Take as long as you like. Your photographs are all of insects and birds?'

'Need a macro lens that allows you to focus on things at a closer distance than landscapes and such. On "the day of the crime" I stupidly left mine out of my bag. Had to return home and collect it.'

Jane took the Chagall book off the shelf. Always useful in a tricky situation. Was it tricky? An old friend up in Eddie's studio. Was Gus an old friend? She liked to think so, but Gus might have other ideas. He was sorry for her and buying Eddie's paintings was the only gesture he could think of that might make her feel a little better.

The book had come open at Chagall's painting of a naked woman in a tree, or rather the woman was part of the tree. Below her, a man held out a hand to a red donkey, or was it a bull? The picture was called *La Branche* and gave the impression it was a dream. Jane was fluent in French, which was why Senegal had been one of the countries she and Eddie had planned to visit. Senegal and Côte d'Ivoire. Had Eddie retained any memory of their plans? Now and again, she had recalled in detail an occasion Jane had forgotten about, the waitress who had dropped a tray and broken some china, or a school outing when one of the second years had been sick and the coach driver had let out a string of expletives. Around that time, Eddie still had a sense of humour and had played a trick on her, showing her a painting she had found in a junk shop that she thought might be an early Cézanne. Jane had fallen for all the talk about what they would be able to do with the money, only to have Eddie collapse in fits of laughter. *Honestly, Jane, it's so easy to take you in.*

'No, this is the one.' Gus had returned to the landscape. 'Sure I can't give you something for it?'

'Quite sure.'

'What's the matter with your arm?'

'Itchy rash. Stupid.'

'Euphorbia. I saw you cutting it back. Well-known for bringing on an allergic reaction, I should dig it up and add it to the bonfire.'

Jane sat down on the chair last occupied by Arthur. 'Of course, how stupid. Brian thought it was my nerves.'

'Typical.'

Jane took a deep breath. 'Rousseau went up to the new loft conversion in your house and apparently it hadn't been the first time. Lee was there and he suggested I had a look round. There's a new sofa and —'

'Once belonged to the Garcia woman.'

'Only I found something. No, it's no good, Gus, I'll

have to tell you the whole sorry story. I opened a parcel addressed to Willa. Yes, I know it was wrong but I'd taken in so many people's parcels.'

'Not mine.'

'I re-wrapped it but left out part of it. By mistake.'

'What was in it? Something you wanted?'

'Hardly.' Should she tell him about the scene in Willa's conservatory? Noel roaring with laughter as he held up the knickers. Maybe that story would keep for a while. 'It's a shame you can't see your daughter and granddaughter more often.'

'She's having another. My daughter. Don't know about you, but I'm not very good with kids, never was. That was one of the problems. Too absorbed with my work. Didn't do enough round the house.'

Jane remained silent and Gus erupted. 'The trouble with you, Jane, you want me to bare my soul while you keep yourself —'

'I've just admitted I opened someone else's parcel.'

'Oh, that! Personally, if I see one of those vans I ignore the doorbell.'

'I was married once.'

Gus put down the painting. 'Really?'

'I had a baby, a boy. He died when he was three days old. A heart defect.'

She expected him to turn away, study another painting. Instead, he stepped forward and wrapped his arms round her. 'What was his name?'

'Edmund. After he died, it was never the same. We

282

tried to console one another but …'

He stared up at the dormer window, firmly closed now Arthur had fixed the catch. 'I wish you'd told me before. No, don't look like that, I'm not good with tears.'

'At the time, I don't think I did cry very much. I was too shocked. Afraid if I started crying I would never stop.'

Gus nodded. 'You know how you and Eddie were going to travel the world?'

'Africa. Australia. Not America. Possibly the Far East.'

'Ambitious.'

'Anyway, it doesn't matter. Now she's gone, I'm free. Free to do whatever … I thought … I don't know what I thought. If you have no purpose in life what's the point of getting up in the morning? You've got your photography. What have I got? A cat, a cat that doesn't care as long as he's fed. An old woman and her cat!'

'I'm thinking of going on a walking tour.'

'Really?' Jane was taken aback at the announcement. 'You never said.'

'You never asked.' He grinned. 'Not sure I could manage a world tour. Too many mosquitoes. Not good in the heat. Coastal path sounds all right. Starting in North Devon, Lynton, Ilfracombe, Barnstaple, and on to Dawlish and Torquay.'

Jane gave an involuntary shudder.

'Well, what d'you think?'

'You'll enjoy it. It will do you good.'

'Come on, Jane, I'm asking if you'd like to accompany

me. Past Land's End and The Lizard. The autumn would be the best time of year. Don't know about you, but I like wild weather. What d'you think? We could stay in bed and breakfast places, booking ahead or taking pot luck. See how far we got, how long the old bones put up with it. Parts of it may be fairly strenuous but we wouldn't be in a hurry. What d'you say?'

'Accompany you?'

'Yes, all right, forget I mentioned it.'

'Separate rooms.'

'Oh, don't worry. Not sure I'm up to any hanky-panky, if you know what I mean.'

'I do.'

'We get on, you and me.' He laughed. 'Yes, we do. We'd make sure we did.'

'What about Rousseau?'

'He can stay with Simmy and Dave.'

'He'll set up home there, never come back. No, I don't think that's very likely. You'll need some new clothes. For the walk.'

'You think so.'

'I do.'

'Right you are, we'll pay a visit to one of those camping shops. No, not a tent. They have boots and thick jackets and waterproof trousers, the lot. Come on then, no not the shopping centre, that'll keep for a day or two. How about introducing me to that Portuguese place you're always on about? Trying to cut down on the cakes and pastries.' He patted his stomach. 'But I reckon this is a special occasion. I took the risk of being turned down flat. And *you* agreed to be taken in hand.'

'Taken in hand? I don't need taking —'

'Yes, you do.' He picked up the painting. 'Going to need some ground rules. No arguing, no bossiness, and—'

'Backpacks with plenty of clean underwear and socks.'

THIRTY-EIGHT

A buzzard hovered overhead, waiting to pounce. Jane stared at the streaky blue sky, felt a sharp sensation in her left ankle, and turned to her companion with a wry smile.

'I've always been susceptible to insect bites.' She searched in her bag for a tube of anti-histamine cream.

'What was it? Not a tick?'

'Ticks don't bite, they suck your blood. A midge, I expect. Or a mosquito.'

'Wrong time of year.'

As they passed through a wooden gate, the whole valley came into view, with its sloping sides and outbreaks of rocks. Gus liked maps, also seabirds, rock formations, and ships on the horizon. Today's walk had started in Lynton, looking down on Lynmouth harbour. The hotel had been reasonably priced and comfortable, and the breakfast large, and eaten at a leisurely pace.

After leaving Lynton, they had followed the signs for the Abbey, climbing between trees, then realised their mistake since their intention was to traverse the valley and, with any luck, spot a feral goat or two. *He shall separate them one from another, as a shepherd divideth his sheep from the goats.* Eddie had gone through a phase of wanting to keep goats, but Jane had put her foot down. *They eat the washing on your line and if they were nannies I know who'd have to milk them.*

'Ragged Jack on the left.' Gus shaded his eyes against the glare of the sun. 'And Castle Rock on the right.'

'You've been here before.'

He shook his head. 'Read the guidebook at the hotel. The goats and ponies help to keep the vegetation under control.'

'It was near here that John Ridd visited Mother Meldrum.'

'Who?'

'*Lorna Doone.* Wonderful book, set mainly on Exmoor, during the turbulent time of Monmouth's rebellion.'

'The ponies are Exmoors. Hardy. Roam free on the moor. Recognisable by the mealy markings around their eyes and muzzle.'

'You've always been interested in wildlife?'

Gus felt in the pocket of his new trousers. 'Isn't everybody?' He handed Jane a strong mint.

'I'm not so sure about that.' She had spotted a narrow path that ran towards the cliff top. 'Shall we go up there and look at the sea?'

'Right you are.'

Urged on by Gus, it soon became a race, terminating in an alarming drop to the sea below. Fortunately, an iron railing had been erected for the benefit of foolhardy visitors. Jane was thinking about another holiday. With Eddie. They had stayed in a bed and breakfast place on the moor, and found themselves sharing the place with a stag party. Jane had found the men a little disruptive but Eddie had enjoyed listening to their escapades, described at the top of their voices. What would she have thought if she had known where Jane was now? Her friend and companion on a walking tour with their neighbour. She smiled to her herself and Gus asked what the joke was and she said she was just imagining what Eddie would think. 'Eddie when she had her wits about her.'

'The two of us on holiday together? She'd disapprove?'

'I expect so.'

They continued in silence, both deep in thought, although it turned out Gus was thinking about the geology of the area.

'Some of the oldest rocks in North Devon,' he told her, 'and the area is known for its interesting fungi.'

'And insects, I expect.'

He bent to look at her face. 'You mocking me?'

'Not at all. With your love of nature and mine of literature, we make a good pair. Sit on that bench for five minutes, shall we, get our breath back?'

'Right you are. From what you've told me, you and the Molloy boy seem to have hit it off. They say it can be like that if you skip a generation.'

'Were you thinking about your grandchildren?'

'No, I was thinking about you.'

'I had a word with Willa, and later with Brian, and they've accepted Arthur doesn't want to be a doctor. Last I heard, he and Simmy had embarked on a new computer game. Not based on Greek myths this time. Birds of prey, I believe, vultures.'

'What d'you suppose Corinne will do? Return to her ex?'

'Arthur says he has a girlfriend but I don't know if it's serious.'

He touched her arm. 'Look, goats, four of them.'

'Oh, yes. I suppose they're so sure-footed, they'd never fall into the sea.'

'It said in the guidebook they used to push sheep over the cliff.'

'There aren't any sheep.'

'Exactly. We'll have lunch at a place I read up about. Grub's supposed to be good. A few miles on, if you can manage it.'

'Of course I can manage it. At first I thought ... well, you know what I thought. I thought Eddie had seen Noel leaning over the balcony and been unable to resist giving him a push.'

'So you did a spot of detective work. Needed a different culprit. Oh, don't worry, I know I was on your list. Well, it could've been me. Not that Noel's departure has put an end to the racket, and God only knows who'll be moving in above me.'

'I'd almost convinced myself Eddie was innocent, then Rousseau ran up to the new loft conversion and when I went to retrieve him I found some pink fluffy handcuffs that had been pushed down the sofa. Oh, it's no good, I'll have to tell you the whole story. The parcel I told you about, the one that came for Willa. It was coming unstuck at one end —'

'So you gave it a little extra encouragement.'

'A teacher's outfit in black patent leather. Not real leather. Plastic. Together with a pair of handcuffs with pink fluff attached to them. I re-packed the parcel but forgot to include the handcuffs so I hid them in a kitchen cupboard and Eddie must have found them.' She paused for breath. 'You've no idea how relieved I was when you said you'd seen Eddie outside Sainsbury's at two-fifteen. She must have gone up to the loft earlier on, when I slipped out to buy her some ice-cream. You see Corinne said Noel only left the house at ten past two and Eddie couldn't possibly have reached Sainsbury's by two-fifteen if she'd been next door – when Noel was there.'

Gus was running his hand through what was left of his hair.

'What? It *was* two-fifteen, wasn't it?'

He nodded. 'You said there weren't to be any lies between us, Jane.'

'Did I? Well, not many. Some lies are necessary. White lies that spare other people's feelings and —'

'Jane!'

290

'What?'

He sighed, staring into the distance at a group of small children running through the bracken. 'Not the big supermarket that's almost a mile away. Sainsbury's local, the convenience shop round the corner. That's where I saw her.'

Jane hugged her knees. She was thinking about Corinne, furious that Noel had lied about his vasectomy. And Dave, determined to protect Simmy from discovering the truth about her dead mother. Willa, the scorned mistress. Brian, terrified his wife was going to leave him. Then there was Nicky, from number twenty-two, who had come to Rousseau's rescue, unaware that Jane had harboured evil thoughts about her woolly hat or, to be more precise, her friendship with Gus. What a fool she had been. No, not a fool – she had wanted to protect poor Eddie and it had affected her judgement.

The fresh air was bracing and it was a long time since she had felt so alive. Gus took her hand. 'Come on then, coffee and cake. Don't know about you, but cake always works wonders with me, makes the world seem a better place.'

THE SISTER'S SECRET
PENNY KLINE

How well do you really know her?

Erin is devastated when her pregnant sister Claudia is left brain dead from a tragic accident. When Claudia's boyfriend Ollie wants to switch off her life support, a desperate Erin finds herself fighting to give the baby a chance.

THE GIFTED CHILD
PENNY KLINE

How do you deal with what comes after a death?

When her partner, William, is murdered, and her beloved stepson is returned to the birth mother who never really wanted him, Kristen's life falls completely apart. The police think the murder was a mugging gone wrong, but did Kristen know William as well as she thought she did?

NOBODY'S BABY

PENNY KLINE

What happens when the past turns up on your doorstep?

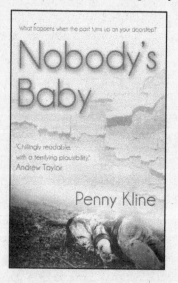

When Izzy finds a baby on her doorstep it looks like the random act of a desperate mother… except that the baby's name, pinned in a note to its carrycot, brings back a striking memory from her childhood.

Proudly published by Accent Press

www.accentpress.co.uk